Trails of Africa

Daniel Nuss

ISBN 978-1-68526-635-6 (Paperback)
ISBN 978-1-68526-636-3 (Digital)

Covenant Books
11661 Hwy 707
Murrells Inlet, SC 29576
www.covenantbooks.com

Many miles west of Babati, as fish eagles perched in the Marula tree and the kingfisher in the fever tree, a Jeep scurried across a steppe in Tanzania. The vehicle crossed behind some tall savannah grass and came to a halt. The driver took out a pair of binoculars and stood up in the Jeep to catch any activity from a distance.

The six-foot driver—with brown hair, a trimmed beard, an outback Aussie hat, a short-sleeved cargo shirt, and a pair of cargo shorts—was a wildlife conservationist and poacher hunter who spotted two poachers in another vehicle. The wildlife conservationist picked up a four-barrel shotgun beside himself and leapt out of the Jeep. The wildlife conservationist ran a modest distance behind the tall grass before he leapt behind a mound of dirt and aimed his shotgun. The shotgun was aimed within range, and he waited momentarily.

The wildlife conservationist fired a shot and hit the backside of the poacher's vehicle. And then the wildlife conservationist stood up partially in the dense savannah grass.

He shouted, "Hey, Charles, are you sure you don't have anywhere else to pursue your grim existence on this planet?"

Charles bellowed, "Lance Clayborne…is that you?" He paused for a moment. Then he said, "Why, I never thought you would tie up my opportunities for me west of Babati."

Lance yelled, "Where did you think I would have remotely found you?"

Charles asked his assistant to fire in the direction marked by Lance's presence. The assistant did that very thing. He aimed randomly at an invisible target and missed by far. Charles turned his vehicle partially and headed in the direction the shotgun fire originally came from.

Lance repositioned himself and cocked his shotgun, aimed, and fired once again. He shattered the windshield out of Charles's Jeep but didn't inflict a wound on either of the two hunched men.

Charles stopped the vehicle and shouted, "I was only taking in the breathtaking vista and the wildlife, Lance!"

Lance laughed to himself about the sad statement and said, "You're a wanted man, Charles! Why would you open fire on me otherwise?"

Firing again from a new position, Lance had repositioned himself out on the savanna. The poacher with Charles fired again and came close to striking Lance.

Lance said to himself, "That was too close for anyone's taste."

Lance changed his location again and fired upon Charles's Jeep. This time, he struck the gas cannister in the back of the vehicle. Flames erupted on the backside of the Jeep, forcing both men to vacate the Jeep.

Lance had put a significant amount of distance between him and his Jeep. By accepting the challenge to capture each of the two poachers, Lance singled out the use of only his shotgun. As Lance tried to bait them by striking fear into both with shotgun fire, he pinned them down in the open.

While Lance waited to apprehend them through fear or a lapse in time, another truck drove up to them. It appeared to Lance there were a few more of Charles's men. Charles and his aide boarded the cargo truck and took flight from further entrapment. At this time, Lance concluded the opportunity to apprehend Charles and his hire had been lost. Lance walked back to his Jeep and drove to Charles's burning vehicle.

While flames partially inundated the Jeep, Lance searched for any miscellaneous clues and items toward future pending stratagem out on the savanna. An itemized list was found with exact poaching targets written out on a document and a hunting itinerary for an excursion on a clipboard. Lance took the material back to his Jeep and drove away.

*****

The following morning, Lance lay in his hammock, which hung in the middle of his Katara lodge-like hut. Its build was similar to the lodge near Queen Elizabeth National Park in Uganda. Wooden posts held the hut off the ground. His Outback Aussie hat hung on the back pole, which supported the hammock while he caught up on his nighttime sleep. Rays of the sun permeated the central room area through the window of his hut where he lay. In the distance, a faint rumbling sound gradually began to grow outside his back window. As it became louder, it woke Lance and the noise provoked him to look out his back window.

Picking up his binoculars on the floor, Lance used them to see the distance between him and the tremor. He identified it as a stampede of wildebeest. Lance jerked violently from shock to the right side of the hammock sharply and fell out onto the floor. Dressed in a white tank top shirt and cargo shorts, he grabbed his keys to the Jeep, put his hat on, and quickly proceeded to vacate the premises. He climbed down a rope ladder and into his Jeep. Thick dust from the impending mass of animals grew closer to his hut.

He attempted to start the Jeep. After he turned the engine over several times, it refused to start. He spoke underneath his breath, "Come on," as he primed the engine. It continued to stall on him. He jumped out of the Jeep and opened the hood. A few adjustments were made while he occasionally looked around the hood to see the distance of the wildebeest. It seemed they had nearly closed the distance by three-quarters. A few more adjustments were made to the engine before he slammed the hood shut, climbed over the front, collapsed in the Jeep, and engaged the motor.

It started for him. He quickly shifted into gear and sped forward from the hut. A hit from the wildebeest busted through the wooden poles and bamboo supports, which broke throughout the hut. Tilting on its side, the hut came crashing down, and the wildebeest infiltrated the interior of the hut. The hooved animals permeated the open windows of the hut as well as the door like a needle through a crevice.

The Jeep kept ahead of the herd. Then Lance spotted a small cliff and drove toward it. Lance parked on it while the herd passed below in front of the Jeep. Once the herd dwindled down, he returned to the remains of the hut.

As Lance rummaged through his belongings, his duffel bags and a backpack were used to store items that remained salvageable at the dwelling. Four duffel bags and the backpack were filled and loaded onto the Jeep. Then Lance set the two supporting posts and the hammock up in the debris and slinked into it. But like a stage prop busted before intermission, the posts, the hammock, and Lance slumped to the ground.

*****

Later, Lance got into his Jeep and drove north of Babati onto a main road into Serengeti National Park. There, his Jeep was parked near a conservation camp with a number of tents that marked the area along with a large canopy rotunda. Lance unloaded his baggage and carried it toward the tent area. Along the path, he joined another Caucasian man with brown hair. The Caucasian man was six-foot-two and wore a traveler blue fedora hat with a navy shirt and brown work pants and surprised and compelled Lance to stop in his tracks.

The man said, "Oh no, now what?"

Lance said, "A brigade of wildebeest assaulted my bamboo hut, Niles. What once was is now no more."

Niles said, "You know, that a bamboo thatch hut can't stand the vigor of any herd."

Lance spoke in a squeamish voice and said, "Yeah, but it was sitting off the ground on stilts, away from the reach of any wildlife—it was such a well-behaved hut for me."

Niles placed his hand on his shoulder and said sarcastically, "Maybe you'll meet one in the not-too-distant future, which will be elevated on a rocky crag and on some remote level savanna plain."

"Don't make any promises you can't keep, Niles." Lance changed the subject and said, "Charles was on the range, and he broke away from me, leaving me west of Babati."

Niles paused for a moment. Then he said, "You tried to shoot him, didn't you?"

"You're happy that I missed, aren't you?"

"It's expected of us to try to preserve all kinds of life as much as we can."

Lance whispered, "My target must have been too evasive for me."

"You did try to shoot him, didn't you?"

"And his hire."

"You are jagged around the edges."

"Mr. Jagged Around the Edges needs a tent to sleep in during the night."

After a brief pause, Niles said, "I guess...I suppose. We'll have to pitch one for you."

"Where's Mason?"

"He's out checking the fence."

"Come on. Let's get this tent set up."

The men spent time setting up Lance's bell tent. Niles finished adjusting the poles and stakes while Lance tinkered with the inside of the tent.

Another wildlife conservationist shorter than Lance, with sandy blonde hair and wearing light-colored work clothing with a blue fedora hat, parked his Jeep beside Lance's.

He walked to the newly established tent and asked Niles, "Whose tent is it?"

Lance heard the question from within the tent and walked outside, glaring with a wide grin at the man.

The man quietly said, "Oh no...oh no."

Lance said, "Yes, Mason."

Mason said, "Oh no."

"Yes."

"What happened?"

Niles said, "Wildebeest took his hut."

Lance put his arm around Mason, led him away, and said, "Are you sure I'm not using your tent?"

Mason swallowed hard and remained silent. Then Mason shouted toward Niles and asked if Lance really got his tent without facing Niles.

Niles answered in a passive response and said, "Nah."
Mason became bewildered at his response.

*****

While using a microscope, Niles cross-examined a slide under the canopy rotunda in the composite laboratory. His specimen happened to be a sample extracted from a giraffe out on the reserve. He observed profiled virus portraits beside the microscope as they are thumbed through on the counter. A stone's throw away, Lance was preoccupied with gear that would be taken out on an operation.

Niles called out to Lance, "Hey, Lance, come here for a second!"

He joined Niles at the station.

Niles said, "Take a look at this specimen."

After Lance viewed the slide, he said, "You've discovered what you should have gotten your grandmother for Christmas."

Niles looked at him sharply.

Then Lance sarcastically said, "You got her a coffee sampler, didn't you?"

Niles, unnerved by his statement, said, "Would you just look at the slide?"

"What am I looking for?"

"It's blue tongue virus. You see?" He directed Lance to an epidemic illustration in the field manual.

"Yeah, that's great." Lance took the papers Charles left behind, which showed the next feasible destination in poaching, out of his back pocket and presented them to Niles.

Lance asked, "So when are you going to rendezvous with Charles?" Lance handed him the papers.

"What reassures you that we're going to find Charles at any designated location?"

"You haven't looked at the material I gave you. It undeniably gives it away in location and assignment!"

After Niles opened the papers and assessed them, Lance watched him carefully.

Moments later, Lance said, "You're still not convinced!"

6

"No."

Lance took the papers back and returned them to his back pocket.

Niles said, "I'm concentrating on what might be a dire effect on our giraffe population as an uncontrolled breakout."

"Go ahead, you compromise the prize. You'll see whether you can smooth out Kilimanjaro with a paring knife," mentioned Lance.

Niles looked at Lance as if he were shady and returned to his microscope.

Mason joined them and said, "Do you need particular vaccinations packed?"

Niles said, "Yeah, blue tooth, skin infection, intestinal parasitism, and hoof disease."

Lance impaled a glare into the side of Niles's head. Niles turned to Lance and saw his reaction.

Then Niles said, "All right, all right, all right, I'll give it some thought."

Lance walked away.

*****

The three wildlife conservationists drove a Hummer H1 Humvee HMMWV through the reserve and administered treatment to the giraffes. They tranquilized one of the ruminant mammals. As the giraffe lay on the ground, Niles straddled its hind legs bound together with nylon while Lance lay on its neck. Mason handled tools and medication as he offered help. Niles examined the giraffe for hoof disease while Lance determined the proper oral health of the specimen. There didn't appear to be any rot at either station. Then the giraffe began to moderately kick and strike Niles in the legs.

Niles said, "I think we need to check the strength of the tranquilizers." The giraffe raised its head in the air, tilted it slightly, and proceeded to lick Lance's face. Lance tried to avert the behavior, but the giraffe was too blatant in its effort. Niles apprehended the feet and double-checked any treatment for foot rot.

Niles administered all other vaccinations that should be applied to the back torso of the giraffe. Lance complied with the giraffe's vaccinations and stood up with a syringe away from the giraffe. Lance wiped the saliva off his face with a handkerchief. Then the giraffe started to butt his head against Lance's body and mimic the action of two rival males.

Lance said softly, "Do you mind?" He gently pushed its head away, but it made little difference because the giraffe's rambunctious behavior was kept up.

"Has the hot-air balloon risen in time out of the crater or are you finished?" scolded Lance.

"The effects of the tranquilizer should wear off completely very soon," said Niles.

Mason packed the equipment and medicine away in the Hummer.

Lance said, "Only forty more to check their substantial health status."

They all boarded their transportation and headed toward their next destination to locate the next giraffe.

*****

Evening had settled across Tanzania since the men had returned to the conservation camp. Inside one of the enclosed canopy tents, Lance handled a Gambian pouched rat and fed it from his hands. He walked out of the enclosed canopy tent and into the open canopy rotunda. He found a park table and took a seat with the rat to continue to feed its voracious appetite. After a few moments, he looked to his right in the darkness, and a silhouette began to appear running toward him. It was Niles, and he was sprinting for fear of his life for some particular reason.

He gasped as he reached Lance and said, "We got to go…now, now!"

Niles grabbed the pouch rat out of Lance's arms and put it into a cage on the counter.

Lance said, "What is it? A casserole got the best of you tonight?"

Niles said, "Come on!" And he pulled him out from beneath the rotunda and to the back grounds. Niles persuaded him to run, but Lance was stagnant. Then a full-grown bull elephant came crashing through the bush, charging at them as it circled the rotunda. They proceeded to run without reservation.

After they had run on foot for a little while, Lance bellowed, "You go that direction, and I'll work my way back to the gate!"

Niles headed around the tents and trees to the gate, which opened to the preserve's boundaries. Lance took an alternative route as he led the angry elephant the best way he could. Obstacles lay occasionally along the winding path. At times, he had to lure the elephant in the right direction, but it seemed as if it stayed continually on his heels.

Niles waited nervously by the gate to see Lance bring the elephant around in anticipation. The tusks of the bull elephant picked up Lance briefly but only enough off the ground so that he didn't topple and become crushed beneath its feet.

Lance said, "Evidently, someone can't duplicate the actions of running while being chased after."

After sixty more feet, he arrived at the partially opened gate as he led the elephant.

He saw Niles holding the gate and yelled, "*Run!*"

Niles did that very thing while Lance led the elephant through the gate.

The elephant barreled into the gate, ripped into the iron and wire, bending it several ways. Both men swung to their right, climbed the fence out of the reserve, and waited until the bull elephant finished thrashing the gate. Once the bull elephant became calm, it slid the gate off its tusks and lumbered off with a commanding gait.

They returned to the gate and shut what was left of it.

Lance was at a loss for breath and said, "That's a dynamite way to end your energy-spent evening, being chased by a rogue bull elephant."

"Come on, let's get ready for tomorrow."

As Niles walked away in the direction of the open canopy rotunda, Lance stooped to his knees and picked up a cut link in the chain, which held the gate closed. It appeared the chain was cut by a tool. Lance pondered the tampered chain and then returned to the open canopy rotunda.

*****

The next morning arrived with the interest to sedate and treat a bull elephant. The three men drove out on the reserve to sedate the elephant with a tranquilizer. They parked the vehicle behind a thicket once they'd identified the bull elephant. Mason remained with the vehicle while Lance and Niles inched their way on their hands and knees toward the elephant. Then they stopped while advancing in the tall grass, and Lance made an attempt to tranquilize the animal. Niles grabbed the barrel of the rifle and adjusted it a little to the left while it was in Lance's hand.

"Make sure you use the scope and hit the right area," whispered Niles.

Lance pulled the rifle in his direction and whispered, "I know what I'm doing. Would you leave the rifle go?"

Moments passed while Niles assessed Lance's aim, and he whispered, "You've got to increase your angle by 20 percent."

Lance became disgusted and displeased with Niles and said, "Your mother came around yesterday and issued you a subpoena to let you know the lionfish you cooked and she ate last night wasn't properly cooked."

"Yeah, totally harmless. Why don't you let me shoot?"

"I've got the tranquilizer well on its way."

Niles decided to leave him alone and gave him an opportunity to shoot the rifle.

The elephant reacted as if he had detected each of them lying in the grass. Niles and Lance both hastily took off their hats and lowered their heads as far as they could in the grass. The bull elephant didn't counteract any further and returned to feeding on some trees. Niles and Lance raised their heads, and Lance aimed the rifle. He took a shot and hit the bull elephant in the rear left hip. The elephant reacted to the cartridge and scurried off.

Niles told Mason over a two-way radio to bring the Jeep to their location. Once he arrived, the two men jumped into the Jeep, and they followed the bull elephant.

A good number of meters away, the elephant collapsed from the tranquilizer. They parked a reasonable distance away and began to examine the elephant. Blood samples and the hygiene of the animal were assessed, and they checked for foot disease. Next, they placed an identification tag on the elephant. Then they took measurements of the bull elephant and wrote it in their records.

Lance celebrated his work and said, "We got another bull elephant. Thank you, God."

Niles looked at Lance in a peculiar way.

Lance celebrated and said, "We found him, and he's in the Serengeti reserve and is *our* elephant…for now.'"

Niles said, "No, that's not it, he might be infertile, and we don't have the means to test him."

"You bringing stress that doesn't belong to the situation on all four of us, especially him. But you don't know if the females will create stress either. Besides, we have plenty of male bulls out in the reserve, and it'll all work out for him."

Niles said with uncertainty, "We'll see."

Mason joined the conversation and said, "Then again, he might end up fertilizing all the females."

Lance said, "You're such a pessimist."

Niles administered the ante-sedative to the bull elephant, and they packed their equipment and medication and climbed in the Jeep to return to the conservation camp.

*****

The three men sat together at one of two long rows of park tables, eating lunch under the open canopy rotunda. A number of prepared dishes were set before them, ranging from crocodile, springbok, ostrich, and wildebeest as entrees. Niles reached for some wildebeest, but Lance slapped his hand with the handle of a two-pronged meat fork.

Niles glared at him with bewilderment and a stern face. Niles said, "What do you think you're doing?"

Lance said, "Do you need to be reminded to hand me your platter so I can *platter* your meat for you?"

"Must we follow some form of protocol such as those at my mother's estate so we can relish the taste of a piece of meat?"

"It's been our routine, which has always been carried out continually. The one who has the two-pronged fork dishes the meal for each person."

Niles objected strongly and said, "Platter?"

"Platter."

Niles strictly implied, "These are plates…and we can *plate* our own meals for ourselves, thank you." He stretched out his hand to retrieve the two-pronged meat fork, but Lance slapped his hand away again.

He stared at him with frustration. Niles said, "You do realize the meat fork is sharp."

"You were mean to your mother over the Christmas holiday by not getting her anything."

Niles explosively said, "I will get her something next year and be the good boy that I am at that time!"

Lance mumbled, "Still isn't good enough."

"*What?*"

"You still haven't given me your plate."

Niles picked up his glass and drenched Lance's face with a drink.

After a few moments and a share of his moderate objectionableness, Lance grabbed the pitcher and removed the lid. He twirled the contents of the pitcher around and bore a vast grin.

Niles shouted, "*No!*" and Lance threw the liquid inside the pitcher in his face.

Niles sat quiet for a moment, soaking wet from practically head to toe.

Lance had seen the earnest necessity to vacate the picnic table, so he quickly rose and ran away. Niles rapidly chased after him.

Mason was left alone at the table, and he said to himself, "More dark meat for me." Then he picked up a leg of meat and dropped it on his plate to eat it.

*****

It was an hour before dusk the next day. Niles had met a new acquaintance unfamiliar in these parts of the conservation camp. Niles said to her, "I believe that a barnyard venue will be an appropriate addition to any child's growth and development. It would be a wonderful experience for them to be treated with such exposure around their community." Lance overheard the conversation with the woman and wanted to reasonably raise a few questions with Niles as he showered outside in the discharge stall.

He turned off the stall and dried himself, put on a white tank top, cargo shorts, and his Aussie outback hat. He walked out and stood beside Niles and the woman who was without hair and wearing a light shirt and utility shorts.

"Lance, this is Jodi. She's a missionary outside of Mwanza, and she came to ask us a favor today."

Prior to any further statement, Lance interrupted Niles's initial conversation. "Can I speak to you for just one moment?"

Niles walked away with Lance and listened to what he had to say.

Lance said, "Can you tell me who's going to look after this barnyard of exotic animals?"

"We have help or staff that will fall into that role, if necessary."

"It's me, isn't it? You're getting me to do it!"

Niles sighed.

"Niles, someone has to give them inoculations. They have to be watched for disease. They have to be properly fed and even nursed at a certain age."

"You're jumping to conclusions, Lance."

Lance stopped briefly and then abruptly said, "You're going to volunteer me to do wildlife tours, aren't you?"

"We'll have the designated job correspond with the appropriate role."

"Am I going to be reimbursed for any of it? What are they going to do when the government finds out I'm offering tours to people? They're going to take my pay as a wildlife conservationist away from me."

"Nobody is going to alleviate anybody's pay."

"That's what happened to Akuchi. He started providing tours for other people while he was a park ranger, and the republic cut him off. You don't believe that will happen to me?"

"No." Niles took Lance by the shoulder and led him back to Jodi.

After a brief moment, Jodi said to Lance, "Well, is your heart in it? Or do we need to find the nearest expert to tie your shoes for you?"

Lance squinted and glared at her. Lance said, "You want to know what my heart is in right now? Relocating a woman's thimbles to Lake Victoria and seeing how well she sews."

Jodi sharpened her countenance and said, "Well, perhaps, then, we could call on God to move both heaven and earth to intervene for your habitual relocation work habits!"

"You can call on God all you want. Feel free to demonstrate that handiwork, which appears to be less precious than, oh, say—"

Jodi stewed and stomped one foot on the ground. Niles pulled Lance the opposite direction and divided them up.

"Yeah, you two are going to do just fine," said Niles as he nodded his head.

*****

It was the middle of the afternoon the next day, and two park rangers drove out of a gate at the game reserve. They hastily stopped at the conservation camp and looked for any trace of someone available. They located Niles and Lance beneath the open canopy rotunda. One hurried ranger said, "There are a group of rangers under fire against an occupation of Charles's men. We need some assistance to properly handle them."

Niles told Lance, "Go fetch our firearms."

Mason joined with Niles, and he was told to bring the other Jeep around back. They loaded up the artillery and followed the rangers inside the reserve.

Within a couple of miles, all three Jeeps began to sustain fire upon themselves, but passengers avoided being shot. The rangers, who had the lead, began to fire on three cargo trucks while poachers, who were dug in, shot from ground cover. Niles drove the middle Jeep into the skirmish while Lance fired his Lancaster four-barrel shotgun at the targets.

Mason followed behind them all as he shot off occasional rounds with an assault rifle on the third cargo truck while he drove with his windshield adjusted flat. The cargo truck's bed full of fighters were partially inundated with fire. It was a relative miracle that most of the targets were finding themselves unscathed. Then Niles drove his Jeep ahead of the rangers, off to the left side of the second cargo truck, and Lance fired into the cab of the truck. Mason broke off from the line and devoted his time to the fighters hunched on the ground. Lance rendered the driver of the cargo truck helpless, so the passenger tried to drive for him.

The rangers sped up to overtake the lead truck that was trying to break off from all the rest. Lance took out a bundle of dynamite, lit it, and threw it on the hood of the truck to hinder the passenger. The passenger ducked, and the TNT bundle exploded upon the hood and inundated the cab. The passenger desperately turned the wheel to the right but unavoidably ventured across a large mound. The passenger upset the truck and spilled out the fighters on the flatbed.

The rangers pursued the first cargo truck, and it recklessly crashed hard into a full-grown tree. Niles and Lance circled around and rounded the reprehensible poachers, with the help of the rangers, with the last cargo truck.

Cautiously and carefully, as Mason made the rounds, he collected ground units that were dug in rather reasonably. While all the field units took the illicit into custody, proper transportation was radioed in to pick up the poachers. Searching through the vehicles to be investigated for evidence, Lance took the opportunity to find Charles's next target sight. He showed the paperwork to Niles and Mason, but Niles said nothing. One of the rangers pointed out to the conservationists exactly where the poachers broke through the perimeter. The three men searched the location and fixed the fence.

*****

It was a few hours before dusk, and Jodi visited the conservation camp upon Niles's request to do so. They met to start transferring the barnyard animals between locations.

As Lance walked beside the tents and looked over his shoulder, he ran into Jodi and let out a guttural grunt. Momentarily, they stopped and looked at each other, and then Lance walked past her and walked on. Before Lance could take a few steps away from Jodi, Niles joined them.

Niles said, "Good, you've caught up with each other."

Jodi said, "Yes, I found your help in the midst of the tents."

"May I see you for a few seconds?" said Lance.

Lance walked away from Jodi with Niles ten feet away and said, "Did you just hear what she called me? I'm the help!"

"Lance, she only thinks the best of you."

"And how did you arrive at this revelation?"

"I was moved by it."

"You were moved by it. I want to know about any other revelations you've been getting in your free time."

Niles removed a few papers from his rear pants pocket, opened them to Lance, and said, "I want you to go to Shinyanga with the truck and load these animals for Jodi's barnyard that they want in Mwanza."

"With Jodi?"

"With Jodi."

Lance sighed, walked back to Jodi, and said, "Come on."

They began to walk to the cattle transport in the back of the tents, and Jodi began to skip with joy toward the pursuit they were about to set out to complete.

*****

As they traveled southwest to their designation point, Jodi said, "This will give the children an opportunity for some exposure to wildlife up close and enjoy it. The variety they'll have to choose from will be exciting."

Lance remained silent and undistracted as he watched the road.

Jodi said, "If we don't find all the animals in Shinyanga, we could go to Tobora and pick the remaining ones there."

Lance objected and said, "Tobora?" They each locked their gaze on the other. He said, "We could have them caged and placed on a cargo plane in Tobora for a more reasonable price."

Jodi hesitated and then sarcastically said, "If anyone told you an aspirin bottle couldn't be opened by you, they should have necessarily informed you because there's a lot more where that came from."

"Yeah, but you couldn't find anyone who could understand your necessary better half."

Without any restraint, Jodi began to swat Lance on his shoulder firmly a number of times after she gave him a disgusted look.

In an hour, Lance backed the truck up after arriving at their destination and, with Jodi's help, loaded some young game animals onto the truck.

She leapt with excitement after they were finished and said, "They're beautiful!"

Lance said, "Yup."

They helped other farmers, wildlife reserves, and others by loading their cattle transport until the last one was on their truck. Then Jodi and Lance headed for Mwanza. After an hour and fifteen minutes, they reached her wildlife closure, which had a fenced area outside her mission's grounds. The cattle transport was backed up approximately three feet from the fenced area.

Lance said, "I left your fence unscathed."

"I would have put it beyond you," mentioned Jodi.

They stepped out of the truck and unloaded each of the animals by hand. Once the animals were off the truck, Jodi whispered praises to God, to herself, and thanked Lance for his involvement. Lance closed the end gate, leaned against the fenced area's gate, and noticed something.

"You're missing something. The zebra and wildebeest go together better with another candidate, a kudu." Lance asked if she would like to trail along.

Jodi accepted, and they drove a quarter of a mile to another house.

Jodi and Lance stopped and stepped out of the truck. Then they walked to the front door of a house, and Lance knocked on the door.

Jodi said, "How do you know they have a kudu?"

Lance made banter and said, "You can pick up a hint of their scent."

The owner of the house opened the front door, and Lance began to speak Swahili to the man.

The man said, "I know how to speak English."

Lance asked him again, but in English, "Do you have a kudu?"

"Yes, I do."

"Is it a young one?"

"Yes."

"Would you like to sell it?"

The man pondered and said, "Seventy-five dollars."

Lance took the money out of his wallet and gave it to the man. Lance and Jodi gave thanks to the man, and he led them to the kudu in the backyard. After they examined its health, Lance led it to the fence, picked it up, placed it on the other side, and Jodi loaded it on the truck. They drove it to Jodi's fenced area and incorporated it with the rest of the animals.

Lance said, "Well, there you have it. Your own closest version of a barnyard for exotic animals."

"I appreciate you going out of the way to transport them here for us."

Lance nodded and said, "Now that every bone in my body is fused together correctly after you broke each one to get me to do it, I'll be looking forward to the next time you'll have something for me to do." Lance got in the truck and said, "If you ever get bigger animals, you'll have to consult the zoo about it."

"I'll have the children round them up and transport them to your reserve."

"Okay. Niles is probably waiting for me back at the conservation camp. I'll see you later."

"Bye."

"Bye."

*****

It was tranquil at dusk on the conservation camp. While he watched an old cinema movie on his television set, Lance sat on his bed in his tent. He cheered on the battle between the cinema monsters while he waited for his favorite movie character to champion his victory. Niles walked into his tent.

"There are three new mothers expecting who will be on the reserve: two elephants and a leopard."

"Yeah."

"Aren't you excited? Take a look at the hormonal analysis results."

Lance looked at the results. "Niles, those are awful test results. The color is off."

Niles evaluated them from different angles and said, "Oh."

After a few moments, Lance became distracted by a smell inside his tent. He meandered around in his tent to locate the smell, but he couldn't find the source. He stuck his head outside his tent, picked up the scent, and followed it. After he followed the aroma to a vent in the back of Mason's tent, it left him in shock as he walked to the front of the tent. He opened the tent and walked inside. Lance saw Mason eating pizza momentarily before he hid it behind his back.

Lance demanded an answer from Mason and said, "What's behind your back?"

"Something."

Lance coyly approached Mason and said, "That's not just an ordinary pizza you bought at the marketplace. You received it by special shipment outside the country. You baked it and are eating it."

Mason rebuffed him as he said, "No."

"You could have reserved a whole pizza for me, but you dismissed the idea."

"It was too late before it crossed my mind. What do you want from me?"

Lance left an impression on Mason to take him likely and said, "Two slices."

Mason gave him a plate with two slices, and Lance victoriously returned to his tent with anticipation.

It was merely seconds after Lance returned to his tent. Niles peeked inside and said, "Where did you get the popcorn?"

"Upper right-hand shelf in the cabinet under the open canopy rotunda." Leaving Lance to his cinema presentation, Niles left to get popcorn from the cabinet.

*****

A week passed before Jodi visited the conservation camp again. She approached Niles beneath the open canopy rotunda and emphasized the need for help on proper supplements, the right feed, the proper vaccinations, and further treatment of her new wildlife animals. They walked in the direction of the Jeep and met Lance on the way. Niles informed Lance that Jodi required help to prepare her for the proper care of her wildlife animals.

"Really!" said Lance in a demeanor that took them off guard, leaving the impression that he may have been already busy.

"We need procedural understanding in full before any visitors may be exposed to the animals," said Jodi in a gentle way.

"Exposed?"

"Yes," said Jodi.

Then Lance stressed, "You mean they could break down with any sickness, suspect to terminal illness?"

Jodi picked up on Lance's confrontational manner and said, "What's your point?"

"It means people might break down with something dangerous. They'll have to be given extenuating care and continual treatment right from the start of a mere transfusion!"

"Didn't I say that? Why don't you talk to me about biological science rather than medicine? Then you won't get yourself into a fluster about a syringe shot!"

"Really?"

Niles said, "I had my share of this in the sciences and college," and walked away.

Lance said, "Well, maybe we should induce your staff into conservation science as opposed to medicine due to the fact that their sport-coats are hung wrong because they're not color-coordinated with their hangers in the closet!"

"Are you proposing colored sprinkles be coated over textbooks, just so you might learn the fine art of becoming a doctor because you're hemorrhaged during a football game's forward lateral in the fourth quarter?"

"Yeah!"

Jodi cocked her head back and vied against him as they glared at one another quietly for a few moments.

"Do you think a man like you could penetrate the surface of the medical profession? You already have a difficult time scaling a bluff with your mountain gear."

Lance raised his eyebrows and showed an appalled look on his face. "I have nothing to show forth when you're off wondering what it's like switching lives with someone else just to get the heads up on another person's mind…as a woman!" said Lance.

"Whatever makes *you* happiest in *our* relationship!"

"I've held up my end of the bargain!"

Jodi rested her hands on her hips as she pranced over to Lance. She stood quiet as she looked at him straight in the eyes. It's a mystery how they inevitably reached the Jeep parked in the back, but it's where they ended up. But they began to hash out where they left off in their debate with each other by silently debating the debate itself.

"Don't even discuss where the pieces fall when it comes to you living in a hut because I'm not even going to discuss those terms with you! You haven't even come to terms with casual clothes dress for men!" stressed Jodi to amuse herself as they squatted on the passenger's side of the Jeep.

"You'll find nothing wrong with the finer qualities of thatch to keep you from overhead marauders and unwanted monsoons! You'll also find everything right with my threads, which wonderfully reveal the silver lining in every one of your clouds!" said Lance with the use of banter.

Being appalled by his rhetoric, Jodi said, "So you're going to just keep on swinging like a fulcrum, aren't you?"

"Well, whenever you tend to flip a scouring pad, darling, it works counterproductively both ways."

Having her share of outrage and dismay, Jodi was fed up and had enough.

Then she said, "Oh yeah," and Jodi rose to her feet after Lance, pulled a handheld confetti cannon out of her back pocket while moving closer, released the pieces, and caused them to surge into the air around them. Lance quickly flinched from the burst after she tackled him.

Moments later, Niles returned from the open canopy tent and searched for both of them with vaccinations and a clipboard to administer to Jodi's animals as he came toward the Jeep.

Niles continued staring at his vaccination chart and said, without putting the pieces of the puzzle together, "Lance, these are the vaccinations that you need to administer to Jodi's animals." By simply supposing that Lance was somewhere around the Jeep, Niles addressed him while he was preoccupied by Jodi's company and party gag. After he rose to his feet with his outback hat tilted back, he was preoccupied with the removal of confetti off his clothing.

Lance surprisingly had a total change of heart concerning following through with all the duties he needed to perform on the animals. He said humbly while breathing deeply, "I'll get on it right away," and walked away.

Seconds later, Jodi stood up and silently walked away inconspicuously as well.

Jodi and Lance jumped into the Jeep and drove to her fenced area and cared for the needs of her animals.

*****

Lance met with Niles the following night beneath the open canopy rotunda.

Lance said, "I want to stress the importance of this voucher, which indicates the location of Charles and where exactly he's going to poach."

"I'll place it under scrutiny," said Niles.

"You haven't even determined exactly when and how you're going to approach this, have you?"

"A clear picture will be painted if and when we converge on Charles at any time."

"I dare you to accept the challenge and sink yourself into these coordinates, carry the baton, and detain Charles and his men."

As Niles busied himself with duties to perform, Lance stared at him for a few moments.

"You can't do it, can you?" said Lance.

Niles walked away, but Lance followed him.

Niles led Lance to his tent as Lance said, "You won't do it, will you?"

Niles continued to remain silent and walked inside his tent while Lance waited near the mesh entry.

A few moments later, Niles stepped out of the tent and frustratingly said, "All right!" and he snapped Lance's papers out of his hand and returned to his tent.

Lance grinned and walked away.

*****

As the Hummer H1 was loaded with an arsenal of weapons, the three wildlife conservationists prepared for the engagement through the designated points on the papers. They departed for the location, which took them two hours to reach. They parked behind a ridge overlooking the camp.

After Lance and Mason climbed out of the Hummer, they stooped close to the edge between two *Combretum imberbe* trees and surveyed the area. They saw large pitched tents and pavilions erected on the savanna.

A small trace of human activity began to stir among the tents. Lance removed his binoculars from the holder on his belt and assessed who the people were. He investigated and identified them to be poachers. They both agreed to a closer estimation.

Mason joined them and lay between them. Then he caught Lance with a wide sarcastic grin as he glared at Niles. Niles turned to his left and realized Lance was telling him, "I told you so," through the grin and became very incensed. He understood his timing was off and that he lacked all the apparent facts to take action. He thought maybe he should value the input of other people.

Lance continued to audaciously bare his grin, which only caused Niles to become more incensed. So he reached out and pushed Lance's face away and began to mumble under his breath.

They returned their concentration on the camp. Lance made a quick trip to the Hummer, placed his shotgun scabbard on with his four-barrel shotgun, and joined the men.

Lance took the initiative to make his descent and head into the camp. As he approached a canopy, Lance pulled out his shotgun and cut a slit through the tent side wall. Inside, there were crates and poaching equipment. Lance examined the contents of the crates.

Lance was made aware of a parked Jeep outside and poured the contents of a fuel cannister across the Jeep and over the crates beyond the side wall. He lit the fuel with his lighter and abandoned the tent.

As Lance ran a stone's throw farther, he met up with Niles, armed with an assault rifle, and they penetrated the heart of the camp slowly and cautiously. After a good number of feet, Niles signaled to Lance to go left while he continued forward. Lance traveled for forty feet but found nothing, circled back, and met up with Niles again while he entered another canopy with side walls.

Inside were endless racks of wildlife skins preserved for the black market, evidence as part of an operation, which both of them needed to witness with their own eyes. They thumbed through as many skins as they could, leaving the tally to the local park rangers who would soon investigate. Lance reached a conclusion, due to the recent curing of the skins, that there must be a pen full of animals to be located at the hunting camp. Lance exited the tent and began to search for a wildlife pen.

Lance circled around tents the alternate direction and took a chunk of distance out of all the outer boundary of the far side of the camp. There he discovered a wildlife pen full of all kinds of species. Before he could close in on it, he spotted an armed man walking toward a cattle transport while a truck backed up close to the pen's chute.

Lance saw that he had a short interval for a window in time. Quickly, the armed man who approached the chute was shot by Lance after the poacher turned in his direction. Then he closed in on the cab of the truck and opened the door because he didn't want to take chances. The driver leapt from inside toward Lance, but he stepped out of the way in what seemed like record time. As the driver struggled to get back on his feet, Lance proceeded to deliver blows with the butt of his shotgun continually until the driver wasn't coherent.

A couple of poachers approached in the direction that Lance reached the pen. So he circled the truck and hid beneath the partial enclosure on the chute. The men searched for the origin of the gunshot. They, however, were unable to find anyone in that part of the hunting camp. So they walked back into the central part of it.

Lance crawled out from beneath the chute and walked to the corral gate, which opened the pen.

All the wildlife was let loose through the entrance gate by Lance. A few of the stragglers were driven out by Lance, and then he stood still for a brief moment.

Shots were fired near him by an assault rifle and ricocheted off a few of the gates' bars of the corral. He ran to the right and then to the left to evade shrapnel until he finally was able to return through the entrance. A Jeep of poachers appeared from behind the camp and attempted to intercept Lance.

The Hummer, driven by Mason, headed them off as he used artillery fire to confront the poacher's siege against them. As Mason utilized the weapon that he brandished, the poachers assailed him with a mounted machine gun on the back of their Jeep, causing Mason to cease fire and take cover at the driver's wheel. After their ammunition ceased, due to a need to reload, Mason saw his opportunity and grabbed a missile launcher in the back of the Jeep. He fixed his sights on the Jeep, fired, and made an impact on the Jeep with an explosion that left the occupants rendered helpless. Mason drove around into the camp to combat any further poachers.

Niles walked to the front of the canopy and was confronted by an armed poacher who crept around the corner. He fired upon Niles and left him grazed in the upper right chest area in the clavicular head, pectoralis major muscle. Niles fired back and fatally struck the poacher in the forehead. He diagonally sprinted to another tent after he spotted two armed poachers who approached the front of the tent where Niles was shot.

Behind Lance, two poachers crept upon him, but he fired upon them before they were given an opportunity.

A very tall Sukuma man slowly approached Lance from behind, then trapped and seized him unexpectedly with his powerful hand. Lance's shotgun was clutched, and the Sukuma man pushed him against the firm, supported, and stable wall of the tent backed by wood panels.

They began to wrestle for the shotgun while the Sukuman stood perfectly still as Lance tried to wrench his firearm from the poacher. The firearm remained under manipulation as the poacher turned it toward the ground and then in another direction. With both hands gripped on the shotgun, Lance frustratingly tried to tug it away and out of the hands of the poacher. As Lance saw it turn upward, he looked above and saw an electrical cable hanging between poles. He mustered just enough strength to maneuver the shotgun toward the cable and fought to fire his shotgun. The cable was severed, dropped, and fell on the Sukuman's scalp.

Enough time was relinquished for the poacher to be slightly electrocuted prior to the cable falling to the ground. Lance evaded any infringement by avoiding all contact in good time. The scorched and marred Sukuman collapsed backward on the ground in an unnerved stunned state. The cable was picked up by Lance, and he laid the severed end of the cable on the Sukuman's chest to bring an end to him. Lance continued farther into the camp.

Niles passed through the tent's opening and was surprised to find Charles and a few businessmen in a gang, making transactions for skins and carcass meat.

Charles said, "I don't stand to lose anything unmitigated by your company, Niles. What brought you out here while you were on such a great journey?"

"Your keen interest in the trafficking of wildlife as well as your taste in a number of things, such as food and how you consume toads during a meal!"

"You arrived here because of my interest in toads? That surprises me, Niles."

The businessmen heard shotgun fire outside the tent.

One gang member said, "We didn't want visitors."

"No matter, they don't need to be here anyway," said Charles.

The poachers drew their pistols and fired at Niles, but he ran into an open path between crates off to his left side and then to his right and then took cover. Crates became lined with bullets, and wood pieces flew in the air. It carried on as the three poachers excused themselves out the front opening.

After a few seconds, Charles stuck his head through the opening of the tent and threw a grenade into the open path between the crates. Then he quickly made his absence. The explosion went off, and it triggered the upper level of the crates, lifting them from those set on the lower level. A few collapsed into the open path and pinned Niles down below. Charles and the men departed the camp in their own Jeeps.

Through exerting great inertia, Niles managed to work himself free after several minutes and crawled to the top from the dark accumulation of broken crates and wood. He left the tent and began to search for any other trace of poachers in his location, but after several minutes, he found nobody.

Lance ran around the back corner of a tent on the outside of the camp near the location where they began and came across a stream partially winding on the side of the camp. After he looked over his shoulder, he spotted two poachers following him around the back corner of the tent.

Lowering himself into the stream, he immersed himself completely while his shotgun rested on the bank. The men dismissed the stream and walked toward the front of the tent. Lance's left arm reached for his shotgun, and he sat up out of the stream. He hurled the shotgun at one poacher's head, struck it, and returned beneath the water.

The other poacher returned to the point where both poachers cornered the tent beside the stream and looked around for anything suspicious. As he looked down into the water, a surprise took him completely as something flung out of the water. But before he could identify the object, he didn't realize it would injure him. He realized it was slender and long, but its sharp edge sank in him only after it was too late. The blade of a machete lodged in his chest and accrued a deep wound. The poacher collapsed to the ground.

Lance rose out of the stream and retrieved his machete out of the poacher's upper body and then his shotgun. The tent where business was forged by the three poachers is where Lance found Niles. Lance sorted through the paperwork to find any existing leads in the form of documentation, body parts of animals, medicines made from poaching, and veterinarian drugs that immobilized hunted animals.

"Come on," said Lance.

They walked to the wildlife corral where Mason waited for further involvement of any culprits as well as the two other conservationists who may have been wrapping matters pursuing poachers. After Lance climbed into the truck, which was backed up to the chute, he removed all the paperwork from the glove compartment and the sun visor. Then he climbed out, and the two men got into the Hummer, and Lance gave Niles the paperwork. They remained near the truck, called the park rangers to investigate the camp, and waited for their arrival.

*****

A couple of days passed by. Jodi had made preparations to offer and instruct for an hour as a missionary to little children outside Mwanza. They began arriving in her shanty after a few hours from the grade school teacher's class early in the morning. Little wooden chairs sat in the teaching room with traces of learning tools, and instruments were found throughout the shelter as they took their seats. Jodi took her place on a barstool at the front of the shelter while a full group of children attended with close attention. The number that showed was common on a routine basis.

She began to speak about the suffering of the Israelites at the hands of Pharaoh. She explained how Moses would not associate himself as a son of Pharaoh's daughter and exposed himself as one counted to be afflicted by suffering. In addition, she recalled how Moses rose up one day to settle a dispute between an Israelite and an Egyptian and slew a man as a result. She explained how he retreated to the desert and lived with the Midianites for forty some years. This led up to the time when he encountered God in the wilderness and was influenced to change before the burning bush.

At this point, Lance walked through the opening of the shanty and joined the Bible study.

Her enthusiasm soared after she saw him join the study.

She continued to discuss how Moses could confidently approach Pharaoh with different miracles as they were shown against him, one after another.

Lance took a seat at the back of the room, and children immediately chose to sit on his lap and around him. He refrained temporarily to rest his hands on them, but then he lightened up. The children rested their heads on his shoulders, and they continued to listen to Jodi.

*****

At the end of the hour, the children were free to visit the wildlife attraction of small animals with supervision.

Jodi and Lance walked a short distance from the fenced area beneath a row of trees to the middle and sat on a log.

"If there's one line you could share with a woman, what would it be?" asked Jodi.

"I would say you do remarkably well with captivating an audience of children and have a tendency to reach out to their sensitive hearts. I would also say you have the native tribal counselors wandering if you don't marshal a friend in far too many acquaintances, such as children, young wildlife, driver ants, mongoose, caracal, kingfisher…koala bear, kangaroo."

Jodi nudged his shoulder. "You'll be in full anticipation, looking for the inside scoop on how I turn trade on commodity upside down in South Africa," she said.

"I guess I need to look into this feat. They still have plenty of land to put a metal detector to use in the United States. Nevertheless, you're coming up with gemstones alone in Africa. You have worked your landowner over for a gemstone detector, haven't you?"

"I might have an entire store, storehouse, or storage that you wouldn't argue to choose from."

"You've been doing far too much geographical surveying by hang gliding…we'll have to keep an eye on you."

"Who could you possibly find to complete that task?"

"Mason."

"Mason?"

"He's the only qualified man I know who's distributed decorative price tags in the color of flags at the marketplace. It'll come as a surprise to you. He gets the job done."

"Should I be more surprised with both of your peculiar habits?"

"Both! Be afraid…be very afraid!"

"I won't take the shining moon for granted on any river ever again."

"Not any bridge?"

"Not even any bridge."

A four-year-old Sukuma girl brought a baby springbok to Jodi and Lance. Her eyes were opened wide in astonishment by holding a baby savanna animal in her arms. She offered the springbok to Jodi and Lance so they would hold it. Jodi took it into her arms while the young girl sat in the middle of them, and they all petted the springbok.

*****

After a number of days, Jodi and Lance drove the Jeep to a lush location a good distance from the school near her shanty. They drove to a secluded location and got off the Jeep. A row of tall trees stood planted near an embankment, which happened to be where they walked. A playful debate played out between them as they approached the bank.

Lance said, "No, I merely said it looked like a cross between a black and a blue impala. I didn't imply they crossbred them."

"You know 'ugly' is what you wanted to say."

"Unsightly. Ghastly."

They've reached the ridge which happened to be a lookout over a wide steady river. Several moments passed by while they looked at the view. Both of them exchanged glances just to see how much each was enjoying the rich foliage and brush.

Suddenly, the large mass of earth collapsed beneath them, and they plummeted down the side of the bank and into the water. During the fall, Lance caught Jodi's hands, and they fell into a cluster of hanging vines. He helped hold her up while his other hand held the vine. With her feet, she anchored herself to a vine.

He encouraged her to start climbing. In the process, she planted her feet on Lance's shoulders and head for support as if it were totally natural to do so. He groaned, shuffled, and turned as she climbed over him.

"Geesh," he said to himself. Then he took hold of the vine farther up, but the strength of the vine wouldn't back his weight. It snapped, and he fell into the river below.

As he made his bearings beneath the water, a congregation of alligators approached him. Once they reached in close approximation of him, he unsheathed his machete.

Having been made aware of the danger below, Jodi saw the reptiles closing in on Lance and cried out, "Lance!"

With all the effort he could muster, Lance swam quickly beneath the closest gator and thrust the machete through its neck.

Another alligator swam directly toward him. He drew his shotgun out of the scabbard and fired upon the gator to render it helpless.

He didn't hesitate to swim to the steep bank to leap out of the water and catch a vine. Several other gators pressed in on him to take close action. After he rose out of the water, his body hunkered upside down as he clung to the vine and held his hat. An undetected gator lunged out of the water and snapped at him. His leg fixed as the target remained amiss by the gator's attempt as Lance did everything to avoid it.

The snap captured both Jodi and Lance's attention, so he wasted no time in climbing the series of vines hanging in front of him. When he returned his hat to his head, he scaled up the vines. Together, they made their ascent after Jodi determined that Lance was fine. After they reached the top, both of them didn't hold back from making ground inward into the land and separated themselves from any possible further collapsing ridge. Once they were in close proximity of the Jeep, they collapsed to the ground, embraced one another, and rested.

*****

In the late evening during a thunderstorm, Lance stepped out of an unoccupied tent and walked around it toward the open canopy tent. Several feet from the tent, he encountered Jodi in the rain.

He nodded his head slightly and said, "Follow me." He led her back to the tent, and they entered it. As they stood inside, she saw a mat sprawled across the ground. Lance took the lead to lie down, face up, and then persuaded her to lie down next to him. She hesitantly waited a few seconds and then lay down.

Once she did, she said quietly, "What?"

"Watch."

She looked up at a red plastic film placed on a cut out section with a plastic transparent film in the roof of the tent, which made it visible outside the tent. Out of the blue, a flash of discharged lightning flashed across the sky. Jodi's eyes lit up, and she was filled in wonderment over the breaking red flash throughout the film and the roof of the tent. They continued to watch the succession of lightning strikes and different types, which lit up the African sky. Jodi asked Lance to hold her hand, and he followed through with her request.

After an hour passed, Lance asked Jodi if she'd like to help him change the plastic color film on the tent above. She said she would be happy to. The film color was changed to a variety of colors blended together in a plastic film. Once they slid it in place over the clear outer film, they laid back again and watched the thunderstorm. They observed the different values found in the color scheme and enjoyed similarities and differences found in the plastic film sheet.

*****

The next day, beyond all the cages and enclosures, Mason drove his Jeep to the solar-powered installations for the camp as well as the diesel-powered backup generator where he refueled and checked all its functions for proper service.

While Mason examined the power sources, he glanced to his right and saw one of the capuchin monkeys staring at a smooth beautifully colored stone outside his monkey sanctuary. When Mason decided to slowly grasp it, he picked it up and placed it and a few nuts inside the sanctuary on the ground before the capuchin monkey. Mason closed the entrance to the hold and watched its behavior. It sat and stared at the stone and refused to do nothing. Then Mason backed up, and the monkey quickly closed in on the stone and nuts to confiscate them with its hands en route to a large flat rock. It was there he began to break and piece apart the nuts with the use of the stone and the rock beneath him. All the other energetic monkeys looked upon it with no trepidation in their usual misgivings.

Mason made a mental note to look in on the particular capuchin with character.

Next, Mason double-checked all the lighting found in the enclosed tents for the animals, which required a light source in their cages, as well as the large canopy tents themselves. Before he ended his chores, an assortment of small animals that were docile enough to accompany him while they watched any change of lighting sat on his shoulders. The simple view from above was embraced by the animals as they lapped up the luxury.

*****

During the evening at the conservation camp, nearly everyone had fallen asleep in their tents. After entering into Lance's tent and shaking him abruptly, Niles attempted to see to it that he was thoroughly awake. Lance made a meager attempt to wake up.

Niles shook him even harder and said, "Lance…Lance!" He did everything he could to wake him up.

Then Lance gave him a detestable look because someone tried to wake him up.

"There's something I need to show you," said Niles in excitement.

After simply yawning half awake, Lance lay back down in his cot, but Niles pulled him up and out of the cot and led him outside the tent. As he bobbed up and down and sluggishly followed him, Niles supported him outside the tent.

"Lance, the man-eating lion that has been recognized over the past months by park rangers is here tonight!"

Lance opened his eyes wide and became very disgusted with Niles on account of the news, unaware if Niles was playing a prank.

Niles turned Lance's head into the direction of the lion, which was standing a short distance to the left of the tent.

Niles said, "It's the man-eating lion!"

"How do you know it's the right lion?"

"Because I identified its whisker spots; it's 148!"

Lance held out his hand all because he expected Niles to be carrying a side profile photo. Niles gave him the profile.

"Wait here," said Lance.

He returned inside his tent and brought a flashlight and his shotgun.

After he shone the flashlight on the lion's mouth, he said, "You're right—that's 148!"

Niles said, "Now you might have one chance to shoot him, so hit him. Are you awake enough to shoot him?"

"You'd better hope I don't hit the tree planted beside him or you'll be detailing cars with whatever remains are part of you for the rest of your life!"

Niles gazed at him, flustered.

Lance returned the sentiment and said, "Don't fret. I might graze him, and then he'll hunt you down by your footsteps or based on a wound from a wandering shot. Show some sympathy."

They set their sights on the lion, and Niles said, "Get ready!"

"How did he pass beyond the barrier? What did you do?"

"Absolutely nothing!"

He zeroed the shotgun in to pinpoint his target.

"This should only take a second."

Lance fired the shotgun and missed the lion. As it roared and led a scampering charge, the lion stormed and cut to the chase.

"Shoot him! Shoot him!" shouted Niles.

"Whoa! Whoa!" shouted Lance.

At the last moment, prior to becoming maimed, he fired his shotgun one more time. The shot struck the lion in the head as it leapt toward Lance.

As a result, the jaw of the lion was left clinched harmlessly around Lance's face, and his entire body was buried beneath the weight of the lion.

"Gross—I'm going back to bed, and the next time, you can handle the man-eating lion because you won't build an appropriate fence around the conservation camp!"

"Oh, what's the matter? Don't you believe in the security of a thatch hut built on stilts?"

"Sure, if you would build a fence around it, yeah!"

Niles helped Lance out from beneath the dead lion.

*****

Lance sat beneath one of the trees near the conservation camp the next morning. In his hands, he held a dik-dik as he wound a bandage around the dik-dik's back leg for a hairline fracture. Jodi and a teen Sukuma girl joined him.

"I'll have him wrapped up for you, and then you can take him back to the cage area if you would like," said Lance to the Sukuma girl.

"How do you know there aren't more of the same in his condition?" asked Jodi.

"They capture what they find, but this one was brought to us."

Then the Sukuma girl changed the subject and asked, "How can I improve myself if I take subjects that don't help me or that I need in school?"

After he heard the question, Lance didn't mention anything for a brief moment.

"Good question. Do you have parents who live by a nonflexible iron fist behavior as opposed to a young girl who has parents that are amenable and acquiescent?" said Lance.

She didn't immediately understand what he had just asked her.

"Let me put it to you this way: do they Lord themselves over you?"

"No."

"Good...will they cooperate with you?"

"Yes."

Jodi explained, "Okay, you can talk to parents about self-directed homeschooling, and if you object or believe your parents are guiding and directing you the wrong way, you could have a discussion with them and others about it. If you attended school, you could take college courses that apply now to your interests and vocations. You don't need to study here. You can study anywhere in the world you'd like."

Lance said, "Then you won't be one of many numbered who were a casualty in a failed search, initial interest, and experience in your endeavor for your vocations. You can optimistically enroll and join a dorm with fellow students if you want to further your education, take pride in parents who backed and supported you, and participate in further expanding your capability to do what's possible in the world by developing your knowledge. You can also anticipate sharing your life with other ladies and men among the student body, discuss the important matters that are trivial to others"—he looked over at Jodi sarcastically—"and even blaze a trail of glory, discussing how much cosmetics disappoint you."

"Are you saying I'm displeased with my makeup or perhaps even wearing too much makeup?" said Jodi, who confronted Lance for what he said and sportively leaned over and, cavorting, tussled with Lance's arm.

Lance tried to fend Jodi off while he held the young wildlife animal in his hand at the same time.

"Careful, you're going to crush the dik-dik," said Lance lightheartedly.

"You need to put the dik-dik down. That's what you need to do."

The young girl simply leaned back in the middle of their banter and giggled out loud because of Jodi and Lance's prodding one another.

*****

Late that evening, Lance and Jodi continued trifling and bantered with one another about diminutive matters.

Then Jodi intentionally physically sparred Lance harmlessly as she leapt by surprise on his back.

"Oh my!" said Lance.

Jodi wound her legs around his chest and neck and fixed her arms around his shoulders. Since Lance saw exactly to what extent Jodi carried herself, he decided to take it upon himself to bite her in the leg.

Jodi bellowed out with a shout and said, "You just bit me!" while she resorted to strengthen her tension with her grip.

Lance said to her with subtlety, "Get off my back."

"No!"

Lance repeated himself, but she said nothing.

Lance resolved by saying, "All right," and began to walk to an enclosed canopy tent. Lance entered, walked to a cage, and opened its door. A grown iguana was taken out and placed on Jodi's head. Jodi began to let out a shrilly scream as a result of Lance's new introduction to her head. She climbed off Lance and ran outside the canopy opening on the other side.

In a slow stride, Lance walked across the inside of the tent and outside to the grounds with a grin on his face.

She returned with the full realization of his grin and faced him with more ferocity. Then he rested his hands on her shoulder and gave her a look of pity.

In a split decision, Lance ran from her toward the bell tents. She immediately began her pursuit of him while she growled and bolted after him.

*****

Mason drove out on the savanna in the Jeep and tracked a baby gazelle as it strode in the tall grass. He stopped a reasonable distance, jumped out of the Jeep with a lasso, and approached the gazelle with stealth in the tall grass.

As he tried to avoid making unnecessary noise, it did next to no good because he was detected by the gazelle as it stared at him in the grass.

So he waited carefully for the unsteady impala to gradually turn around and linger off with undetected attention.

After the gazelle took the bait, Mason quietly tossed the lasso and looped it around its neck. Mason allowed only a little lapse of time for the gazelle to wrestle with the lasso. A cover necessary for the eyes calmed it down gradually, and it opened a window of opportunity for Mason to administer veterinarian medicine. Once the completion of the treatment was made, the gazelle was let loose again.

After Mason returned to the Jeep and placed the medical equipment and supplies in their proper place, he grabbed a pistol and broke out his lunch pail. Then he sat in the grass behind the Jeep and began to eat his bologna sandwich.

After a couple of bites, the very gazelle that he treated approached the sandwich and sniffed the scent. The gazelle unhesitatingly tried to take a few bites, but Mason held his hand away and denied the gazelle an opportunity.

"No, you're given the privilege of eating the gritty, tasty stuff," and he pulled a handful of grass from its roots and fed the gazelle. "How come everyone wants my food? First, Lance wants my pizza, and then a gazelle hones in on my bologna sandwich." After a few bites of grass, the gazelle aimlessly wandered off.

*****

As he stood in the midst of the bell tents, Lance waved a red flag in the wind.

Jodi approached Lance and questioned his premise, "Why are you waving a red flag?"

"Because our camp hasn't been entirely taken yet."

"Oh, and are you certain you're not using the wrong flag? Maybe you want to call your attention to the white flag."

"It hasn't reached its zenith yet."

Jodi wrestled the flag out of his hand humorously in frustration, threw it to the ground, and chased him again. Obviously, she reached a decision in her mind that Lance was simply pranking her for no reason at all whatsoever.

*****

As he traveled along the border of Kenya, Mason stopped beside a fenced-off area to that country. He took an assault rifle from the Jeep and approached the fence. He scaled the chain-link fence up and over and crouched close to the ground as he crept forward. The area was under his scrupulous investigation as he surveyed it. Once he reached a tall tuft of grass, it was his intention to remain there patiently.

Mason looked around for any poachers participating in any activity on the open range. As he looked closer, two poachers were currently in pursuit of a kill within their reach. Mason was unable to see exactly what they'd fixed their eyes on a number of meters away.

Minutes later, he had the confidence to conclude that a white rhino was in the thick brush. Several minutes more were used to identify any more species, and the final conclusion was two more white rhinos at the location. The apparent conduct of the poachers was placed under close scrutiny. The poachers waited for a viable opportunity to slay the white rhinos if they could close in on them.

They refused to waste time any longer and raised their rifles.

Rising to his feet, Mason secured his crosshairs on them and fired his rifle. He shot and snagged the leg of one poacher, and he fell to the ground. The remaining poacher attempted to give assistance momentarily to his wounded partner but ended up abandoning him. He ran to his Jeep and made an attempt to hightail it out of town by starting the engine.

Another shot rang out, and Mason struck the last poacher in the leg through the driver's door and left him startled with incapacity. As he tried to free himself from immobility, the two rhinos the poachers were pursuing spotted him and charged his Jeep. They lifted the left wheels off the ground, lunged it sideways, and toppled it on the ground with the driver still in the driver's seat. Mason made certain to drop to the ground immediately.

Suddenly, someone touched Mason's shoulder, and it filled him with strong fright. He turned immediately to discover Niles lying next to him.

"What are you doing?" said Mason.

"You do realize you're doing conservation work across the border."

"I know...but there's killing in the wild taking place."

"All right...let's try to round them up."

Thrashed and pierced by the thrusts of the white rhino's horns, the pair was still making substantial damage to the truck. Crying and yelling out loud, the poacher beneath the Jeep was frightened with intense fear. The remaining poacher hoped he would remain undetected while he lay in cover.

Mason rapidly sprinted near the rhino that was butting its head in the rear of the passenger door, and then the rhino charged after him.

Losing its interest from multiple crashes and butts with its snout against the Jeep, the hesitant remaining rhino looked to its side and eyed the poacher in the grass a few times. Then its attention was drawn to his scent, and it turned to the poacher in the grass. One foot after another, the rhino slowly began to advance toward the frightened poacher. Then the rhino began to pick up speed, but Niles stepped between them momentarily to draw the creature off guard. As a result, Niles led the charging rhino in an alternate direction similar to Mason.

Critical distance fell between Mason and his rhino; however, the stride had growth as he picked up the pace. After a number of meters, Mason looked behind him to see the distance he had between the rhino and himself. Mason collapsed, however, into an empty brook before he had the opportunity to look in front of him. As Mason tried to writhe around to a position where he could step up, the rhino toppled down into the ditch and made the furious attempt to stave Mason in close approximation. Mason tried everything he could to avoid being gored by the rhino. Trying to evade the long horn of the rhino, Mason scrambled and shuffled to his feet and at times on his knees.

Niles put some necessary serious distance between him and the rhino because the gap left between the rhino and himself was serious. He made a turn over a long distance toward the fence and quickly headed for a post as part of the fence. His hands scaled the wire mesh and post immediately, one hand over another, to the top of the fence. The rhino closed the gap quickly and abruptly presented itself strongly as a dominant presence to be reckoned with. Its eyes and scent-gathering nose fixed on Niles as he remained critically out of reach on top of the post but still presented a hazard to himself in his situation.

The brook narrowed for the rhino. Once Mason could permanently keep his feet on the ground and could break into a narrower path, he could anticipate having left the rhino behind and any susceptible harm for him.

The rhino that cornered Niles reached the decision that there were better circumstances to tend to and abandoned him on the fence. Niles gradually descended from the fence and returned to the Jeep where he joined Mason.

*****

Back at the open canopy tent, the pant legs of Mason were lifted up where both Niles and Mason saw the remainder of existing red marks by the rhino that successfully rubbed up against Mason. So they treated any marks or cuts on Mason's legs. Contact was made with the local authorities to report the two poachers while the two conservationists held them until the lawbreakers could be taken into custody.

*****

The next day, beneath the open canopy tent, Jodi and Lance concentrated their efforts to play the card game, Slap Jack. Lance laid a card down and accidentally slapped it. Jodi laughed in a sinister way by egging him on while she collected the stack of cards. His eyelids squinted, and he questioned in his mind whether she was playing by the rules while picking up the stack. So he decided to check the instruction book and picked it up. She deliberately knocked the book out of his hands in objection to his action.

"Are you suffering from a broken gland?" he said.

"Well, if you need therapy because you don't know how to wield chopsticks, I wouldn't be looking for it in a medical book about glands." Glaring at Jodi with an agitated reaction, Lance remained speechless until he decided to continue playing along poised.

"Well, at least I don't get caught up falling into the intricately woven design of a strainer in the kitchen. And please tell us how you're going to redeem yourself for an overdue medical book with notes based entirely on takeout rather than actual existing medical material."

"Well, it's because boys like you try to muster enough courage to try to break themselves free from simply reading the table of contents."

"Well, my concentrated efforts aren't left fixed entirely on dozens of artificial sweetener packets being filed disorderly and being concerned which one to choose."

After being at the height of being provoked, Jodi crawled across the table and decided to kiss him because of the provocation.

They stopped briefly, and Lance said, "This carries a need for the both of us to avoid research." Then they kissed each other briefly.

Then Lance said, "And I won the card game."

*****

Later, beneath the open canopy tent, the teen Sukuma girl with a basket of food approached Mason. He looked at the kinds of food she carried in her basket.

"Oh no, this is the wrong food. You have Belladonna or death cherries, Sodom apples, and Sausage fruit from the Kigelia tree. You'll have to throw these out. They're very toxic. I'll help you find the right food. Let's go."

They drove away from the camp a good distance to a rather large lot located with abundant fruit and vegetables planted as an effort to grow produce.

"Whose lot is this?" said the Sukuma girl.

"It's a co-op joint effort between villagers, tribes, and us. You're welcome to choose anything you want."

She picked papaya, bananas, eggplant, tomatoes, spinach, and maize as a selection of food to fill her basket.

As they were enjoying the lot filled with produce, a Caucasian man approached the girl and said ruthlessly, "Why do you have a basket of our fruit and vegetables? This lot was meant for someone else."

Mason said, "We're part of the co-op that works with the people to grow it. You may even ask the women who work it with us."

Cackling wickedly, the obstinate man said, "I don't think you realize where your place should be."

"I believe you're mistaken."

"I'm afraid you have no other choice but to turn your basket over to me," and the man threatened by approaching Mason.

"Do you find anything wrong with the spot you were standing in? You can return to that spot." The man continued to advance, but he saw persistence and boldness in the eyes of Mason. He stopped and stepped back to the place where he was standing.

"We have a sense of giving and flexibility as you can clearly see."

A middle-aged Tanzanian woman approached the dispute and listened in on Mason.

"You're neither alive…and you can't live with others nor stand sight, vision, nor sharing."

As abruptly as she came, the Tanzanian woman started to reprimand the man in Swahili, and she pulled out a long thick stick hidden in her dress and began to beat him. Deeply alarmed by the beating, the man took flight but was unable to shake the Tanzanian woman for a duration and long distance. His stubbornness and obstinance resigned him to want to pick up his threats where he left off, but he had a difficult time shaking the Tanzanian woman.

"There, now you have the right food," said Mason as they climbed in the Jeep again and returned to the conservation camp.

*****

Jodi was preoccupied with equipment at the conservation camp as she fixed and cleaned it in front of a counter in an enclosed large tent. As he walked into the tent, Lance intentionally brushed up against and ran across the back of Jodi. She looked up, puzzled, while she was shuffled to the right against the counter. Lance broke free and stood beside her.

Then he said, "You're always getting in the way. It seems you're constantly in the wrong place. What are we going to do with you?"

Jodi showered a grimace on her face while she rested a hand on her hip.

"You simply take it upon yourself to wake the entire pride by brushing up against them and wiping your unsightly scent on them, don't you?" A second later, she said, "I don't even need a market to buy any fragrance when I'm granted a priceless antique bottle filled with the best imported perfume after I visited a foreign country from afar myself."

"You have a priceless laundry detergent vase, and you didn't tell me about it?" said Lance amusingly.

"As a man, you're so preoccupied with determining in your mind how anything could be made out to be junk that you've chucked it before you realized its value."

"You're not about to use it as a bottleneck that holds spaghetti noodles or a plant, are you?"

"Is it any different than every other kind of basin in your collection?"

Seconds later, Lance said, "You forgot to rinse your vase out with Clorox, didn't you?"

"It just stands to reason, just exactly what you use to bake that award-winning casserole."

*****

At the other end of the open canopy tent, the Sukuma girl began to walk in the midst of the bell tents. She spotted a stray young Jack Russell terrier dog and tried to catch it. As she chased the dog, Mason saw her between the tents. He decided to help her. As he circled the tents to head the dog off, they didn't seem to have any success. The dog would double back and slip by the girl.

Calling the girl's attention, he recommended to her that she stand still to see whether the dog would approach her.

The dog, who was out of sight, slowly began to walk around a tent and toward them. The Jack Russell terrier stopped and peered at her from a short distance.

Mason told the girl to draw him toward the open canopy tent. The dog slowly heeded and was drawn inside the tent. Under the tent, Mason looked for an empty dog dish among the cabinets. After Mason found one, he filled it with water and offered it to the dog. After the Jack Russell terrier slowly approached the dish, the dog lapped the water and allowed the girl to pet him.

"It is a stray after all, isn't it? It has no tag," she said.

"Yes."

"We have to turn it in to the animal shelter to provide an opportunity to be found by its rightful owner, right?"

"Right."

"If we turn it in now, we could claim it sooner if nobody showed up. He could stay here."

"True."

"Can we turn the dog in now?"

"Yes."

The next stop they made was the Mbwa Wa animal shelter in Tanzania.

*****

At night, Lance was seated on his cot, studying paperwork in his tent.

Jodi walked in and said, "I want to see you at your earliest convenience tonight."

Lance looked with a solemn face toward her, returned his eyes to his papers, and said, "You can find me by the brook on the south side."

She walked out of the tent and stopped out front to speak with Niles. They engaged in conversation for a few moments until Lance stepped out behind them and stood there, watching them.

Then Jodi gazed at Lance and said, "Lance seems to always play mind games."

Lance said, "Well, you will have to receive authorization to choose from any of the other company directives. Second, you'll have your kitchen dramatically altered by someone else. Concoct a new cocktail that passes criteria with someone else and the rest of the tribal neighborhood and find a remote watering hole that animals haven't contaminated to wash your and your husband's laundry."

"I don't have a husband!"

He lifted her arms up and placed a stack of paperwork in her hands and said, "Here's the paperwork. I hope the best for you." He walked away while she spent her time throwing the papers to the ground.

*****

Niles, Lance, and Mason traveled deep into the savanna. They stopped the Jeep and began to walk on foot. Lance and Mason headed in one direction for a short distance while Niles walked a considerable distance the opposite direction.

After he reached a lookout point on a ridge, he spotted a number of shining objects in the dirt below. He crawled down the ridge and picked up a few historical coins out of the dirt, which dated back a few centuries. Niles called Lance and Mason over his two-way radio to point out what he had found at his location.

The two other wildlife conservationists located Niles, and they studied the coins together. He pointed out the coins in the dirt left a trail to a shallow mound in the dirt. What crossed Niles's mind was the need for someone to fetch a few shovels in the Jeep. So Lance retrieved the shovels and, after he returned, they unearthed the mound.

After they dug a foot into the ground, they came across a hard surface. They dug around the find and pulled out what appeared to be a chest.

"We need to find a way to open the lock."

Mason's hand grabbed the lock, and he yanked on it, and the lock worked free.

Niles and Lance briefly glanced at Mason in shock and removed the lock.

Once the lid was swung open, numerous assortments of shiny gold coins lay inside the chest. The men concluded that whoever came across such gold from earlier civilizations wanted to plant it where it would be hidden from others. They questioned why they found it in the middle of Tanzania.

"This may have originated easily from the northeast or been brought here from the coast," said Niles.

"Mason, would you be the lookout while we dig deeper into the chest?"

"Yes."

While Mason stood on his feet and began to keep an eye on the surroundings, Niles removed his shirt, placed it on the ground, and they began to empty the chest on the shirt. A variety of gemstones, silver, and jewelry were found deeper in the heart of the chest.

"It's necessary to return to camp immediately so we can call an archaeologist to study its legitimacy and value. It's not safe out here with this in our hands."

*****

The next day, Lance drove the Jeep to the southeast of Shinyanga. He brought the Jeep to a stop because fuel ran low. After he climbed out and walked to the back of the Jeep, he lifted the reserve tank but found no fuel in it. He dropped the tank in the back of the Jeep and moaned to himself. Then off to his right, he saw a few impalas out on the savanna. A coalition of cheetahs not far away rested and sat upright and observed the impala.

Lance decided to tag one out of the cluster of cheetahs and took out his tranquilizer rifle and medical kit. After putting some distance between the Jeep and himself, he closed in on the cheetahs and lay down in the grass. He placed a dart into the chamber and aimed the rifle at a cheetah.

He shot the rifle and pegged one of the cheetahs in the cluster.

Lance spoke softly to himself and said, "Now as long as it doesn't venture far."

The cheetah jolted a few times but came to accept the dart in some dense bushes where it took refuge. It's there where the tranquilizer took effect, and the cheetah dropped to the ground.

Lance caught up with the cheetah and began to take blood samples, vaccinations, and gave a tag to the cheetah. Lance also took measurements from the cheetah.

Before he completed his examination, Lance heard a noisy distant rumble from afar. He took his binoculars and looked into the terrain. It was a herd he couldn't identify as four-footed creatures stampeded closer to him.

Lance collected his equipment and ascended a small modest ridge overlooking the terrain. The herd gradually turned as they reached the ridge; they clearly may have been seen as a variety of hoofed animals. After they all drove through the area, Lance spotted a leopard that chased them from behind, meters away. The leopard spotted him, however, and directly chased him.

Lance yelled, "Whoa!" and headed for a tree.

He scaled the tree as fast as his limbs would carry him, and the leopard pursued right behind him. It tried to clinch Lance's boot with its teeth, but Lance did his best to kick the leopard away.

Once Lance had kicked the leopard a number of times, the leopard fell from the trunk to the ground. It wasn't apparent to Lance whether the leopard chased the herd to improve on its stealth or picked up his scent and chased him. He also wasn't aware if there was a reason the leopard fell to the ground and why it suffered sudden arrest.

He climbed out of the tree, examined the leopard, and carried out a postmortem examination. He also took blood tests on the leopard once it appeared to have troubled symptoms, which bothered Lance, so he expanded his work further by writing notes in his journal. Then he returned to the Jeep, stored all his equipment away, and began to head for the conservation camp, which was a long way in distance.

*****

A few hours later, Niles noticed that Lance hadn't returned from his assignment. So he stocked the Jeep with extra supplies and equipment in the Hummer and told Mason he was about to go search for Lance. After he made his departure, he did what he could to find the designated route that Lance took.

An hour had elapsed, and Lance's canteen was dry.

Another hour had passed. Dehydration had set in, and his muscles suffered from pain.

As he traveled the dirt road Lance took, Niles remained on the lookout for him but hadn't found him. Then the bending dirt road came to an end, and Niles stopped the Jeep.

"All right, where do I go from here?"

Seconds later, the Jeep started up, and he continued on.

Twenty minutes later, as Niles drove his Jeep, he looked off to his left and saw a figure slowly walking in the far distance from the Hummer.

He drove toward the person, stopped the Hummer, and ran toward the person.

Niles yelled, "Lance! Lance!"

Once Niles reached Lance, he collapsed against him.

Niles tried to get a response out of him, but there was no response as he shook him and gently slapped him.

His attention had been diminished from dehydration, words he sputtered carried on, and he couldn't enunciate at all. Niles removed his shotgun scabbard and dragged him backward to the Hummer. After he pulled him into the back of the Hummer, Niles radioed dispatch and told them to look out for an abandoned Jeep that belonged to the three conservationists. Niles drove Lance home and confiscated all the medical research from Lance's cargo pants and equipment. He opened up Lance's journal and read his findings.

*****

Niles called the local doctor, and he treated Lance at home for any possible field medical emergencies. He put an IV in Lance's arm as he lay on his cot.

After a few days, Mason slowly passed Lance's tent. His arms were full of food he'd bought special from the market. With the IV pole by his side, Lance walked outside his tent and confronted Mason. Lance stared inquisitively at Mason.

Lance said, "Why do you go to the market and not buy any of this imported food for others and myself? We could have reimbursed you for it."

"Because they ship it for me exclusively."

Jarred from his place, not knowing what to think, and a little perturbed, Lance said, "Place your food in your tent and meet me at the Hummer."

Mason took the food to his tent, and he joined Lance at the vehicle.

As they prepared to jump into the Hummer, two park rangers returned the Jeep Lance left out on the savanna.

"Thank you for returning the Jeep!" said Lance.

"Thank you for your work," said a park ranger, and they left with their transportation.

"You are going to drive me to the market."

Mason got into the Hummer after Lance, who made sure his IV pole was in a secure spot as he placed it near the transmission shifter.

Once they reached the market after the long journey, they met the market manager at the front entrance.

Lance asked the manager, "I want to know where you order your imported food for Mason in your market?"

"It comes from a special shipment from trucks through various routes."

"The pizza and the Chinese?"

"Yes."

"This is a special list of Mason's acquaintances who could use this food from you. Can you get it?"

"I have nobody to deliver and set aside this much produce for me."

"Hire someone as a manager/driver/deliverer to set aside the food, and we will pay you for it."

"Oh…I can do that."

Lance handed him a list and said, "Do you have that in stock?"
"Yes, I'll show you."

Mason hunted down a cart, and they followed the manager. They walked to the back of the market, obtained the food, and returned home after they'd paid for it.

*****

The following day, the three conservationists drove south of Serengeti National Park toward Lake Manyara. They stopped meters away from the lake's shore. There was an abundance of wildlife surrounding the lake, so the men took the opportunity to take a closer look at the shore with their binoculars.

After some time, they spotted something trivial on the other side of the lake. They returned to the Jeep and retrieved raptorial gloves and walked to the location. Their new location appeared to have two large fowl in some trouble, separated some distance from each other by a number of feet.

Niles and Mason walked toward a flamingo hobbling on one leg while Lance examined a fish eagle grounded on the shore. The flamingo seemed to have fractured its leg while it made no attempt to fly or shuffle away. A wing on the fish eagle appeared to be broken.

Each of the men wrapped his bird in a towel to keep it calm and steady and from hurting itself. They picked up the birds gently and transported them to the Jeep. Two door hatches opened on a set of wire cages, and they slowly placed them inside. Afterward, they brought the birds to a wildlife animal rescue for treatment.

*****

That night at the conservation camp, Lance read a book on his cot with the light on upon his nightstand. He heard a particular but familiar sound behind him outside his tent. After rising from his cot, he listened closely at the mesh opening in the back of his tent. Then he left his tent and walked to Mason's tent and entered inside. Mason gave him a scowl while he sat on his cot as Lance looked at Mason's television set.

Lance said, "You're watching one of my cinema movies which wasn't broadcast at all tonight." Then he looked down at the bowl Mason was holding and said, "You used the rest of the peanut butter to make that peanut butter popcorn."

Mason didn't say a word. After finding a seat beside Mason, Lance asked if he could help himself to the peanut butter popcorn. Mason gave him permission to share his snack.

Lance scooped up a handful and said, "We're going to need more than an ample supply of peanut butter on popcorn night."

Mason muttered, "Yeah."

"At least you're at the good part in the movie."

As he gasped for air, Niles ran into the tent frantically. He said, "There's an animal out there that's within the perimeter of the camp."

"How many times have I told you to build a fence around the conservation camp?" said Lance.

Niles exhaled and said, "I need somebody to help me identify the animal."

Lance moaned and expressed disapproval at the request because it found its source from Niles at a satirical level. Niles left the tent with the two other men following him.

"It's over here...in the bushes," said Niles.

"What? Your imaginary eluding relative? You know, you really need to build a fence around this camp," said Lance.

Niles abruptly said, "I would need supporters to furnish the funding before we could follow through with it."

Lance moaned out loud.

After Niles and Mason stopped meters from the large bush, Lance continued to close in on the location and stooped down in front of it. He looked around in the bush and saw a pair of eyes glimmering from the reflection of what little light existed from his flashlight. A number of questions rose in his mind as he looked at the creature. *What is it? What size animal could it be? How are they going to draw it out from its location?*

"What do you make of it?" asked Niles as he joined Lance.

"I think it's an animal that found its way into our base camp and is hiding in some bushes."

Niles pushed Lance over onto his left side. "And not a word about this fence again."

Lance stood upright again, walked toward Mason, and said to Niles, "Well, it's cornered in the bushes, and it's a wild animal that's breathing down your throat. I'm going back to my *Godzilla* movie." Lance began to turn and walk away, but Niles caught up with him and pushed him on his side once again.

Niles retorted and said, "Would you determine what we have in our midst?" A second later, Niles said, "What do you think, Mason?"

"I can't make it out from this distance."

"Me neither," said Lance.

Niles pled and said, "Come on, Lance, what do you see?"

"I see an animal with its backside backed up against prickly, thorny brush, asking the question, 'Why can't I enjoy peanut butter popcorn or caramel popcorn, for that matter, at 10:30 in the evening?' It never entered my mind that the deciding factor would cause reluctance.'"

Niles continued to stare at Lance, speechless but repugnant.

"Wait here. Watch the animal," said Lance. Then he walked to the Jeep and pulled a net from the equipment and tools. He returned to the bush and gave two corners to Niles.

"Now do it correctly because you might be given only one chance," said Lance.

They approached the bush with one set of corners hung above the creature while the remaining corners were held low to the ground. Once the slack was pressed firmly into the tree, the animal sprinted into the net. They enclosed the open end, lifted the center off the ground, and held the creature up while they walked it to a large cage behind the open canopy tent.

It was a merciless caracal who put up a fight against the net and the lengthy journey to the cage. Niles and Lance made sure no harm would come to the cat nor succumb to stressing itself out. After he ran to the Jeep, Mason grabbed the tranquilizer rifle and joined the two conservationists to induce the cat.

Jodi and a local Tanzanian woman arrived at the conservation camp and joined the three men. They observed the partially sedated cat as it moderately squirmed inside the net.

"This pattern of behavior bears a resemblance to those who continually put up a fight in their life. You can call it rebellion, but you couldn't paint any clearer of a picture," said Jodi from her perspective as a missionary.

"It would be no different if you were a sailor established for days while you were out at sea on thrashing waves that caused you dispiritedness throughout the voyage. You raised questions concerning when you would arrive on land. But when that moment arrived and you saw solid ground to walk on from afar, for you and the crew, every passing minute left in the voyage was unanimously welcomed," said the Tanzanian woman.

Minutes later, the caracal discontinued struggling, and Mason removed the net as it lay in the cage.

Then Lance pointed out to Niles outside the cage, "You need to get busy building a fence around the compound, effective immediately."

Niles wrenched his face with his hands, growled out loud, and walked away from Lance.

Lance shone a flashlight on the caracal to see any prevalent conditions that may reside with the cat while Mason petted him. They planned to run a full cross-examination for him early in the morning.

*****

The following week, in one of the enclosed canopy tents, Lance checked off evaluation results for wildlife in two-week intervals before the local veterinarian examined the animals.

Niles entered the tent, wearing a colorful ceremonial tribal outfit made in Tanzania.

Lance said, "Let me guess, you offended someone again."

"Yup, your stock broker."

Lance cackled at him sarcastically and wanted to understand about the clothing.

"I'm going to a wedding ceremony, and I'm the guest of honor."

"Oh, take the reins of two animals at the same time while straddling both!"

"Why don't you come to the wedding with me?"

"Why?"

"I would welcome the company."

"What's going to take place? Is it going to be a simple ceremony?"

"No, there's going to be a tribal ceremony, dancing, and a feast."

"Feast?"

"Yes."

After a brief moment of silence, Lance said, "This better be some remarkable feast."

"If that's all that compels you, I'm sure it won't leave you disappointed."

"When does it begin?"

"Within the hour."

"Let's go."

"Is that what you are going to wear?"

"I'm not the guest of honor."

*****

They attended the wedding along with Mason after an hour's drive and parked beside a number of canopy tents in single file. After they passed all the closed tents, the last canopy tent in the series stood open to the public. There, beneath the shade, were several carvers and artists who worked on arts, carvings, and crafts. The three men stopped to admire the work.

A carver told them a majority of the profits would be given to the bride and groom and the guests.

Lance said, "Jodi would have enjoyed this."

"Jodi is here at the wedding."

"Jodi's here?"

Niles nodded his head.

Lance looked at the merchandise and saw a table of wooden rabbits that stood by the numbers. He removed his wallet and purchased a carved rabbit on a necklace and one that stood a foot tall.

Once they had finished browsing, they walked out to the open grounds and joined the festival underway. A fire was found in the center of the grounds with dancers circling the fire, which was part of a village. After the three men walked to the tribal chief and his daughter, who was getting married, they sat to his left in front of a rondavel and observed the festivities.

Niles asked the tribal chief whether his daughter had been given in marriage.

"No, here they come," said the tribal chief.

The minister and the groom arrived at the center of the village grounds while the bride joined them. The village congregated as best they could to listen to the nuptial rites.

Two seats were taken by a Caucasian and an African man just to the left of the three conservationists. The rites continued to be recited before all the witnesses, and then the minister tied a cloth around the couple's wrists, making the marriage official. After the completion of the ceremony, the couple left the center of the grounds and sat with the rest of their family.

The two men introduced themselves as conservationists to Niles, Lance, and Mason.

Niles pointed out, "They have some of the most unique types of marriage rituals in Africa."

The African man said, "Everything from jumping a broom and preserving it in the couple's house to crossing two tall wooden sticks."

"Where are you from?" asked Mason.

The Caucasian said, "Zambia."

"We're border neighbors. How has the fight against poacher hunting played out?" asked Lance.

The African man said, "It's as proliferate today as it was yesterday."

In the middle of their discussion, a rock pelted Lance in the chest. To the left of the dancers, a young boy was practicing with an old-fashioned slingshot. Lance watched him as he armed the sling-shot one more time, and it ended up hitting him in the chest.

When he stood up and walked over to the boy, Lance asked him, "What are you trying to hit?"

The boy pointed to a metal gong sitting near the conservationists' seats.

"Try again," said Lance.

He unloaded his slingshot once again, but it misfired and sharply turned to the left.

"Come on," said Lance, and they walked back to the Jeep. The equipment chest was opened, and Lance dug through the items inside. He pulled out an up-to-date slingshot and handed it to the boy. He took it slowly in his hands and relished the make of the slingshot.

"Is it for me?"

"Yes."

The boy saw a tree as a target and practiced his first shot. Since he missed the target, Lance guided the boy's arms and hands to hit the target easier. He released the sling and hit the target. The boy told Lance he wanted to continue practicing on the tree, so Lance took a number of steps away so he wouldn't seem as though he was interfering. Once he saw the boy was successful, he rejoined the celebration.

After Lance took his seat, he glanced at the dancers circling the fire and saw Jodi. She was dressed in a colorful ceremonial wardrobe and wore a mask as she shuffled around the fire. Lance entered a rondavel after he had been given permission to enter and donned a ceremonial wardrobe and mask. He joined the circling dance, right behind Jodi, and held onto her as they continued the dance. On occasion, they broke from the circle, and both of them twirled around as a couple and then rejoined the dance.

After a couple of minutes, they came to a stop, and both exchanged a glance toward each other behind the masks. Lance removed the wooden rabbit necklace from his pocket and put it around her neck while she reflected on his gift.

She removed her mask to reveal a joyful smile, and she hugged Lance. Then she lifted up his mask and discovered Lance beneath it, which gave rise for her heart to be glad. Later, she was filled with more joy and gladness after Mason furnished the large rabbit to Lance, who gave it to her afterward.

Outside the circle of dancers, Jodi and Lance stood in an embrace for a period of time.

*****

Nighttime fell upon the ceremony, and Jodi sat down beside Niles.

"Did you have an enjoyable time at the wedding?" asked Jodi.

"Yes, I did."

"Are you ready for the feast?"

"I have to admit, for me, that's one of the hallmarks of weddings."

A skewered hog was carried around the circle as they inaugurated the thanksgivings to God for the meal they were about to offer.

Jodi asked, "How is the game safari with the children looking for you and the conservation camp?"

Almost immediately, Lance walked into the village and said, "Excuse me, game safari…game safari! Have your capillaries in your head seized up?"

Niles sarcastically said, "*Absonna admiss affiss anolloia amoniss.*"

"What?"

"The facets of my mind are just fine."

Lance ignited once he said, "Do you know what the institution will do when they find out we're conducting safaris? What if they find out we're using fuel to run these excursions?"

"They are not about to do anything nor is it in their interest to find out about it."

"You really want to volunteer me to field children on wildlife safaris?"

Niles, at point blank, said, "Yes."

"Oh, come on!"

Lance gravitated away from the group, gripped his hat frantically, and then walked back to both of them and said, "It isn't going to work!"

"Oh?"

Lance growled to himself and looked at Jodi. "Sure, she has something to smile about now."

As she stood up, jumped repeatedly, and twisted her arms back and forth in a dance, she wore a big grin with glee and excitement in her expression because her Bible study students might participate in a safari. Niles and Jodi left Lance and attended the ceremonial feast to have dinner. Lance remained standing exactly where they had left him.

*****

The next morning at the conservation camp, all of Jodi's students huddled around a safari truck in anticipation of an expedition. Jodi mingled among them while Niles and Mason waited for Lance. Surfacing slowly from the tents, Lance walked toward the group with a scowl on his face.

"All right, let's get this defilement over with," said Lance.

Niles said, "Now do you know which route you're taking?"

Mason lifted a clipboard in front of Niles, who began to provide instructions to him.

"You're taking the route involving a curve in this direction, and you take the loop," reinforced Niles.

Lance bent his head down and moaned because he didn't intend to take that route.

"You have to be kidding me!" Lance snatched the clipboard out of Niles's hands.

Niles spoke to himself, "I'm sure I left something out."

Lance looked sharply upon him.

"Oh! If you come across a significantly sized herd, travel around it and gradually avoid riding through them. The rangers don't want us to do it for a temporary period of time." Niles took the clipboard away from Lance and wrote it on the paper.

Once Niles had finished scribbling, Lance swiped the clipboard away from him. A few moments passed while Niles's mind continued to dwell on matters.

"Oh, one more thing."

"What?"

"Make sure you have fourteen children at all times, and include Jodi." Niles took the clipboard again and wrote down the number. Once he had finished, Lance quickly snatched the clipboard out of his hand again.

A young boy with an elongated Ghana mask approached Lance and tugged on his cargo shorts. In spite of having gotten Lance's attention, the boy said nothing.

"Isn't the mask a little too long for you?"

"It fits around my head just right."

Lance unrestrainedly tossed the clipboard in the cab of the safari truck.

Jodi yelled out, "All aboard!" The children cheered and started loading onto the truck.

After he removed the shotgun scabbard off his back, Lance placed it near the shifter on the safari truck.

Lance mumbled to himself, "The resourceful occupation of a wildlife conservationist becomes endangered at the plight of eavesdropping on animals during its precedence."

He took a count of the children, started the truck, and began the trip.

*****

After several miles, the group saw their first exposure in the form of a small herd of kudu. Lance apprehensively picked up the receiver and spoke over the intercom.

"Ladies and gentlemen, the male kudu can be found in groups of males but can live a solitary life. When males face off, they lock horns in competition to determine the stronger pull. Sometimes two kudus are unable to unlock horns, and they will die of starvation or dehydration."

They passed the kudus, traveled some distance, and saw a herd of elephants in the thick vegetation.

"Elephants can reach thirteen feet high and weigh 15,000 pounds. Their incisors can serve as weapons, tools for moving objects and digging. They prefer to stay near water. Elephants can live up to seventy years in the wild."

They kept a reasonable distance away from the animals at all times. The safari truck creeped onto a herd of giraffe.

"Giraffes range from Chad in the north to South Africa in the south, from Niger in the west to Somalia in the east."

The children looked closely at the giraffe and the bush to the right and began to see an animal emerge from the midst of it. Everybody's attention was captured, including Lance's. Overwhelmed with immediate concern, Jodi saw the imminent threat of a lion from her seat.

Immediately, Lance began to struggle to get a grip on his shotgun, but it fell sideways. Closing in rapidly on the safari truck, the lion picked up speed with intensity, growing in its behavior. The lion leapt up on the windowsill and began to climb up.

The shotgun came into Lance's grip, and he ran to the middle of the safari truck and closed in on the lion. The children either maneuvered out of their seats or lurched back beside one another. A few reacted with great sensitivity in fear of the unrestrained animal. He pointed the shotgun off to the side of the lion, let one round off, and prompted the lion's temper-partial paralysis in its tracks. The lion, however, didn't subside in its aggressive threat.

Lance let off another round, spooking the lion again, and it settled in its mind not to surmount an attack on the people in the safari truck that day. The lion relinquished its grip on the side of the safari truck, rerouted his path, and paced off into the trees diagonally from the safari truck. Jodi took a deep breath, and Lance lowered his shotgun. He asked if everyone was okay and, everyone nodded. So he returned to his seat and returned his shotgun to the scabbard.

The safari continued as Lance took the loop where they came across a substantially large herd of zebra and wildebeest. Giraffe and elephants dotted the outside of the herd as well. The children were taken by the large numbers and appearance of the wildlife in the herd. It topped their interest at the heart of the day.

*****

Jodi, Niles, Lance, and Mason attended a church service near Mwanza. Jodi found one of the remaining seats in the front row. The three men walked to the back of the large closed canopy tent where three very large rocks sat parallel to the side wall of the tent. They each took a seat on them as opposed to any empty chairs and waited to listen to the associate pastor. Two attendants set up a projection screen and left from the front of the room prior to the associate pastor's discussion.

"Many of us are aware of the increased heightened aggression which has taken place in our land. A number of assemblies or churches have been torched recently, and questions have been raised concerning the security of our future site. If we built the structure only to have it burned down, the point of using our finances to break ground may be meaningless. The finances may easily be used for something else, which has the security that it requires to follow through. What we need to do together is resolve to understand exactly what we'll be doing by further developing the right choice."

As the three men sat on a rock, Lance's seat began to roll backward, and he fell in that direction.

One assistant ran the projector while the assistant pastor showed which churches had been torched at their location on a map.

As the meeting commenced, Lance continued to struggle with the stability of the rock. Then he moved one of the sides to another angle, which came more to a point. So he turned and reestablished the rock in that position and sat down.

Mason whispered, "Why don't you sit on the floor?"

"I can't see from there!"

"Sit up front."

"I'll get in the way."

"Participate as an usher."

Lance looked at Mason with a frown he bore across his face.

The associate pastor offered the option of taking a vote by ballot or by a show of hands to settle the issue of security. So they took a vote.

The assistants asked for a vote by a show of hands, and then they passed out ballots.

Then the rock Mason was sitting on rolled sideways as well from a lack of equilibrium.

"Well, look at the folding chair waiting to sprout feet and sit perfectly still for you," said Lance.

"That's because all government buildings are automatically furnished with a seat for you. It's not my fault, Lance."

"What about fire stations? Fire stations, Mason!"

"You don't know whether they're lacking a place to sit or whether they're government buildings."

Lance ruminated and then said, "I still think they could have used a slide rather than a brass pole to suit up...far less injuries."

The associate pastor said, "Okay, we'll count the tally and provide the results after the end of the sermon. Thank you."

*****

On Monday morning, Mason prepared breakfast for himself under the open canopy tent. A dispute was brewing between Niles and Lance as they walked toward the open canopy tent.

Lance distinctly stated, "You're going to place your dependence on whom in order to confirm information about the activity of Charles and his men?"

They reached the tent, and Niles poured himself a cup of coffee.

"Who has some vital information concerning up-to-date progress Charles has been making and has been undertaking lately?" said Niles.

"Ya know, it's not like we're depending on some winged parrot to come and break the news to us! What's transpiring, Niles?"

"A winged parrot."

"You are one disturbed man, Niles."

After a few seconds, Lance said, "You know, it would be like you to take information from Applebury for some irrelevant desolate site out who knows where, just to engage in archaeology."

"My information is relevant, and I will have none other than relevant information because it will come through—for me!"

*****

An hour later, the three men got in a Jeep, which hadn't been started at the conservation camp. Niles took his place in the driver's seat while Lance sat in the passenger's side, and Mason sat in the back seat.

After a few seconds of staring forward, Niles turned to Lance and said with a firm tone, "Are you ready?"

"Don't talk to me!"

The Jeep's engine was started, and they drove south on a highway for forty-five minutes to a secluded village.

They climbed out of the Jeep and met with a number of tribal elders who sat outside their huts. As the men greeted one another, they obliged the conservationists a seat to sit among the villagers.

The witch doctor let the three conservationists in on some information in his native tongue as they listened carefully.

After the witch doctor finished his first statement, Lance quietly asked Niles a witty question: "He wants to introduce me to his daughter so I can have her hand in marriage, doesn't he?"

Niles strictly said, "Would you listen and understand the local dialect correctly?"

He rerouted his attention to the witch doctor and said, "Were these acts of unlawfulness? Or did you hear about them from a questionable informant?"

The witch doctor continued to speak about the actions at a poaching area. He elaborated on Niles's previous question, which the conservationists did not understand.

Then Lance told Niles, "Ask him if anyone helped themselves to the teeth of a live leopard to make jewelry or if they got them off a dead leopard?"

"Do you mind?"

Niles told the witch doctor to proceed. Minutes passed as the witch doctor cued Niles in on evidence concerning the degree of corruption and involvement in a camp's wildlife trading and poaching.

"Tell him we're looking for people who tear down ruins too," said Lance.

"We won't today because that's not our line of conservationism. That's left in the hands of other people!"

"I'll remember that when you want to listen to Applebury again."

Niles sighed beneath his breath and returned to the conversation with the witch doctor.

*****

Later, the three conservationists set out for three hours to the poacher camp by following the directions the witch doctor had given to them.

Lance looked through his binoculars outside the area from a lookout point and discovered canopy tents in between the trees. The conservationists, armed themselves, permeated the boundaries of the camp undetected and infiltrated a large and long canopy tent. They discovered it filled with all kinds of crates and home merchandise, anything from all kinds of decorative rugs to antique relics.

Lance enthusiastically said, "Africa is such a large continent where anything that can be discovered on it will be."

As they opened a crate, the three of them found an endless assortment of unfinished gemstones. Lance opened a sachet and found one particular kind.

He gazed at the rock with heightened excitement and said, "Rainbow obsidian! That's my favorite!"

Niles convinced him to return the rock to the crate, and they closed it.

They slipped outside the side of the tent on all fours and snuck into the tent next to it. Inside, they discovered all kinds of pelts and wildlife head mounts with an assortment of stuffed animals and animal relics.

There wasn't any possibility of advancing to the front part of the tent because a group of poachers were huddled around a table. So the conservationists climbed out of the tent and ran deeper into the camp to a large thatch facility and circled to the front entrance.

Inside, countless numbers of bunk beds and accommodations that made up living quarters for poachers stood in single file. As walking sticks leaned against the side of the tent, each of the conservationists took one and wrapped his own handkerchief around an end. They lit them with their lighters and spread out to different sections of the living quarters. Then they set the walking sticks against the tent, and it lit on fire. The fire spread along the fabric covering to the thatch roofing and continued to be consumed in flames. The conservationists regrouped and left the living quarters.

They ran across the farthest side of the camp and its entire length to see if they could find a corral holding wildlife. After sprinting the stretch, they discovered a corral filled with wildlife. The conservationists carefully opened the entrance gate, and they set the wildlife free as fast as they could. A short distance diagonally to the corral, a company of vehicles sat parked in single file. At that location, the conservationists witnessed a number of poachers reacting to the news of their living quarters.

Exactly from where the three conservationists stood, a humming sound from a good distance resonated behind them. They looked to investigate and discovered a cargo plane slowly crawling away but picking up speed in the other direction. As he looked in the back of one of the parked Jeeps, Lance quickly picked up a grappling hook and ran toward the plane.

After the two remaining men saw Lance head for the cargo plane, Niles said to Mason, "Come on! Let's go check the major tent." Niles and Mason ran to the outside of the tent where a great number of poachers were assembled. As they took precautions to slip into the tent, they used a camera on the table to record documents.

As fast as his feet could carry him, Lance's distance picked up behind the plane.

Then a poacher with an assault rifle appeared in the back open hatch of the plane and fired on Lance. Quickly, Lance headed diagonally toward the side of the plane from his straight course to avoid shrapnel. An ammunition round lined up accurate enough strategically to graze Lance in the leg, causing him to momentarily hobble, but he kept running forward. After removing his shotgun, Lance aimed at the poacher while the poacher was zeroing in on Lance. But Lance fired on the poacher who didn't get another shot off as Lance struck the poacher across his chest. Collapsing to the hatch floor and no longer showing any lingering movement, the poacher lay dead, indicating no threat to Lance.

He diverted to his original course and made up for the distance. The cargo plane, however, was reaching its necessary acceleration to take flight, causing a lengthy stretch to reach.

After he unraveled a little of the grappling hooks rope, Lance swung it above his head, released it, and hooked it upon the cargo plane's hatch cable. While he held the rope, he fell to the ground clumsily. By speedily rising to his feet and leaping for the rope, he started gradually climbing toward the hatch. Once he reached it, he pulled himself inside where two armed poachers waited near the cockpit.

Since they were not entirely prepared, however, their aim failed to strike as they fired. Time was on his side as he hid behind a large crate. Multiple rounds were shot into the crate where he stood, but Lance remained unscathed.

As time ran out, the need to locate literal communication was growing very important before Mason discovered it by going to great lengths with a communications crate. He pulled out a radio, but Niles didn't want others to possibly listen into their party. So he pulled out a field phone and made a call to the local park ranger.

Lance placed his shotgun on the crate. Great curiosity grew in the two poachers as they began to hear wood being pieced apart behind the crate. So one poacher persuaded the other to close in on it and investigate what was taking place. After he approached it while banging sounds of tin were heard, he stopped for fear of what was transpiring.

Suddenly, a long trunk duct thrust against the side of the low fuselage skin, creating a loud tumbling noise. Surprising the poacher who was closing in on the crate, the trunk duct shook him rather erratically. Taking him even more unexpectedly was another trunk duct of the same size that landed above the other disorderly. Heaping on top of the other, the clutter was enough to cause the approaching poacher to stop several feet from the back of the crate.

Instantly, there was complete silence and inactivity behind the crate. After waiting for any sign of Lance, the poacher nearest the crate began to lower his assault rifle. Several seconds passed while no sign or movement had seemed to take place.

Proceeding to take a few steps back with paint splattered over him, the poacher hastily wiped paint from his eyes for a few seconds before he collapsed against the side of the fuselage.

It was merely another few seconds before another paint can was splattered against the same poacher again. Then the furthest poacher raised his assault rifle and fired several rounds into the crate. But once the poacher ceased fire, the only sound that could be heard from behind the crate was the sound of liquid splashing into a container.

Slowly taking a few steps toward the crate, the farthest poacher fixed his aim toward the side of the crate. Spilling out a medium-sized box of nuts as far as Lance could, he spread the hardware across the floor. The poacher who was on his feet stopped approaching Lance slowly behind the crate. With paint on his face, the poacher closest to the crate tried to find balance on his feet with little vision and footing, which was unhinged by the nuts.

Then the liquid poured out into a container behind the crate was additionally splashed out onto the unfortunate poacher as well. Irritation and burning set into the poacher's eyes as he frantically collapsed again against the lower fuselage skin.

Throwing the empty paint can aside, which was filled with turpentine, the other poacher gradually made a safe effort to get close to the crate while he aimed his assault rifle.

Once he closed in on the crate, the poacher quickly looked behind the crate for Lance but found nobody. The four-barrel of a Lancaster shotgun gradually moved toward the side of the poacher's head. Realizing that something threatening was pointing at his head, the poacher decided to freeze exactly where he stood. After Lance had crawled to the top of the crate and looked down, he made an attempt to make an opportunity against the poacher. Lance's attempt had made good, and he apprehended the poacher. He led the captive poacher to the edge of the hatch.

The dazed poacher said, "Why are you putting my life in danger?"

"Are you carving up wildlife?" asked Lance.

"Yes."

"Are you using an assault rifle for the wrong reasons?"

"Yes."

After a sharp butt with his hand, Lance sent the poacher over the hatch floor to plummet at a high elevation.

Then he approached the cockpit, looked inside and waited until the pilots made eye contact with him.

Sarcasm certainly was in full swing when Lance began to engage in conversation when he said, "Hi, where are we going? It's so pleasant to have such close acquaintances with men like you. I'll be right back."

Lance stepped back into the cargo deck momentarily, then brought a rope to the cockpit, and said to the pilot on the right, "Tie him up."

The pilot questioned, "Why is he supposed to be tied up?"

"It's because you kill."

Lance pointed his shotgun barrel at the pilot so he might tie him up.

The pilot began to follow through with Lance's requirements in the midst of his darkened bewildered confusion.

Then Lance abruptly said, "No, tie him right so his arms are tied and he doesn't reach the wheel!" The grief-stricken pilot followed through with the orders, and then Lance told him to sit back down. Lance tracked down another rope, and the remaining pilot was tied as well.

"I want to thank you men for attributing to more than just the usual formal acquaintance to be such a rich indelible experience."

Lance slowly walked away, out of their sight, picked up a parachute rig, and jumped out of the hatch.

The pilot screamed, "We are going to die!"

As the plane plummeted toward land, the endless descent for the pilots seemed tortuous throughout their closing demise. The plane nosedived into the ground and crashed with severity against some trees.

At the conclusion of his descent, Lance packed his parachute and returned to the poacher area.

Upon the discovery of a one-story building in the heart of the camp, Niles and Mason entered the expanded structure with their hats removed and stashed them behind their clothing to avoid detection. Workers began to walk by them without asking them who they were.

They walked into the main facility and discovered that it was a slaughterhouse for wildlife. Rails and hooks were suspended from the ceiling to move carcasses around to butcher.

It brought great relief that Niles and Mason called in assistance from the park rangers.

They investigated the entire length of the facilities until they reached the back exit.

Mason and Niles ran into Lance from his return trip, while using GPS and tracking, walked to the parked Jeeps and welcomed three park rangers. They prepared for a late group of more park rangers who would engage and investigate the camp.

*****

After having found a seat beneath the open canopy tent, Lance enjoyed his lunch as Niles and three men in the conservation field sat at another picnic table beside Lance. Niles and the three conservationists were discussing certain discoveries based on what was concealed at one of the poacher sites.

Niles made a statement to Lance that one of the men said out of the blue, "'They had a corpse amongst themselves.'"

Lance turned to Niles, looked baffled immediately, and spent a little time staring at him.

"Quartz?"

Niles sat quiet for a moment and then said, "Corpse!"

"'They had quartz amongst themselves?'"

Niles stuttered words at first and then stressed, "Corpse! Corpse! Don't you hear a fraction of what I say?"

Lance said, "Highly unlikely," and then Niles dropped his head to the picnic table.

*****

Nighttime fell upon the conservation camp, and Lance had found his way to his cot. With his eyes closed as he lay awake, a sound of rustling was heard at the front of his tent.

As he pushed a mop bucket into Lance's tent, Mason was incognizant of his doings and surroundings. Lance's head rose to look and see what it could be. He identified who it was after he shone his flashlight on Mason.

Mason slowly took the mop out and began to mop the ground in the tent.

"Oh no, no, no, no, you're not going to wipe up dirt on the tent floor. You're sleepwalking again, come on."

Mason, disposed with sleep, continued to mop the floor in the tent.

"Are you getting anywhere with it? Okay, give me the mop, and let's push it out of here." Lance guided the mop bucket and Mason by the shoulder out of the tent and began directing him to his tent. He lowered his head through the flaps of his tent and led Mason to his cot.

To make absolutely sure he wouldn't wander again, Lance watched over Mason as he sat in one of his chairs on the other side of the tent.

*****

Early evening the next day, Jodi and the three conservationists were invited to be guests at a wildlife conservation banquet held in Mwanza. A driver drove them to the banquet in a limousine as they sat in back and engaged in small talk.

"Are you sure you've singled out the right location for the banquet?" said Mason while Niles filed through directions on a map.

Niles said, "Yes or we're attending a janitorial meeting, a law enforcement banquet, and a quilting convention."

"I didn't hear a piano recital on the list," said Lance.

"We'll go next week," said Niles.

"I was only kidding. We went the week before!"

"Sure!" said Jodi.

They arrived at the banquet, and the maître d opened the limousine and helped Jodi out of the car. "Good evening, madam."

Mason stepped out of the car and discreetly mentioned, "Are you sure the list of guests has been secured…searched?"

"Yes, sir," confided the maître d.

"Let me see your list."

Mason kindly asked, "Okay, who is this group of men?"

"That's the Anderson group. They're here to turn the dial for zoological interests between parks and zoos."

Mason suspiciously and critically mumbled beneath his breath. After overhearing the conversation, Niles stepped out of the limo and told Mason to bring both lists.

They joined the banquet and took their assigned seats. Adjacent to their table sat another seating arrangement with assigned name cards labeled "Anderson" and a group of men who glanced at Niles. Beneath their table, they passed a picture of him among themselves.

The award ceremonies were underway, and the nominees for conservation work in the north region were recognized. As the last nomination was called, Niles's team was named one of the best preservation camps near Mwanza.

Niles signaled to the conservation leaders that he wouldn't accept the award due to the conspicuous company. Two of the men opened suitcases beneath their table, assembled compact assault rifles, and held them in seclusion. Then the two men covered their assault rifles with cloth napkins and walked over to Niles's table. They removed the cloth napkins and held up everyone at their table.

"We've come to congratulate you for your work. Now it's time for you to depart."

"What kind of departure?" said Niles.

"This was not a good time for me to leave my shotgun in the Jeep," said Lance in a plausible way.

"You left your shotgun in the Jeep? You left your shotgun in the Jeep?" shouted Niles while he rose to his feet and swatted Lance on the table with an empty roaster pan, sending him backward to the floor.

After a while, Lance stood beside his seat and said, "That's the best you can do when you raise an argument?"

Quickly, Lance turned around to a gunman who had his assault rifle partially lowered and took the opportunity to strike him in the face. The conservationists had portrayed part of a ruse to throw the gunmen. Niles and Mason rose to their feet and got involved as well. Niles and Mason made a hit against the other gunmen as they began to hurl plates at the "Anderson" table. As a result of that distraction, Jodi took the staves off the food cart and leapt on one of the stooped men behind the "Anderson" table.

Lance became preoccupied lifting his gunman high in the air and crashing him hard to another banquet table. He repeated the same to the gunman over a stack of chairs as well. Niles struggled with his gunman as he wrestled hand to hand as his adrenaline picked up, and he threw him across the banquet table, knocking him unconscious on the floor. Niles stopped for a few moments to catch his breath.

"How come I'm working on the first criminal, and everyone else is on their third or fourth?" said Niles to himself. Then another thug tackled him from behind.

Seeing two thugs who were closing in on him, Lance jumped up on stage and ran stage right where nothing was placed for the banquet.

Niles overthrew the aggressor who was a bother by leaning backward on a table and then walked toward the wall. Niles removed a fire extinguisher from the wall, and after he returned to the table, he emptied it into his opponent's face. The thug gradually backed up against the table as he resisted the chemical agent. Then Niles tossed the empty fire extinguisher to Mason, and he pelted the aggressor with the side of the fire extinguisher's tank, producing a light hollow ping sound. The aggressor fell to the ground in a daze.

Preoccupied with a thug as she hung on his back, Jodi tried to stave a skewer into his chest, but she wasn't succeeding at all.

As he tried to wrench her arms off and away from him, he found her closing his jaw on his head, twisting his head left and stabbing him in a jugular vein. She pulled the skewer out, and he bled and ran frightfully on as he shouted from the sight of blood and pain.

After he found a magician's chest and opened it, Lance took out a set of throwing knives and threw them at the thugs. They saw the knives and saw how imperative it was to leave the stage. So they leapt down and crashed to the floor. They dodged more than one knife but then hunkered down and rolled off the stage, and, as a result, evaded the target range.

"I can't hit anything today. It's this tuxedo I'm wearing. It won't allow me to close in on anything," said Lance to himself.

He left the chest and scaled up the stage ladder on the back wall. Then he traversed the scaffolding and beams across the stage and began loosening ellipsoidal lights on the frame; some had been hung carelessly above.

He freed a light, and it toppled unaware on one of the thugs following him. Moving out of the way and to another location altogether, the other thug avoided being struck by a light. But the thug lost track of Lance hunched down in the scaffolding because Lance simply vanished out of sight. Everything the thug could do to track down Lance turned sour as he searched for him. He looked to his left and then to his right, but he couldn't catch a glimpse of him above.

Then he picked up the perception of movement behind him. He turned around, and an extension ladder dropped down onto his forehead. The whole weight of the extension ladder was brought down on him, and he toppled to the floor.

Traces of any remaining guests were reduced as a result of the skirmish. The conservation leadership had already placed a call to the authorities.

As the four guests from the conservation camp regrouped, Niles said, "We didn't find out whether they were involved with Charles or not at all."

"You hit me," said Lance.

"Call me a realist."

A moment later, Lance said, "You're a suspension bridge which they paint every year to avoid corrosion!"

"So where do you hide all your suspension cables?" asked Mason on Niles's account.

"Oh, shut up," said Niles.

Jodi and Niles began to walk out of the building.

Lance turned to Mason and said, "Why don't you put some face paint on and make yourself more presentable? People are going to start talking about you." And Lance followed Jodi and Niles. Mason stood still and looked provoked, but he looked around to see if there were any people who happened to overhear Lance's banter.

*****

Late in the evening the following day, as Lance lay in his cot at the conservation camp, Mason, wearing pajamas, entered Lance's tent and got his attention.

"Yes?" said Lance.

"Look what I got. Hot Tamales candy, Lance," stressed Mason.

Lance stretched his hand open since Mason was offering.

"Ah, you've got to do something for me first."

Lance sat up in his cot and said, "You know, I could squeeze margarine through your sinuses, and then I'd acquire the candy for myself."

"It's just a simple request."

Lance slowly reached for his mini fridge, opened it up, slid out a stick of margarine, and developed a scowl on his face.

Mason persisted with enthusiasm, however, and he persuasively shook the box while he was filled with excitement.

"Ugh…what is it?" asked Lance.

"I'd like to meet a woman, and it doesn't seem to be happening yet."

"You realize the job doesn't provide much exposure on a conservation camp."

"We attend a few social functions, attend church, and go to banquets."

"The social functions and banquets are few, if any. You may have to visit Mwanza and try harder."

"Okay."

As they walked outside Lance's tent. Both of them ran into Niles in his pajamas, yawning and groggy.

"Is everything all right?"

"Yes," said Mason.

"You weren't sleepwalking again, were you?"

"No."

Mason looked at Lance, handed him his Hot Tamales candies, and returned to his tent for the evening.

"What is it? Is there something wrong?"

"He's longing for a companion," said Lance.

"Ah, there may be a need for him to relocate and search for the likes of such a person, the same methods we use to search for wildlife. We may have to discontinue appetizer checkers, our own devised gameboard."

"Why you sopping opened floodgate. He may find someone. It'll be all right."

"Okay."

*****

A couple of days later, two hours before dusk, as he walked beside the clothesline, Lance discovered how loaded it was with clothes. He stooped beneath the clothes, moved to the other side, and met up with Mason.

"Where did all this laundry come from?" asked Lance.

"Jodi is here. She's accommodating a spare tent for a little while, so she's here to stay."

"Why doesn't she stay at her residence?"

"She's offered her residence to another unfortunate family, so she's staying here for a while."

Niles joined them and said, "I want everyone to know that if we have any more company to stay, we will have to accommodate more tents. Most of them are reserved for disclosed reasons."

After a few moments, Lance creatively said, "We'd love it if you'd posed with the wedding couple after you're finished placing icing in the bride's shoes again."

Niles glared at Lance.

Then Lance said, "You've just been slap-hammered."

Niles grumbled, pushed him forward, and made sure he was sent on his way.

*****

A couple of days later, in the afternoon, the four residents stood outside among their tents at the conservation camp.

A large cargo plane that had smoke erupting from its engines and fuselage made a descent during a troubled flight. As he looked through his binoculars, the frightful occurrence played itself out for Lance while the others watched the incident. It dropped from the sky almost gradually and crashed a quarter of a mile away from the camp.

After they unanimously reached the decision to investigate the crash site, Lance drove the Jeep while Niles placed a call in the Jeep to the authorities. They arrived at the crash site, and Lance volunteered to open the cargo compartment. Lance removed the fire extinguisher and flashlight from the Jeep for use, opened up the bay door, and entered the plane. After Lance walked back half the length, he threw a lever, and the cargo door opened up. With it came a flood of smoke that billowed outside.

After they let the smoke ventilate, Niles entered the rear and discovered three large crates in the docking area. Niles proceeded to the front and joined Lance in the cockpit who extinguished it only to find two severely burnt dead pilots. Both men hacked from the smoke randomly over time.

Lance looked around and said, "Where are the papers?"

"They should be with either of the two pilots." They both dug in the pilot's pockets and pulled out partially burnt papers. Watching Lance tear into documentation as it spilled out to the floor caught Niles's attention. "You have a methodical way of keeping them in a tidy neat stack or—"

"Hey, I'll have you know that the maître d will find them before you do!" Then Lance broke a band overhead and removed a clipboard from a small compartment.

As they walked back to the crates, Niles said, "I'm unable to determine from this itinerary whether this was a shipment for poachers or en route to another company."

"These papers say it was en route to Mozambique's zoo," said Lance.

"If it's a zoo, we need to open the cargo."

Mason hunted down a crowbar from the Jeep, and he began to break open the wooden crates.

As the last crate farthest from the front was cracked open, they found a red panda inside a cage. The second crate held drill monkeys in their cage. They broke open the last wooden panel of the remaining crate and discovered a Sumatran tiger in the cage.

"Who's going to get these?" asked Lance.

"I don't know. We could or the zoo in Mozambique. Or they can go to Dar es Salaam or Bahari Zoo in Tanzania," said Niles.

"You don't have the necessary facilities, an enclosure, to house a Sumatran tiger?" said Jodi.

"We could improvise…or manage," said Niles.

Mason enthusiastically said, "Let's try it. Let's keep them!"

Lance stressed, "You're looking after them."

"All right."

"We need to get a truck lift and get these cages out before the plane explodes, flames spread, etc."

"I'll contact someone to bring the equipment," said Niles, and he placed the call for all the necessary assistance that afternoon.

*****

Inside the large enclosed canopy tent, Mason sat at a cart table with a stack of boxes sitting off to his right. He had been at work sculpting an African craft made out of wood of a couple hugging. Once he saw someone's silhouette shadowing the tent, he quickly put the sculpture in one of the boxes with wrapping inside.

Arriving inside from the outdoors, Jodi approached Mason and his folding table and kidded, "Waiting for a volunteer to step forward and play Yahtzee with you?"

"There were so many who voluntarily threatened to play that I had to fend them off and tell them to go back where they came from," said Mason.

"That be some Yahtzee game! It takes seven boxes to set up?"

She began to curiously inquire by staring and wanting to know just exactly what might be in the contents behind the boxes.

After she delayed, Mason broke down, aggravated, foiled by the lack of surprise, and said, "All right, they're gifts that I want to give my future girlfriend. I've even written what her personality should be according to my interests and established them in a bust of her."

"You have a bust based on how she's supposed to appear?"

"That, plus six other items, which she should enjoy. I'm making an estimate to see whether she'll, in all likelihood, enjoy them."

"Did you sew some exotic tablecloths for her?"

"Better…a colorful tin can pot for starters." A pot full of decorative tin cut out with flowers was on the table. "A book on collective poetry based on our love type we share together." He brought out a red journal he kept to gather his own prose, poetry, and sayings. "A large wooden beehive that splits open in the middle, and you place a real piece of honeycomb in the heart of a plastic center inside. A few 1:100 small scale wooden ships and some artifacts Niles and I discovered on an archaeological expedition in the Mesopotamian area."

Unexpectedly, Lance slapped his hand on Mason's left shoulder by entering the tent and took Jodi and Mason by surprise.

Lance said loudly, "How is the new cable installer job going for you, Mason? I see you've picked up a new hobby—infiltrating parts for colorful kiddie pools! What else do you have to show to us?"

Mason said, "A future love interest."

"Who is she?"

"You'll see."

"Ah, a rare botanical species found from a remote region of our hemisphere, most welcome with so many other recognized kinds that populate the area. Would this be the extent of your showcase?"

"A bust." Mason removed a large white bust of the woman he envisioned would exhilarate his interests.

"Ah, a plaster of Paris. What is it you do? What do you have stored in your tent?"

The head of the bust had been sculpted looking up, capturing the exquisite beauty of her appearance with semi-curly shoulder-length hair and shared goodwill highlighted in her expression. She exhibited a strong sense of fascination accentuated from herself toward others as one looked into her eyes. Her cheerful, without reluctance, kind of spirit shined through the work of art in its depiction.

"It would appear you'll do a terrific job with cable hook-up as well as cutting up more kiddie pool parts."

Marching directly toward Lance, Jodi put an immediate front up against him and backed him up while Mason carried on looking at his masterpiece bust.

Lance said with sarcastic defensiveness, "I never brought up how Mason put the hot air balloon into storage last month."

"That was you who handled that undertaking, not Mason."

*****

The following day at the market in Mwanza, Niles grabbed a cart at the entrance, and Lance followed him. As Niles entered an aisle behind two ladies with carts, Lance stopped and watched two more ladies with carts box Niles into the aisle. Back at the entrance,

Lance grabbed two baskets and began to pick up items in the aisle to Niles's left.

A young Tanzanian girl farther down Niles's aisle, beyond the two women, began to climb the shelves to the left that were standing four tiers or fifty-four inches. Once she courageously reached a particular shelf, she began to reach for a bag of candy. Her grip wasn't fully secure, so she brought her hand back and tightened her grip. But when her attention returned to the bag of candy, it was gone. From the next aisle, Lance had reached deep for the same bag of candy, took it, and placed it in a basket.

Niles made an attempt to push his cart farther but realized he was blocked in by two women in the aisle. As he looked behind, he encountered the same trap and understood every set of four women stopped to browse products. Niles was left no other choice but to wait.

As the girl held on to the shelf, her bottom lip began to quiver, and she became very sad. She climbed down and ran to her mother and wept out loud.

Moments later, she turned around and saw someone offering her the bag of candy. She looked up and discovered it was the man who had taken the candy himself, the same person who had helped himself to it. She stopped crying immediately, gasped with exhilaration, and accepted it like only a child would know how. She broke a heartfelt smile across her face while Lance ruffled her hair, greeted her mother, and filled his baskets while he walked toward the two women in front of Niles. He loaded both his baskets full of groceries, squeezed past both women behind Niles, and set them in his cart.

"You know, you never seem to take advantage of the passing lane in an aisle or else you'd be done. To say the least, you have difficulty advancing beyond toll booths, don't you?" said Lance.

"Why should I have to take questions when all four women, who were clearly indecisive for fifteen minutes, never allowed me to spread my wings either direction of the aisle? And there wasn't one of them who had a grocery list!"

"You think lists still help or benefit them any longer?" Pausing to think for a brief moment, Lance decided to make another point. "Maybe they were working for Charles," he said dubiously.

After a few seconds, while Lance stared at Niles, Lance said humorously, "But seriously, you have more paperwork on him, don't you?"

Then Lance began to search Niles's shirt pockets for the paperwork, provoking Niles to grumble and try to fend Lance off as best he could. "Would you stay out of my pockets? And if you search elsewhere, you're going to embrace a long hard winter here in Africa or I'll simply pelt you!"

"It was there the last time I searched for it." Then Lance discontinued searching and looked closely at him. With one swift quick swipe, Lance took it out from one of his thin jacket pockets. Niles objected again as Lance walked toward the checkout counter while he left Niles with the cart full of groceries. Niles refused to leave his cart, so he sped the cart around and out of the aisle toward the checkout counter at the front of the store.

As Lance approached the front door beside the magazine stand, Niles struck him against the back of his hat, causing it to tilt forward on his head.

"You hit me in the back of the head with my box of caramel popcorn!" said Lance.

As a few feet separated each of them, Niles confidently stood still until he had to drastically flinch when eight magazines were flung at him from different angles, flopping around in a few places.

"You can't do that. You're going to get in trouble with the management!" emphasized Niles.

A check-out cashier approached Lance from behind the magazine stand. He pulled out a few bills from his pocket, gave them to him, and then he returned to the cash register.

"You bought off the manager! You can't do that!"

"I paid for the magazines."

"Oh, in that case, I'll just throw the rest of the groceries at you!"

"I'm not the one who has to pick them up." Lance turned around and walked farther toward the entrance.

But before he exited the market, Lance looked back and said, "I paid for the caramel popcorn."

Niles stood still and pouted until he had fully released all his frustration, and then he checked out with the groceries.

*****

Two days later, as the three conservationists drove through the community of Mwanza, they stopped before a tall building and parked on the other side of the street. The three conservationists investigated a parked livestock transport to see what was inside. It was filled with wildlife while it was backed up to a chute. They entered the building and climbed the stairwell. They came across nobody as they approached a floor that opened to a remote slaughterhouse for wildlife. There, in a chilled room, a few butchers could be spotted at work. They reached a decision among them to leave Mason behind on that floor. Niles and Lance climbed the steps to a door where Niles remained to investigate as Lance continued upstairs.

Once Lance climbed two floors above Niles, poachers spotted Lance and immediately made an advance against him. He used the butt of his shotgun to engage a few of them. Then he tossed a few free-standing furnishings in the lobby against them to use as obstacles. Lance shot two of the last poachers because he was left with little to defend himself.

Niles opened the door to a room filled with Charles's poachers. They immediately recognized Niles, stood from their chairs, and rushed toward him out to the lobby. He tripped and toppled over two of the poachers down in the stairwell but then climbed to the next floor. Niles was overwhelmed by the poachers as he confronted them as best he could.

Two poachers followed Lance to his designated floor. They subdued him at once on the floor's lobby area as they carried him toward the large window panes. They inevitably saw that Lance began to be more than a handful, so they settled to place him against a wall. Lance made every attempt to free a roll of rope from a poacher as they attempted to tie him. After he seized the rope, their heightened degree of aggression and conflict worked against Lance's favor.

As an interval of time was given to Lance while the two poachers held him face first against the wall, he slowly and awkwardly was given the opportunity to lower the rope over a piece of furniture while he began to suffer blows. He climbed on top of a poacher from the chair and tied the rope around his open jaw.

But the poacher took Lance to a reckless extreme and broke through a windowpane to attempt to send both of them to their deaths. The chair scurried across the floor and caught against the bottom window frame. Falling to his death, the poacher thumped hard on the ground. Lance rebounded and hung on the rope outside the building and saw Niles through the window as he continued to defend himself. As Lance swung himself against the window three times to shatter it, the force wasn't enough to break the windowpane. So Lance decided to get Niles's attention while he was preoccupied with fending poachers off him.

Lance made an attempt to contact Niles, but he sounded muffled as he said, "Hey, break the windowpane! Break the windowpane!"

As poachers captured Niles's attention, he looked back at Lance while Niles struggled with a poacher and heard him.

So he picked up the poacher and threw him as hard as he could against the windowpane. But nothing changed, and the window stayed intact.

Lance reacted with embarrassment that conveyed all his emotion. He turned his head sideways, sighed while his inner eyebrows raised, and flinched in disgust. Then he looked up and began to climb the rope.

"I'll just climb the rope into a broken window!"

As he swung carcasses against poachers, brandished hooks into their stomachs, and dealt a blow to several as well, Mason gained the advantage. Then a tall, muscular, authoritative man who thought Mason was out of his element struck him in the face and caused him to slide beneath a few hanging carcasses. Mason climbed the nearest manageable carcass and unwrenched a hook hung from a rail in the ceiling. The carcass toppled to the floor, which stood nearly as tall as the muscular man and collapsed on top of him. Then Mason struck him with the blunt end of the hook but didn't seem to get anywhere. So he struck him with his fist, and the muscular man blacked out.

Above Lance's head were two openings in the floor and the site of construction underway. He headed for the stairwell and climbed two stories. On a dark floor, he found a pallet jack parked beneath a pallet filled with construction materials. He wheeled the pallet jack over to an opening in the floor, took out the pallet jack, and slowly began to push the pallet over the opening.

"This is what happens when you call the authorities and take things into your own hands. You fall out of buildings, you take the initiative to kill people, and you mindlessly climb steps and push construction materials over the edge of building floors."

He utilized his two-way radio and informed Niles to stand in the stairwell. Niles pushed the poacher, who was wrestling with him down one step, while the others stood by and crowded the lobby.

Lance watched as the materials were pushed over the edge and toppled down two floors and crashed through the third and onto the fourth floor. The result crushed four poachers on Niles's floor, leaving three. Two took flight, and the reminder tried to square off with Niles but were dealt with by Lance and himself once Lance descended to Niles's floor.

"Did you see what someone did to the building? They're building onto this very site, and then someone nearly went on a rampage to condemn the very structure singlehandedly!" said Niles, wound up.

Since his investigation on his floor was completed, Mason joined the two conservationists before the rubble and was shocked to find what he saw as well.

Mason said, "Who could have done such a thing? How dangerous."

Lance stood quietly and rubbed his disgruntled face from their reaction, sighed, and took a few steps from them.

"I wonder if someone's going to bottle my tears and use an eye-dropper during the process," mumbled Lance sarcastically.

As they descended the steps to leave the building, all three saw the arrival of the authorities.

"Did either of you call the authorities?" asked Lance.

"No," said both of them simultaneously.

Arriving out on the street, Jodi met with Lance near the wildlife transport who planned to haul the wildlife off to the wild.

"You've been here waiting since we've arrived, haven't you?" said Lance.

"You made me late because you botched up the lattice top on your cherry pie crust," mused Jodi.

"The views and opinions expressed by the host do not state nor reflect those of the company and its management."

"Parental guidance suggested. So may I tag along?"

"You'll have to try a bite of my casserole. It'll put this shady cherry pie lattice work in its proper perspective. We may need to take two trips."

The wildlife transport was taken out to a remote location, and the wildlife was released after Jodi hitched up a ramp to set them free. Niles and Mason returned to the conservation camp.

*****

On the coastline of Tanzania between Pangani and Sandani, Charles and a few of his men accommodated themselves on their unknown crudely built seaport. They all enjoyed a drink beneath an umbrella over a table. Niles and Lance walked up to them and took a seat with Charles.

"I assumed you narrowed your trace of us to our luxurious hideaway with ease from all the square miles this continent has to offer," said Charles.

"Actually, the vultures were found circling above after we followed your trail of dead animals," said Niles.

"A secretary bird came up to us and whispered in our ear and told us exactly where we could find you. Then we followed your aroma. That's where the vultures came into the picture," said Lance.

"I'll make you aware of how I'm going to capitalize on my new seaport operation that will capture the grandeur of any kind of species I want from Madagascar. I'll sell them at a remarkable price in my market. You won't mishandle it with your filthy hands as an enterprise," deterred Charles.

To the farthest point from the inland, Mason planted explosives on the dock at the seaport.

"Are you sure?" said Lance.

Suddenly, Mason's explosives went off, and large pieces of debris and chunks of wood blasted violently into the air. The conservationists captured Charles's attention once again. The farthest extending portion of the dock was obliterated into pieces, but the plank to one of the cargo ships remained intact.

Pulling the tablecloth to his side of the table, Lance took a sip from Charles's drink. Charles stewed in disgust at each of the conservationists.

"The scales are in my favor and your endeavors...cut off. I can assure you!"

The table and umbrella were tipped over upon Niles and Lance as Charles began to run toward the plank walkway.

Niles crawled out from beneath the table and umbrella and chased after Charles. Only seconds later, Lance maneuvered out from beneath the two pieces of furniture but was confronted by one of Charles's men and was delayed once again by violence.

Charles crossed across the walkway and remaining plank and boarded the cargo ship. Mason blew up the next section of the three-story structure, and the plank to the ship fell into the water. Niles scaled to the end of the structure, just short from where the plank sank while Charles cackled from the ship.

"I guess you still can't wager the right bid when it comes to any of my steps, Niles Wilson!"

Taking a running leap, Niles soared toward a harness that hung from the side of the cargo ship but missed grabbing it and fell into the water. As a result, Charles made sure Lance's opportunities were cut short with the harness, which offered Niles a way to climb the ship, so he cut off the harness.

Lance pulled out the umbrella from the table, struck Charles's aggressor with the metal tip, and stuck the tip into the eye of the other man. He dropped the umbrella and ran for the platform.

Niles swam his way to the opposite side of the other cargo ship resting behind Charles's ship and began climbing a rope ladder dangling from it.

Lance found the start to the first story platform in the center and began climbing to the third story on a rickety stairway. Two men came out of a small shack on the second story and pursued Lance. On the top were a stack of small pallets that were set off to the side of the platform. Lance removed one and slid down one level of stairs into one of the men climbing the steps. They toppled to the floor. Then the man got hold of a chain and swung it at Lance as he tried to take the second level of steps up to the third story. Lance stooped out of the way and struck the side of his stomach. The swing caused the man to double over in pain.

A tall robust Tanzanian man with a patch over his eye and unkept teeth emerged from the shack and confronted Lance. He seized Lance from the front of his shirt and pulled out his shotgun from the scabbard. Then the Tanzanian lifted Lance against the woodwork platform above his head and pushed him into the individual boards.

Niles engaged the cargo ship and turned it into the path of Charles's ship as he made an attempt to leave port. Charles's ship was gradually overtaken, and inevitably, Niles slammed into Charles's ship. His ship was diverted toward the port's direction and was pinned against the land. Charles leapt off the compromised ship with Niles following him.

Lance took a running start to leap against the chest of the Tanzanian man's chest, but there was no sign of progress made against him. After Lance was back on his feet and removed from the Tanzanian in distance, the conservationist ran toward him, scampered beneath his legs, and headed back for the shack. The Tanzanian followed Lance and cornered him outside the shack.

A sledgehammer sat off to the side on the platform. Lance picked it up and pummeled the Tanzanian in the side as he attempted to strike him. The Tanzanian lunged toward the shack and was thrown through the window. Lance entered the shack door with the sledge-hammer and struck him on the head and the side a few times. Lance drove him with a hard blow through the tattered remains of the window and onto the platform outside.

"I need to see what other tools lie idle on the ground more often," said Lance to himself.

The section the Tanzanian lay upon was suddenly taken out by Mason's explosives, and the Tanzanian came crashing down with that part of the platform. The only section left standing was the one with the shack.

But it only took a few moments before that section was compromised by an explosion as well. It sent Lance and the second-story shack hurling to the ground.

A driver drove up in a Jeep to the bank, then stopped and waited as Charles rose out of the water, hopped into the Jeep, and rode off. After he swam out of the water, Niles realized he missed his opportunity to apprehend Charles as he rode away. After Lance had collected himself, the conservationists regrouped and reported the area to the authorities for investigation, and they headed home.

*****

Several hours later, Mason drove a Jeep across grasslands along a high raised band of land, which broke off relatively steep on the right side with rocky terrain and a very steep valley to his left. As he drove, the land was soaked from previous rains within the region. Its left ridge caused him to swerve erratically, placing him in danger with his car tires repeatedly over the ridge. The Jeep was momentarily involved with spinouts occasionally over time. The ridge made a gradual descent over a long distance, which worked more as an obstacle to the location where Mason was headed. As he came down the bend and the ridge ended, large, smooth, embedded flat boulders served as another obstruction in the path where Mason was headed. The Jeep went airborne several times while Mason sat calmly in the driver's seat, maneuvering it.

After he drove several miles and the terrain became less rocky, Mason came across a tract of open land in the middle of some thick acacia woods. He stopped the Jeep, climbed out, and removed a reasonably large crate from the payload of the Jeep and approached the land with a number of markers in the ground. He knelt down, cracked the crate open, removed the remains of a dead animal, and laid it on the ground. He fetched a shovel from the Jeep, dug a hole, and placed the remains inside the grave. The site was none other than an animal cemetery.

The broken ground was used to cover up the hole once again, and a grave marker was placed in the ground. Mason spent his remaining time checking the upkeep of the rest of the cemetery. He recalled the past of many animals and their personalities of many kinds from the remembrance of the inscriptions on grave markers. A particular name stuck out on a grave marker, and it found appeal with him. He pulled out a notepad and wrote the name "Aisha' on a piece of paper and then looked upon it in admiration. He returned the notepad into his back pocket and then returned to the conservation camp.

*****

Out on the savanna, Niles and Lance provided treatment for a wounded aardvark out of action. They applied antibiotics, wrapped its leg, and moved it to the back of the Jeep to a cage.

"That went down smoother than emptying the inside of a broken egg," said Niles.

Suddenly, a dark red smooth coating in the form of fluid ran over the front of Niles's hat and brim. Niles abruptly became repulsed, developed a scowl, and touched the fluid to determine what he could make out of it.

"Cough syrup!" said Niles.

"I wanted to help you along in such a smooth transition," said Lance.

"You stored cough syrup in the medicine chest!" berated Niles.

"It'll remove the hot dry treatment from the sun off your fedora, you know, if you want your own corral, chute, and enclosure for special animals. You're also going to inevitably need to join a fraternity too. You do realize that, don't you? Let alone improve your bowling average. Or people are going to start talking about you."

"Oh, shut up!" Niles snatched the cough bottle out of Lance's hand and threw it in the back of the Jeep.

"You know, I proposed an idea once to put a bowling alley—"

"Would you like to know what I've recently discovered? Women go to far less war than men when they engage in conversation with each other."

"There's a reason for it because they don't see the need for any cheese slices to be dispersed around the dinner table in a mismanaged way. They just toss them like a deck of cards until everyone has a slice. Have you ever watched a woman serve cheese slices? Men may not capture it when a woman sets the table."

"Women still avoid war over it! That's no excuse!"

"You think there's less war because of women per capita?"

"I think they face more driving hazards on the way to the store as opposed to preoccupation with preparing food for others. That's what I think!"

"You don't want to tell that to a sanitation truck driver who's a woman."

"No, you don't. And they won't initially put up a fight over fringe benefits. They'll take it as a grain of salt unless you change the flavor of their gum. Then there's an initial conflict! I'm still trying to solve that mystery. Does that answer your women per capita question?"

"Yes. We need to solve the gum mystery now."

"Oh, okay."

*****

Out amongst the Ngorongoro, Mason busied himself following a sporadic caravan of motor vehicles while traveling through the hill country. As he sped through spotted cruising vehicles, Mason questioned whether each journeyer he confronted had permits and licenses to hunt. A cluster of particular vehicles were traversing to start a new ranch from the appearance of their possessions. There was another collection of vehicles that trekked on the outskirts of the group. A number of outstanding facets caused them to stand out as poachers from a considerable distance from Mason's Jeep in front of him. He made the decision to keep a safe distance from them. As he looked at the scarce company left around him, Mason discovered another conservationist who was a Black African actively involved in pursuing the conspicuous party.

Breaking away and passing over a bridge in single file, the poachers traversed to another uneven valley sporadic with vegetation and trees. After the gap had been made, the two conservationists crossed the bridge and stopped beside each other thirty feet beyond it.

"The trees and brush become thick, so it's best to give them space. It presents complications, so we have some time," said the African conservationist.

Both of them watched to keep a close eye on any activities from the poachers in the distance.

It was mere moments, however, when Mason sensed the presence of something to the left of his vehicle. After he looked left, he saw the presence of a hippo, which posed a risk because it was far too close to his Jeep. The African conservationist leaned forward in his seat to see the threat and temperament of the hippo.

"Don't bat an eye if you can help it," said the African conservationist.

There was no lack of lost untrained concentration by either of them as they looked upon the hippo glaring at them.

Then the hippo took a few short steps forward, unhinged its mouth open, and began to grunt. Mason reached over to secure a grip on the center console and lifted his leg toward the passenger's seat. The hippo began to slowly inch forward and close in at a rising rate of speed. Swiftly and abruptly, the aggravated hippo rushed into the cab of the Jeep and lunged at Mason. Its jaws immediately began to attempt to maul Mason, who was scrunched tightly and firmly against the passenger's side door. Its head veered to the left and the right as it made every opportunity to pinch a piece of him while he was pressed to the side of the Jeep.

Mason wrenched the handle of the Jeep door, but the door was stuck and wouldn't swing open at all. The entire Jeep was being rocked by the livid hippo, and it wasn't in Mason's or the conservationist's understanding whether the driver's side door was about to buckle effortlessly. Gradually, he slipped both hands upon the top of the passenger's side door, slid up the best way possible, and dropped over the top to the ground. The African conservationist told him to hop into his Jeep, and they sped off very quickly.

The two conservationists found a small remote area several miles ahead and located among the buildings vehicles they had identified earlier as notorious by their plate number. The two men parked their Jeep some distance from the camp. Hunched behind rock and a few trees, they analyzed the camp and discussed how they would discover the validity of the camp's involvement in any serious corruption.

"We don't have a complete overview of those inside the camp, what their tactics and operations may be according to any type of monitoring through field work prior to today. Since this is the territory I cover, the next move should be initiated by me. I know what to do," said the African conservationist.

The African conservationist ran behind his Jeep to evade detection and climbed into the cab. The horn was engaged for a lengthy time, and then he stopped while remaining hidden below the windshield.

One of the drivers of the poacher's Jeeps heard the vehicle make a honking noise out in the brush somewhere, but he couldn't consistently pinpoint any location. So the poacher made a decision to investigate the boundaries.

Minutes later, the poacher came across the conservationist's Jeep but didn't find any trace of anybody belonging to it. He circled to the back and looked around into the open-top Jeep.

Mason spotted two men who crossed between two buildings in the camp. They carried a stretcher stacked with wildlife pelts on top of it.

All at once, Mason clutched the shirt of the suspected poacher and said, "Do you see exactly what was carried in the midst of this camp? We want to investigate it!"

The African conservationist said, "We have a duty for you to perform." He began to fit a metal brace around his leg and said, "We are about to question and incarcerate you if you don't cooperate by tracking the camp for us, and this homing device will tell us whether you do it or not. I want pictures taken on this digital camera to be used to determine the slaughter of any wildlife on this camp. Is that clear? We will be watching where you are going and what you are doing!"

The suspect returned to the camp, and he left the two conservationists waiting.

"What was it that you put on his leg?" asked Mason.

"A stainless-steel pipe repair clamp. Don't worry. My plan will work no different than it did last week."

"How do you know he won't spill the beans?"

"Because I have a hidden microphone installed on the camera. The earpiece is in my ear."

"How do you know he won't ditch the camera?"

"Because he is on the monitor on the Jeep as we speak, and it'll work no different than it did last week."

Surprisingly, the digital camera was put to use snapping shots of the illegal slaughter facilities and the neglect that took many forms of evidence in skin pelts and trade. In naivete, other oblivious workers were unaware they were being photographed as participants in a link to wildlife poaching. It didn't faze the photographer that he was singling out detailed locations with the camera and monitor, only that he was happy to take them.

The freewheeling poacher returned to the two conservationists with the digital camera and returned it.

"Now I want you to walk in the opposite direction of the camp because we're going to investigate it. We'll be following through by allowing you to go free mercifully, but be very sure you stay on that heading because we'll be watching you!" said the African conservationist.

"Aren't you going to remove the homing device?" asked the suspected poacher.

"No because we're going to keep an eye on you. Go on!"

Like a man setting out for a calling, the suspected poacher went without reservation and aimlessly meandered in the direction of the hilly brush and grasslands on the Ngorongoro.

The two men infiltrated the camp and then walked among other poachers on the outset of mingling with them to pose as poachers. It was only a few mere moments when an armed man found someone who displeased him and was seized by the armed man to be taken to those in charge of the camp. So both conservationists kept a close eye on their surroundings and exactly who they met on the grounds.

They discovered many facilities through pictures of their LCD screen and continued to take photos with the camera throughout the camp. An understanding was made fully aware between both of them that no action could have been taken today because they were unprepared to address the camp. In that particular case, more men would have been needed in order to take the camp according to what they knew, and that was what they intended to do another time.

Their exploration brought them to the epicenter of the site's corruption as they discovered in a three-story building in partial ruins the involvement in poaching and terrorist activity. The images, documentation, and assorted papers collaborated the basis as they littered a table in an enclosed canopy tent.

Due to growing noise outside the tent, they found themselves enclosed seemingly by a number of people. They hurried and crawled into a crate standing behind the table and closed the top quickly.

In a short amount of time, a pallet jack was placed beneath the crate, pulled out of the tent, and pushed across the grounds of the camp. Inside, the two men were unaware where they were headed.

They were pushed into a tent for storage to check inventory.

Mason said, "What's in these smaller rectangular crates beneath us?"

The African conservationist cracked one of the lids open without being heard. Once one of them was opened beneath them, firearms were discovered.

A mob of men busying themselves with smuggling purposes peered into the crate and pointed their assault rifles at the two conservationists.

The two men were hurried out of the crate and given unloaded weapons to defend themselves while the mob mocked, made sport of them, and were closely shot at with rounds. As minutes went by, the serious intentions of the act didn't hit home until one of the shots struck the African conservationist in the shin, causing him to collapse to the ground. During the moment of misfortune, Mason made an attempt to catch him but wasn't fast enough. Grief filled his heart as his friend was afflicted with pain. Those who had inflicted the African conservationist had done next to nothing to relent from their confrontational behavior, with both conservationists finding no solace. They were hemmed in and had nowhere to go.

A dark stout figure entered the tent and began shouting orders to the men. Some of the men resisted him, but he made himself quite convincing in their native tongue. The mob left them alone to carry out the orders, which seemed to take precedence over their current objectives.

Once they were alone, the man pulled out a task force ID as he operated as an undercover investigator and showed it to the two men. He removed the thin fake beard while he kept a close eye on the entrance.

"I want to make you aware as quickly as possible that you'll find under no circumstances that any of you or your men will take this place. There will be long-term consequences as a result in the event you'd like to take this place into custody," said the investigator.

"We won't keep you if you're doing surveillance. You need to leave now," said Mason.

"If you escape this place, please give this to my wife. She will be wondering how I am doing. This will keep her up-to-date."

"When are you being relieved?" said Mason.

"You must understand that I can no longer leave, and I'm in harm's way."

Heart-stricken and bewildered without any awareness of what they could do, the two men tried to search out the matter to see how they could help him.

"Go now! You must be on your way!"

As they broke outside through the tent-fly, the two men tried to maintain their composure and support the hobbling leg due to injury as they made the quickest route to the Jeep. Their gait proceeded to scamper as fast as it took them. After they crossed beyond the tents, out into the open area beyond the grounds, the men shuffled slower to the Jeep.

They hid behind some brush near the cover of a tree.

Then, when Mason cracked the passenger side door open on the Jeep, he saw a poacher who had an unraised pistol chasing after him from a distance. Mason's knee-jerk reaction was to draw his pistol; however, he knew it would only create a reaction across the camp and possibly place the task force investigator in danger.

He reached into the back of the Jeep, lifted a spear out, and hurled it at the poacher. It found a target in the poacher's torso, lodging it into his chest and causing him to collapse to the ground.

The two conservationists climbed into the Jeep and sped off through the hills.

Watching from the narrow footpath through two large enclosed canopy tents, the task force investigator watched as they hustled away from his detrimental assignment, waiting out the duration and knowing just how many days he could be left alive.

Mason's Jeep made a stop, and both men returned to their camp.

*****

A few days later in the early morning, Niles approached one of the cages, which held the caracal. He was there to run a few tests on the cat. He assembled a tranquilizer gun, loaded it, and shot a dart into the caracal. The dart was embedded into its thigh.

It only appeared to be a couple of minutes before the drug had inundated the cat's system. Niles opened the cage and entered inside with his medical equipment. He closed the door behind him and laid the tray out of a medical tote. The cat was placed under assessment.

In a matter of moments, the caracal, which seemed to be sedated, leapt on top of him, then clawed and bit him on the shoulder. He began to immediately beckon out loud as the cat mangled him.

As he stood in the middle aisle a reasonable distance from the cage, Lance heard Niles's cry where he stood with his share of hand tools. As he glanced over his shoulder, he saw Niles in the enclosed caracal cage, trying to set himself free from the caracal by hand. Lance set the shovel and pitchfork aside and ran toward the open canopy rotunda.

In a steel storage cabinet, he grabbed two thick gloves, and from other storage, a medical kit. Then he ran to the caracal cage, opened it, and entered the cage. He closed the door behind him and put the reinforced gloves on. At this point, the caracal had shifted from his shoulder to crawling to the calf of his leg. Lance immediately pried the jaws off his leg and wrestled with the caracal toward the other side of the cage. He spent what seemed like an eternity subduing the cat while it clawed and bit his gloves. Then the cat took a swipe at Lance's face, and the wildlife conservationist screamed, "Aah!"

"All right, lights out," said Lance as he placed a cover over the caracal's eyes.

The cat let out a high-pitched, "Err," and proceeded to bite Lance on his gloves. The gloves actively did the work they were supposed to do; they protected Lance from any cuts the cat might have made on him.

Suddenly, the caracal broke free, leapt over Lance's head, and crawled rambunctiously over him. Lance let out a cry and pursued the freed cat in the cage.

Moments later, he quickly apprehended the caracal again while Niles lay out of the competition because of injuries. Lance braced the front paws on the ground as the caracal bit him in the gloves again.

Mason showed up at the cage.

Lance said, "Get the tranquilizer shot out of the kit and inundate it with a dose."

Mason grabbed the drug, scrambled into the cage, and administered the shot after closing the door. After a few minutes, the drugs reliably took effect, and the cat fell asleep.

"Those that Niles used were the third in a series that turned up ineffective. We need better tranquilizer darts."

Niles abruptly said, "You think?"

Lance and Mason helped Niles to the open canopy tent. Niles removed his cargo pants and discovered a bloody bite mark on his leg. After he had removed his shirt as well, he discovered bloody gnaw marks throughout his left shoulder.

Lance told Mason to treat Niles as he broke out the first-aid kit without any expense. Lance returned to the caracal cage to complete the tests on the caracal.

Once Mason had given Niles antibiotic shots and bandaged him up, Niles lay back to rest on the picnic table.

Mason said with subtlety, "It could have been a Sumatran tiger."

Niles said, "Shucks."

"It could have been a black mamba."

"All right with the formidable suggestions!"

*****

A day later, Mason was in Mwanza and in a suburban neighborhood across the street from three shanties connected with one another. His pistol was drawn as he hid in seclusion from the residences, observing and waiting for any activity. For twenty minutes, he waited for any spur-of-the-moment arrivals and departures through the door, estimating and trying to determine when he could approach the house.

But there didn't seem to be any live activity occurring at the front door of the house. So he took advantage of it and stormed across the street, through the yard, and stood behind the closed door. The sheet-metal-covered door swung open while he carefully tied the door back with a hook and secured the entrance. He proceeded in through the door.

There was stark darkness inside, and the light didn't seem to strike or permeate throughout any rooms. He searched the kitchen, but there didn't seem to be any occupancy involved. So he walked to the back door and opened it, but little light was let in because of an enclosed side porch to the kitchen.

As Mason started to walk back to the entrance between the kitchen and the small foyer, he was jumped by a thug from the other entrance to the right of the dining room.

The tackle sent him crashing against kitchen items on the front counter, and then he was shoved diagonally across the room onto a one-basin sink with a left and right porcelain drainboard.

The thug used restraint upon Mason to rivet him to the sink until he could edge a kick toward the thug to set himself free. Then Mason proceeded to drive the thug numerous times into the wall and slam him on top of a chest freezer in the far-right corner.

The thug suspiciously ran into the dining room from the kitchen. Mason trailed after him through the entrance of the foyer toward the front living room. Another thug leapt on Mason and delivered two blows to his back.

Mason delivered a strike and initially threw him out the large living room window. Once the second thug crawled back into the house through the window, he leapt on Mason. Twirling around once in motion with the poacher on his shoulders, he threw the poacher backward onto the dining room table.

Then Mason jumped out of the dining room window, but the poacher followed and leapt on him again. A third poacher outside swung a chain whip around his legs and caused him to fall immediately to the ground. Two more men struck him in the back and head, and one inevitably stabbed him.

*****

Later during the night, affluent men and those of high status involved in poaching assembled at a makeshift club café, dancing to music out back while tables sat out front.

To the far right along the wall, Mason was sitting in the middle of a row of booths running perpendicular to the wall, across the seat from two of the poachers who had kidnapped him.

While he was in cuffs and not allowed a refreshment, the two poachers indulged in their assortment of mixed drinks that sat strewn on the table. Mason sat downcast as he suffered from the untreated penetration of a pointed object in his back and additional roughing up due to the accumulation of time spent with the poachers.

Lance walked toward the booth, had a seat on the outside on Mason's side, and expected him to stay seated in the inside of the booth.

The Caucasian lead poacher in a white suit and Panama hat with a black band said, "My faculties weren't in dire need of suffering from repercussions due to any existing growing health problems. What do you want?"

"On account of pending critical circumstances and required life-sustaining medical treatment, there's no disadvantage of incorporating the likes of equipment, instruments, or procedures and, for that matter, anything else," said Lance in a scathing manner.

"How do you know the critical state and conditions of our circumstances?" said the second thug.

"Why, it all doesn't simply fall under the categorical identification as a gradual squirt of blood, which behaves copiously. It may be erratic and unsustainably unpredictable and indeterminable," said Lance.

"He's telling us he's going to try to undermine us in some way," said the second thug.

"How unsettling it must be on your nerves to know that your set of circumstances, which may unfold, are engraved in your life, and you know what might certainly take place," said Lance.

Lance slipped out a set of three-by-five-inch index cards and started to spread them in both hands.

"You brought a stack of three-by-five-inch index cards to negotiate for your colleague's life?" said the second thug.

"Why, you've come to the misfortune of dropping the entire set of medical instruments on an unsanitary floor without any replacements. Now you're without an alternative," said Lance.

"Maybe it'll be a second stack of three-by-five-inch index cards wrapped in cellophane," said a slightly angry Mason.

"Choose seven cards from the stack," said Lance.

"Magic?" said the second thug, exasperated.

"Not magic. Reality…or is it real estate? I can't seem to remember."

With an angered expression on the lead poacher's face while his head tilted forward, he became offended at Lance's statement about real estate and squirmed around restlessly.

"Pick a card!" said the excited enthusiastic second thug.

Out of a medium-sized nylon sack on the side of Lance's waist, Lance removed a bundle of explosives with a timer on it beneath the table. Mason saw Lance remove it from the sack.

The lead poacher picked a card with reservation. He flipped it over and the depiction of thorns and thistles in a briar patch which grew in a wilderness representation.

"Ah, now if we could only distinguish between those animals who could traverse through this kind of habitat," said Lance.

"You are in a harsh environment," said the second thug, leaving the lead poacher irritated by his remark.

"Pick another card," said Lance.

The lead poacher chose another card, and Lance said, "Ah, not merely just a debilitating disease but a wide-spread epidemic. It permeates everyone through and through. What could it be? How will it impact others?"

"Again, another card," said the second thug, leaving the lead poacher even more angry.

"And this card leaves you with widespread destruction. You see, this is what tarot cards won't leave you with."

Both men began to look at him with strong soberness and seriousness as if their lives were in danger.

In heightened anger, the lead poacher said, "This couldn't possibly involve a stupid conservationist's hope on behalf of someone else's freedom, could it?"

Having an obnoxious sarcasm that he's primarily known for, but frisky, Lance continued to follow through with another outfielder. He said, "Ah. You see, that's where you must play the role of one who is resilient, similar to many plants that can withstand any storm, whether or not the storm is fierce and you survive the occasion. You simply hope you haven't left the storm door open in front of your wife."

Instantly, Lance, with full awareness of good timing, pushed his booth backward with the gap left to move around and tilted the table down toward him to the floor and onto its side. Then he dropped down and pulled Mason down with him between the table and his booth to take shelter. Far before dynamite could detonate between him and the two poachers, Lance and Mason tightly embraced each other.

An abrupt explosion shattered booths, leveled wooden and glass panels, and sent poachers lethally through debris as a result of the blast. Guests were thrown off their seats, tables were overturned and broken, and virtually everything was left damaged and unspeakably scarred. The table between Lance and the poachers had busted into many chunks and large splinters. The wide metal support of the table base helped protect Lance and Mason to a great degree from the explosives.

Lance came out of the occurrence tattered and without multiple life-threatening injuries as opposed to many of the others involved in poaching at the social establishment. Couples straggled while others struggled to get to their feet. As Lance stood to his feet, large distinct parts of the roof fell to the floor in various places. Mason rose to his feet and proceeded to walk to the front of the club.

The bartender pulled a compact assault rifle on Lance, but a triple-barrel shotgun was pulled from Lance's shotgun scabbard, and he shot the bartender before he got a round off on Lance.

Behind a stained-glass window, a silhouette randomly moved behind it near the entrance of the club, which got Lance's attention.

He fired on the subject. Glass shattered, and a man aiming a weapon behind it was shot, and he collapsed to the floor.

Mason turned to Lance and whimsically said, "Don't you ever make sure...deem it necessary that a threat may lie behind something?"

Lance said, "Why would you want to do a thing like that when you have a stack of index cards at work for you? Besides, they're doing rather well."

"Let me pull one," said Mason. He chose one and read it. "Values and principles" was what it read. Mason tossed the card at Lance and said, "Whatever."

He insisted on looking at the rest of the cards, and they revealed four sets of cards titled "Disease or peril," "Harsh environment," "Destruction," and "Values and principles."

Then he found one card that read, "Mason is put in harm's way." He shook his head and walked out of the club behind Lance.

Two women entered through the clubhouse double doors.

As the last woman who wore a sun hat passed through the middle of the double doors, Lance said, "Isn't that hat for daylight hours and before your curfew?"

She took the hat off and immediately began to swat him with it. Once she stopped, he removed his hat and said, "You see, this is a more reasonable hat for the sun."

As she chased him out the door, she lifted her foot up and pushed him out of the door.

The two conservationists walked out to the curb where Jodi sat behind the driver's seat of a Eurocargo bus with Niles in the passenger's seat.

Lance told Jodi in advance, "No more!"

Jodi said, "You'll do more safaris for us!"

"No, I won't."

Mason muttered to himself, "He'll ask you to install a thermostat for his tent made of fabric, but he won't do a safari."

Lance said, "It's warmer in my tent as opposed to a watering hole...and a Eurocargo bus. Besides, a safari just doesn't qualify as any imperative matter. It's no different than thawing chilled dough in extreme heat."

Jodi said, "Oh whine, whine. What else?"

Lance carried on and said, "Long-lasting chewing gum…a long-lasting shower…long-lasting cologne, and long-lasting fresh breath…people who call you by name to flatter you when it gets them nowhere!"

Niles said, "It's only after Lance discovered those things may have already been improved or may have been handled properly."

*****

A week after Niles's mishap in the caracal cage, a farmer approached the three men to discuss problems about his farm.

"My crops have been targeted by wildlife's appetite, after they've built a new trail, which encroaches and draws itself closer to my crops. I don't know what I'm supposed to do."

Niles said, "May we look at your crops?"

"Yes."

The farmer gave the three conservationists a ride to his farm.

The three conservationists analyzed the crops the farmer grew on his farm.

Niles said, "All the types of plants you grow here are open season for all herbivores. They won't last very long here."

Mason said, "You'll have to build a special fence around your field."

Lance said, "You still haven't made any effort to build a fence around our camp."

Niles growled to himself.

Mason said to the farmer, "The rangers with the government will help you build just the right type of fence to keep all the wildlife out of your field."

The farmer took a big sigh of relief and said, "I see. That's great."

Mason said, "You'll have to drive away the wildlife until the fence gets built. If any are too much for you, call us or a ranger, and we'll help."

"It should be okay. I have Okbo, my dog, to fend them off most of the time," said the farmer. The farmer took the men back to the conservation camp.

*****

The following day, a Tanzanian conservationist from the central part of Tanzania, came to visit the conservationists. He sat with them beneath the open canopy tent.

The conservationist said, "We're facing an obstacle involving the central part of Tanzania. There is an old mine in operation, which was formerly active during a prior period of time, cutting off the trail of a major wildlife path, which has caused a diversion for plenty of migrating herbivores."

Lance said, "Have you talked to the park rangers?"

"I would, but each of you have developed a following about yourself as a group of conservationists who can handle it in the wake of their absence. We thought maybe we would allow you to manage the negligence."

"What kind of mine is it?"

"Oh…copper, nickel, or silver from what I understand."

"Could you ask the authorities whether we have their consent?"

"Sure. Have you ever faced an untamed mining company before?"

Niles said, "I have, but Lance and Mason have not. You're invited to stay at our conservation camp and inspect the wildlife while we address the matter."

"I may take you up on the request…until your return. I'll carry out any of your responsibilities that need to be watched during your absence."

An hour later, the Tanzanian conservationist roamed around the cages at the camp and casually cross-examined the wildlife in the holds. He stopped and noticed a particular animal that had symptoms of a disease.

The conservationist walked up to Niles and said, "Have you been made aware that a few of your ostriches are suffering from dehydration?"

Niles saw Lance nearby while he walked to the cages, carrying a feeding bucket and a pitchfork. After Niles called him to ask a question, he said, "Are you aware that our ostriches have come up with an illness inside their pen?"

"Yes," and Lance made the attempt to blatantly walk on.

"When did you come down with this estimation? And what did you do about it?"

"If you checked the medical log on the clipboard, one would determine such an illness would exist."

The three men checked the examination papers beneath the open canopy tent.

"Oh…it's been documented, and the ostriches are now inoculated with medication."

Lance gave Niles a coy smile for a few moments and then waited for any other continuing matters that Niles might address.

Niles quietly said, "Oh, all right…I guess you can return to your activities." Lance left the two men while they remained behind and observed the charts.

*****

The next day, the three conservationists took a Jeep to the central part of Tanzania to the mining location. They parked off an angled precipice where activity seemed to be taking place and creeped out of the Jeep. Behind two sets of large rocks, they investigated for any suspicious activity and watched the activity involved with the migration site. All three men armed themselves for a confrontation and quickly shuffled up the gradual incline along the path toward the front of the mine. Lance led the way to cross into the mining grounds as he scampered toward a conveyor belt.

Immediately, the attention of an armed man was captured in a watchtower, and he opened fire on Lance. He hunched and remained secluded while he bent beside the conveyor belt. A square dump bin that stood off to the side of the conveyor belt became the next point where Lance quickly relocated.

Niles ran around the entire conveyor belt approached the entrance and opened fire with his pistol on two men. They took flight into the mine and didn't anticipate returning shots themselves. Niles headed for the watchtower and began to climb its ladder.

Lance leapt onto the active conveyor belt and ran back to the entrance of the mine. He drew the attention of three more men inside, provoking one of them who had climbed onto the conveyor belt. Based on their naivete, they decided to attack him, one after another. The first attempted to make an opportunity against Lance with a shovel as the miner, none other than a poacher like all the rest, swung and struck Lance with the shovel, grabbed the miner in the chest and abdomen, and threw him behind onto the conveyor belt. Then Lance ran toward the mouth of the mine while the same miner followed him.

As the man, armed with an assault rifle, reached the halfway spot on the watchtower's ladder, he fired upon Niles. Niles lurched to the left to avoid any rounds. He removed his pistol and fired upon the armed man. He missed his target.

Lance reappeared at the mouth of the mine in front of the same miner on the conveyor belt and swung the broad side of a pick at the poacher. He missed, so he tried a few more times but continued to miss. Then he drove the point into his side, and the miner collapsed to the conveyor belt. Another miner climbed onto the conveyor belt and pushed Lance into the square dump bin filled with rocks and mud, but the second miner followed him in the dump bin.

They immediately began to struggle as they pushed one another in the mud. Lance used the pick to push the miner away, but the miner reciprocated the gesture.

So Lance reached the decision to turn the pick around and club him. The miner dropped partially disoriented in the mud. Lance returned on top of the conveyor belt and ran toward the entrance. But the next miner met him beside the square dump bin and pushed him in again. The struggle seemed to carry on in the mud for Lance, and he tried only what he knew how to do by avoiding the circumstances but found none. The miner got the advantage and pushed him under. He remained under for a lengthy time. Then Lance reached up, laid hold of the miner's shirt, and pulled him into the mud. After that, he lifted his legs into the air and triggered a moment for suffocation to follow.

Mason climbed into a tractor loader and began loading and pushing freestanding mining equipment onto a dump truck across the open area on the trail in front of the entrance to the mine. Part of the mining equipment was dumped onto the truck, which was sent over the steep cliff in front of the mining area. He followed through with the square dump bin as well after he emptied it. Next, he removed a vacant conveyor belt adjacent to the one Lance remained in motion upon.

After there was no other opponent, Lance stepped off the conveyor belt, and Mason removed it as well. Next, the dump truck vehicle itself was sent over the cliff.

A few park rangers and the authorities stationed themselves behind the rock's edge to the mine and waited for an opportunity to take it. Mason saw Niles was actively involved in making an attempt to get an opportunity against the armed man.

Niles reached the top of the tower, stepped inside, and struggled physically and combatively with the armed man.

"Do you need help?" shouted Mason.

"No!" hollered Niles.

After several minutes of physical confrontation, Niles became indignant and struck the armed man several times to remove the fight out of him and refrain from being shot. Niles turned the armed man toward the open door on the watchtower. Then Niles struck him, and he fell on the floor of the watchtower, partially hanging out of the door opening.

Niles caught hold of the armed man in place and shouted, "Tip the watchtower over on its side, quickly!"

Mason determined through comprehension what Niles had in his mind as a request.

Shifting the tractor loader into gear, Mason dug up the outer foundation of the watchtower and toppled it to its side.

Inside the watchtower, Niles took careful precaution to take a firm grip with one hand on what he could find to secure himself. The other was used to hold the miner in place. Everyone present was concerned about the reason Niles had made such a request, which could have put him in harm's way. Crashing down abruptly and hitting the ground hard, the watchtower made a thumping rustling thud.

The leader of the two conservationists, however, climbed out on his own from the watchtower window opening facing up.

He slowly hobbled toward Lance, who stood in the middle of the open mine area, raised the miner's assault rifle, and said, "Look at the unearthed mined souvenir I uncovered from a makeshift watchtower knocked over carrying its own armed man."

"Quite an amusement park ride, too, huh?" said Lance.

Mason pulled out the watchtower, and then, using the implement, pushed the watchtower over the cliff. Last but not least, the loader tractor was sent over the cliff as well.

Niles said, "The junk pile will be used for scrap or melted for iron."

After the mine was taken by storm, rangers and the authorities rendered their services to take the mine in under their custody. Once the armed man was freed from being pinned beneath the watchtower and his health examined and cleared, he was arrested with any other miners found at the mine.

Afterward, the location was vacated, and they all stood behind the group of boulders near their hidden vehicles. They waited and watched to see what transpired with hopeful confidence for the wildlife far beyond the other side on the open trail beyond the mine to see if the wildlife would reclaim the trail winding in front of the mine and rugged area.

The group of people watched as the herds of wildlife did that very thing. The herds all began to stampede and cross the trail as the group of conservationists and authorities stood within close proximity behind the large rocks and celebrated together. They were all reassured that the migration trail had been opened to the wildlife in the grasslands.

*****

111

As the three conservationists returned from the mining site, they drove through a partially forested area. They ran into a caravan, which brought them to a stop.

"Scavengers?" said Lance.

"Marauders perhaps," said Niles.

One of the men from the caravan walked up to their Jeep.

"Are you people who work with animals?" said the man.

"In a way," said Niles.

"Yes…yes. Come with me."

The man walked back to his caravan while Lance looked at Niles and said, "It's your turn" to indicate whose turn it was to listen to the request.

"Is not!" said Niles.

After they got out of their Jeep and followed the man to the caravan's wagon, inside was a dog who was lying on the floor.

"He's been lying around without any motivation of any kind for many days and has no appetite, rigorously pants, acts lethargic, and is listless."

Lance examined the body of the dog and rendered a diagnosis. "He's suffering from tick infestation. If he doesn't get treated, he'll die."

By returning to the Jeep, Mason volunteered to retrieve a medical kit out of it. Once he returned to the group, Lance gave injections to the dog when the man suddenly became angry and pulled a firearm on the men.

"What are you going to do to him? Try to put him to sleep?" said the frantic, furious man.

"No, I said he has to be treated. Then he'll live," said Lance.

After he grabbed the gun out of his hand, Lance set it aside.

"How long will it be before we see change?"

"Give it a couple of days."

Mason turned to the Jeep and discovered two men of the caravan scrounging through the equipment and supplies in the back of the Jeep.

"Scavengers!" shouted Mason as he walked to the Jeep. "What are you doing?"

The men continued to rummage through the Jeep.

Lance walked back to the Jeep and said, "All right, all right, all right. I'm the one who has to get the supplies from town." And he shut one of the lids on one of them.

One of the men grabbed a syringe gun out of the remaining open kits and showed it to the other man. They admired the medical tool as if it were meant to be held in awe.

"You can have that syringe," said Lance.

"Should we take the needle off?" asked Mason.

"Nah, they can reach an understanding based how long it would take to jab each other...maybe gouge something out in all their infatuation," said Lance as he returned to the covered wagon.

Niles shouted, "What's wrong with that syringe?"

"It's no different than your bath amenities you've worn out over the years from bathing."

"If you'd learn how I properly take care of it right, it would work like a smooth oiled machine."

Niles said to the man, "Is that all you need?"

"Yes, thank you."

With the syringe, the two men who ransacked the Jeep climbed onto their caravan, and the entire group rode off on horseback. The conservationists returned to their Jeep and headed home.

*****

Jodi spent time in a small town and met up with a disfigured child who tried to tell her a group of raiders were attacking shanties and starting them on fire. When he tried to make it apparent, she failed to understand him. Another woman who walked toward them on the walkway knew him and helped translate on his behalf.

The boy showed Jodi two maps that comprised two rather elaborate drawings. The maps were very detailed, three-dimensional, and consisted of the town map and a neighborhood sketch, which were the locations under attack.

Jodi said, "There's got to be a far greater way of understanding people with special needs than relying on a translator. Come on, let's go look into it."

They climbed into her mini truck, drove through town, and used the maps to search the streets to locate the area. The boy did his best to relocate the specific designated spot where the houses were being raided. Difficulty happened to knock on their door, however, and they couldn't make a connection to the location of the attack.

After driving around so many blocks, she stopped the minivan and said, "We need the help of other people. We'll return in a little while." They headed an entirely different direction to return with help to the route they were originally headed.

Fifteen minutes later, Jodi drove out to the same location and picked up where she had left off. It was just one block short and at the end of the block to the right to the outskirts of town.

She accelerated straight toward the group of raiders circling around the shanties. A number of vehicles broke off from the rest of the raiders and began to head toward Jodi. She carried on and wasn't about to relent, striking the appearance that she was playing a game of chicken.

She headed for the first driver in the broken group as they ran in single file toward her. One hundred feet behind Jodi, park rangers and law enforcement units drove around the end of the same block and joined Jodi.

She continued to cease from flinching from the very direction she took and drove the first raider off course and forced him to make a sharp right turn into another compromising vehicle. It was beginning to be apparent that no one was about to cause her to deviate from any course she took. She passed four other vehicles that didn't stand up to her and broke away from her as well.

She set her crosshairs on another driver. The rest of the group continued to break into shanties, burn, and circle them.

The disfigured boy was shouting sounds and cheers from his highly adventurous side as a sign of cheerfulness.

Mason drove around the corner in a Jeep and quickly joined the raid. Niles followed with a cargo truck while Lance followed behind him on horseback.

Mason rammed into one of the raiders circling a shanty, pushed it into the yard, and drove the Jeep against its side, very close to a shanty. Its rickety shape caused it to stall and break down in its spot. Mason stopped and backed his Jeep out and pursued another Jeep.

Then he reached another pair of poachers in a Jeep and drove by the Jeep's side. Mason simply kept eye contact while he drove.

Mason leapt into their open-top Jeep Wrangler Sahara, seized the driver's head with both arms, and pushed the passenger against the door with his feet.

In seconds, the driver's foot withdrew from the accelerator to abruptly stop the Jeep. But keeping the vehicle in motion to divert the two raiders' attention remained important to Mason. As Mason tried to keep the Jeep from coming to a stop, he quickly pressed his foot down on the accelerator. Preoccupation with a misdirected moving Jeep and the threat of striking an obstacle posed more of a problem to both raiders than a stopped Jeep to Mason. As the accelerator was under constant friction between the raider and Mason's foot, either to speed or not to speed up the Jeep, the steering wheel was forcibly preoccupied by both men.

By predominantly getting the upper hand, Mason wrenched the steering wheel in the exact direction toward the line of marauders trailing one another around the house. As he overpowered the steering wheel and maneuvered it methodically to his leisure, Mason swerved the Jeep into the convoy of vehicles and butted into them one by one in their reckless storm.

Seeing Mason growing resentful and impatient because of the diversion, the two raiders tossed Mason in the back of the Jeep to avoid a crash and a contradictory route. Both raiders, who were filled with heightened aggravation and hostility, canceled out in their minds whether their distraction had been properly handled and disposed of.

Half a minute later, Mason rose up in the back seat, looked at the two raiders, and picked up two bottle bombs he had discovered on the floor behind the front seats.

He lit the fuses on the bottles and prepared to throw.

The driver glanced back and was struck with fear at the threat from the bottles.

The driver screamed, "No!" and tried to seize one of the bottles from Mason's hand.

The raider in the passenger's seat was immediately struck with fright as well from the driver's scream. Instantly, he turned to see what had the attention of the driver.

Mason threw one bottle bomb toward the top of the driver's side dash and then the other bottle on the passenger's side of the dash. Ignited fuel splattered over the dash and the occupants in the front seats. Smoke and flames erupted from the dash and rose behind the windshield.

Both raiders screamed as parts of their clothing and their skin burned from the fuel. Filled with stinging sharp pain and overwhelming dread, the two occupants in the front seat raised their arms in the air and let out growing ongoing screams.

As a result of their bodily burns, they hurried out of their doors to meet the ground and roll in the dirt to end the pain and flames. Mason crawled to the driver's seat and resumed his campaign against the other drivers who continued to press the shanties hard.

Jodi pushed another Jeep with the edge of her mini truck by clipping the bumper and made no sign of steering away. Nevertheless, turning the vehicle at a ninety-degree angle, Jodi continued to aggravate the driver who couldn't maintain course.

Niles ran into a few stragglers breaking off from the main group, upsetting one Jeep and driving it into the other Jeep. Niles spared neither of the two Jeeps as he pushed them over a remotely deep embankment.

Lance rode ahead of a car a number of meters, but the driver accelerated and caught up to him, so he put a bullet in the front right tire. The horse was guided to the right side of the car, and immediately, the passenger shot several times through his window with a compact assault rifle in Lance's direction. His drew his horse back and swerved across the back end of the vehicle and struck the window with his machete. The window was completely broken out in the car.

Then Lance rode near the rear of the car to loosen the tire in the back of the vehicle. He led his horse to gallop behind the vehicle as he inserted the tire into the window. He stuck the blade of his assault knife into the tire to build a punctured hole. He placed a stick of dynamite into the tire, lit it, and rode away.

An explosion took place, which sent the tire into the back of the front seat and threw the driver through the front windshield. The vehicle ran over the driver on the ground in front of the vehicle and swerved into other oncoming traffic.

One raider mounted on a horse near a shanty while another joined him and was obliged by fellow followers to raid homes.

They charged headlong, however, toward Lance who rode in their direction. One of the riders ahead of the other drew a machete in the air and threatened Lance with it.

Several feet before they met, Lance drew a Cavalry sword and lopped off the hand of the rider. The cut was swift with precision and took place before the rider could act against Lance. The dismembered raider toppled to the ground, and the second rider chased Lance.

The park rangers and law enforcement officers had let gunfire loose throughout any opportunity they could make against the raiders.

After circling away from any disruption, two raiders in Jeeps tried to pile-drive into a law enforcement vehicle. Niles abruptly drove into them by circling and cutting into them from the side. The officer merely joined the rest of the enforcers by cutting into a few cars from circling and possibly breaking into more shanties.

As Lance rode toward the other rider on horseback, he accidentally banked him, and both horses toppled to their sides. The men both rose to their feet, and the raider drew his pistol, lifted it in the air, and pointed it toward Lance.

The raider tried to fire his revolver into Lance, but the cylinder was free of bullets because they were lying on the ground.

The raider looked at his gun and discovered the cylinder loose and unable to lock. Baffled and filled with disappointment, the raider looked up to Lance to see his reaction.

Immediately, with a grin, Lance drew his firearm and made himself ready to fire and said, "Worn-out revolver and not a properly maintained cylinder."

Then he stopped smiling and decided to see whether his clip was loaded. He took it out, examined it, returned the clip to its place, and shot the man in the shoulder.

Moments later, one of the raider's vehicles unsuspectingly drove beside Jodi while lagging to a particular degree. The truck they were driving had a winch in the front of the flatbed. The passengers crawled onto the flatbed, placed the eyebolt in the socket of Jodi's cargo bed, and then hooked the slip hook on it.

He returned to the cab, and the driver began to jerk heavily on the side of her mini truck, causing the left side to become slightly tilted on the opposite side.

Mounds found in the terrain, which both vehicles encountered, acted as a continual constant menace as she tried to stabilize the truck.

As they rambled on, the disfigured child told her to apply the brakes or turn left. When the brakes were applied, however, there were little results because the brakes were weak. If she had turned left, they would simply have leaned and remained braced to their original course.

Then Jodi's truck unsuspectingly approached a large grass mound in the lot near the houses. The raiders took drastic measures to veer toward the mound.

The mini truck was turned on its side.

While the cable on the mini truck remained intact, it twirled the vehicle and dragged it behind the poacher's truck. Inside Jodi's truck, Jodi and the disfigured child struggled to remain steady in the cab while being bruised and banged up.

The poacher gradually circled around to drag Jodi's truck even farther. Plenty of deep concern about Jodi and the disfigured child's well-being reverberated in the hearts of the three conservationists, but Lance was no exception.

As the poacher's truck was completing the circle, however, Niles's cargo truck hit a mound and lifted off its right corner axle. It lunged on the left corner of the raider's truck, diverting and busting it into a construed wake of partial wreckage.

As Mason made a pass by following Niles, he fired on the poacher's truck with an assault rifle and penetrated it with bullets. He struck the driver with a round, but the poacher drove on while firing a pistol at Mason.

Mason remained untouched as he followed Niles's lead and led the charge to set Jodi's mini truck free from constraint. Niles made a pass to deflect the raider's truck off his bumper but missed entirely and nearly clipped Jodi's truck. Mason made a second pass as well, and clipped the frame, throwing the truck in a separate direction. Then Lance rode along the driver's side of the raider's truck and leapt onto it.

In his hands, Lance carried a crowbar and busted the slip hook off on the eye bolt. Then he used the hooked crowbar to break through the rear of the cab window. He braced the crowbar around the driver's chest and pulled toward himself. With both hands, the driver grappled with the crowbar around his chest as he tried to set himself free. Lance tugged back on his chest and began pulling him through the rear window.

With the removal of his own pistol, the passenger fired upon Lance where he squatted and worked the crowbar, but the poacher's clumsy shot missed him.

A strong backlash came from the driver because his shot was far too close to leave him unscathed. The passenger wouldn't have it any other way because of stubbornness, so he aimed his pistol at Lance again.

The driver blurted out words, which were enunciated incorrectly because of the squeeze, and he continued to try aggressively to work himself free.

Lance removed his firearm from his holster, and he fired on the passenger, striking him in the back of the chest. Lance pulled the driver out of the cab and struck him against the shoulder with the crowbar. The blow left the driver unbalanced, and he fell aside to the flatbed.

Seconds later, Lance realized the truck was headed for a shanty. He turned the steering wheel into the oncoming traffic of the circling raiders. As he angled the truck correctly, it headed straight into the front of another raider's truck. As he saw his time narrowing closer and closer, Lance leapt off the back of the truck, making impact, and rolling across the ground. Both vehicles struck head on, crippling both of them and impeding the flow of a few raiders circling the shanties.

Jodi and the disfigured boy, both of whom had crawled out of the mini truck, walked around its rear and were immediately confronted by a raider on foot.

As she stood beside a slightly full portable gas tank that found its way on the ground, Jodi took it and swung against the man repeatedly without holding anything back.

Within moments, the man was lying on the ground and put out of his senses.

Then Jodi looked into the distance near the shanty and spotted the driver whom Lance confronted with the crowbar.

She fiercely started to pick up a hurried gait toward him. Her feet picked up speed, and she approached the driver. Once she reached him, she furiously and energetically used the portable gas tank to put him out too.

After she brought it to a conclusion and exhausted herself with heavy breathing, she saw Lance standing ten feet from her. Then the agonizing driver showed a little movement, but it left her compelled to use the fuel tank on him a few more times.

Then Lance said, "Oh, just shoot him for everyone's sake. Above all else, put him out and get on with it." He threw his shotgun in his scabbard to her, and she discovered the empty chambers in the shotgun.

He pulled out a rubber projectile shell in his hand and held it.

After being agitated and aggravated by the ride she had with the driver, Jody bluntly said, "Give me the shot!"

Lance threw it to her. She loaded it and shot him in the chest, nearly leaving beyond a shadow of a doubt the potential to kill him.

Then she walked over to Lance and handed him the gas tank, took some of his shells from his scabbard, and began to walk ahead of him toward the raid while she kept the shotgun.

Minutes later, Niles drove toward Jodi and Lance in the cargo truck and picked them up.

It didn't seem as if an impact was being made on the raiders and shanties as numerous vehicles were beginning to circle them.

Mason brought his vehicle in the circle and found himself inside of it and not allowed to break free. He understood that he was hemmed in as they roared by him, and there was no way out.

As Mason looked on the initial interest of the drivers, he saw their intentional inclination to harm. So Mason stepped out of the Jeep and took shelter with what little there was to offer for protection outside of the vehicle.

Around the end of the other block, more law enforcement officers and park rangers who were throwing their support arrived and surrounded the circle of vehicles around the shanties. The enormity and size of the circle's growth had caused the authorities to question whether they would break off into more circles.

The authorities heard a loud exhaust noise from a cargo truck driven by Niles, and he backed it into the pervading nonstop circles and brought the vehicle to a screeching halt. The vehicles that followed made no attempt to stop and crashed into the vehicle in order ahead of them.

The authorities got out of their vehicles and began to arrest all those involved in occasional pilfering and burning of the shanties.

The conservation team, disfigured child, and missionary who showed fortitude with the authorities and rangers all gathered as they looked at what they had before them.

Jodi lifted up the disfigured boy and said, "I would hold onto those two maps because of the surpassing quality that lies in you as a hero. Let's hear it, ladies and gentlemen, for this town's true hero of the day!"

The crowd applauded him, rubbed his head, cheered, and celebrated by congratulating the young boy. The rest of their time was spent enjoying his and each other's company for the rest of the afternoon.

*****

The following day, Mason was decorating a few cowhide leather vests in an enclosed canopy tent. Spread out on a cart table were a number of craft tools and 3D stamps utilized to design beautiful styles in the leather.

Lance entered the enclosed canopy tent and said, "Boy, you're hosting an all-star lineup. You've taken pointers from busy ant colonies and demonstrated details in all their pointers. Who is this for?"

"I'd like to give it as a gift to my lady acquaintance and the rest of the vests to other people as donations."

Lance remained silent for a few seconds and then said, "You're going to make an entire wardrobe for her, aren't you?"

"Hey, you're right! I could, couldn't I?" said Mason with excited anticipation.

"Just let us know when you move into the executive suite on Fifth Avenue. Seriously, would you like to use gemstones in your designs?"

"Yes."

"You know, if you're that precise with details in arts and crafts, you could carve her a rose instead of growing one for her."

Jodi walked into the tent and with surprise on her face from what she saw before her eyes said, "Wow, Mason, your craftmanship follows a design that's one of a kind. That's rare...no different than a gem."

"Would you like to incorporate those gems now?" said Lance.

"Yes," said Mason.

Niles joined the group and said, "If you have a knack with arts and crafts, perhaps you're a jack of all trades with construction too. We have a thatch hut and a fence to build around the camp."

Lance changed the subject entirely and said, "We want to talk about details! You're the one who tools around with the thermostat in everybody's tent constantly."

Niles abruptly jabbed, "I've told you before. It has nothing to do with details since you have a bent on the temperature inside your living accommodations."

Lance said, "Like I said, you're the one who tools around with the thermostat constantly."

Niles said, "Well, we've drawn such a familiarity with your personality being right at home with being inhibited that we thought you'd welcome the heat."

Lance said sarcastically, "You do realize the contagious sense of humor I have."

Then Lance left the tent, and Jodi looked closely at the decorative make of the jacket.

She said, "Wow, Lance may never do a leather jacket like this for me. Could you provide one for me?"

Mason said, "He could surprise you."

"Maybe you could add more patterns to it than any vest from him?"

"Perhaps."

Niles said, "Have you ever had the experience of putting a stained-glass electric or oil lamp together?"

"I have all the pieces cut, but I haven't assembled one. It's almost a jigsaw puzzle to me. I love the challenge it presents to me. It's no different than Sasha, our female harbor seal pup, whom we visit routinely on a regular basis."

Jodi said, "Where is this seal?"

Mason said, "She's part of an aquarium we are involved in, a contributive effort to care for in the city. It only holds a few animals in captivity that we're trying to get on the right foot."

Niles said, "If we see them flourish, backed by funds and kept reasonably well with the help of sponsors, great! If we don't get backing, it will be suspended."

Jodi said, "What age is the pup?"

Mason said, "There are two seals, a mother and her pup."

"Is the pup full of energy?"

Mason said, "Yes, they have their own secluded stomping ground out of the aquarium."

"How near is it?"

"Mwanza."

"May we see it?"

"Absolutely."

*****

Making the aquarium their desired destination, they made a trip which seemed so soon. Jodi, Niles, and Mason visited the solitary seal exhibit with the mother and female pup in an aquarium.

"The seals were given a spacious aquarium to roam freely and an open semiaquatic land area to roam."

Jodi watched through the glass enclosure to see a very curious, young, healthy female seal pup staring back at her.

"I hope if I participate in childbearing, my child will have the same temperament as you do," said Jodi.

Moments later, Sasha swam out of an opening and inched forward across the surface by pulling herself forward toward Jodi. The outer boundary refrained her from crossing and advancing within five feet of Jodi. There she stood, resting her chin on the edge of the outer boundary, actively staring at Jodi, enjoying Jodi's presence.

A Caucasian young girl walked up to the land exhibit and mentioned nothing to Jodi until she had Jodi's undivided attention at her side.

Jodi looked down and said, "Would you like to see Sasha the seal?"

The girl nodded her head and Jodi lifted her so she could have a closer look at the lively young seal.

Moments later, Jodi gave it some thought and asked the young girl, "Hey, would you and your mother like to go to Shooter's Grill?" while her mother watched several feet away.

The quiet and shy girl said, "Let's ask her."

Much later, the conservationists found a booth while the ladies sat separately in a booth of their own.

Jodi led a conversation with the mother and begun her question, "What kind of interests generate revenue to build a solid building for children's teaching classes for the purpose of missions here in Mwanza? It simply seems as if it would be a hurdle to complete. It would seem that nothing would comprise a greater challenge for us, according to the size in scale. It would be great to have a three-class division or group system in study."

"Festival," said the young girl.

"What could get people to come and enroll their children in the study groups?" said Jodi.

"Festival."

"And what would convince and give confidence to people to invest in a project like it?"

The young girl took her fork, stuck Jodi's steak, pulled it from her plate, and placed it on another plate. Jodi's attention was captured immediately.

"Festival!"

Jodi reacted to her response with shock and surprise as it entered her mind and said, "Festival!"

A popular familiar festival, which was thrown on a biweekly basis, always drew a crowd for the entire group who had attended Shooter's Grill and the public. They set up booths to raise funds for Jodi's building. As the crowd mingled around the stands and booths, the group had set up small wildlife exhibits picked from Jodi's young animals in her fenced area near her residence. The booth was set up beside the exhibit to help fund the building.

Jodi stood in front of the booth and said to Mason sitting behind it, "I hope we can build a structure out of this."

He said, "We could postpone building it and do some more fundraising or look for alternative methods of raising money."

Niles appeared before the booth in a master of ceremonies costume and began to proclaim to those around the booth, "Ladies and Gentlemen, there's an offer and an opportunity for those of you who may want to volunteer for an opportunity not to be missed."

Lance joined Niles in the same costume and said, "Step right up, folks. Look at what we have here! We have a woman eating cheese out of her very own pressurized can. Right before your own eyes! It's my understanding that it's one of the leading causes of shrinking your height. If you'll find your way over to the booth, we can address that problem effective immediately."

Embarrassed by Lance's words, Jodi abruptly pulled him aside and said, "What are you doing? Would you stop behaving like an astrologer, prognosticator, or soothsayer from the past?"

Lance said quirkily, "You do realize if nonprofit organizations exist, businesses can provide us with vouchers. Then they won't have to send anyone into space."

Jodi pushed him back from behind the booth and began giving him an earful. She said, "You are gone! Are you lending me your ear? You are gone!"

Niles continued to speak to the public. "Don't ask me to bring in a circus performer when we have a wonderful wildlife exhibit for the entire family right before your eyes. Come one, come all. Anyone can be entertained by a vender in Marrakesh or a crop duster from Fulton, but you and your children could attend an exotic wildlife exhibit."

A half an hour later, a group of children ran out of the wildlife exhibit and joined their mothers contributing at the booth to the fund.

After they had left, Jodi was left stunned by the amount they had contributed. She leaned over to Mason and gave him a hug for helping her.

Then Lance carried on behind the booth and said to Jodi, "You know what I need to do? There's this nagging need to point out all those disgusting batter lumps that you left on your corndogs!"

Jodi pounded her fists down on the booth, growled, and said, "Come here!"

He immediately started running away from the booth.

Jodi immediately took to the chase as Lance made certain he carefully weaved through the crowd.

As Lance and Jodi reached the far side of the festival, the mother Jodi invited to dinner stopped her and said, "Come here."

She led Jodi to the second of three booths they had set up for Jodi on the grounds along with two other wildlife exhibits beside them.

As Lance continued to sprint straight forward, he bolted beyond the festival while he held on to his hat and cane.

As Jodi approached the booth, the mother said, "You have made a generous amount from the crowd that was willing to give. I guess a person finds more than just fruit and shade beneath a tree. They have you covered."

Jodi took a seat behind the booth and counted the contributions at the first booth. Then they checked the second booth and combined the amounts.

"I have to pay my fees or any additional amounts to the festival, but we're going to be reasonably close. This is great!"

Then Jodi decided to pick up where she left off and resumed her quest after Lance and chased him.

*****

A few days later at the conservation camp, one of the twenty-by-forty-foot closed canopy tents was struck by lightning.

The surrounding brush around the camp was lit on fire in spotted locations. The flames put the wildlife in the cages on edge throughout the camp. As the rain drizzled, uncaged spooked animals wandered around in the midst of the smaller bell tents as Jodi walked through the middle of them. She saw a kudu and a lioness, but they didn't give her any attention.

She met Niles, who happened to be carrying a stack of towels out in the rain.

Jodi asked him, "What are you going to do about the wildlife roaming free through the camp?"

He said, "I think we'll be safe for now." Then he continued to walk away.

She walked in the direction of the climbing flames from the enclosed canopy tent.

Before she reached it, Mason approached her coming from that direction.

He said, "Do you know where Lance is? Or have you seen him?"

Reacting in an inconspicuous and predictable way, Jodi answered, "No."

"A few hands have showed up with extra fire extinguishers out back by the vehicles. I could use his help to bring them to the enclosed canopy tent."

Mason continued to his tent with fire extinguishers in his hands while Jodi went to Lance's tent.

After a brief stop was made at his tent, Mason stopped out back at the vehicles and picked up charged fire extinguishers and left the discharged ones behind.

With tattered fabric flapping in the wind, the rain continued to gradually grow over time as it fell through the top of the enclosed canopy tent during Mason's return. He took the precautionary measures to keep any small traces of fire spreading toward any caged animals left behind.

After her head stuck through Lance's tent opening, Jodi found an unoccupied tent. She left the tent and went out back to the vehicles and helped one of the park rangers carry more fire extinguishers to the burning tent.

They strode to the enclosed canopy tent through mud and soggy rain, which grew during the lightning storm. Inside the tent, they saw another park ranger hard at work putting out the fire. Jodi approached Mason as he had his back turned toward her while she thought how she could help.

Mason closed the small door to a cage, turned toward her, and was covered with small furry animals from his head to his stomach. Due to the elements around them, the small furry animals hung tight to his body. He began to walk toward the entrance and left the tent.

But before he could take a good number of steps, Jodi hastily asked him, "Do you know where you're going? Are you able to see?"

He said, "I know it by heart," and he left the tent.

Jodi asked herself, "Why did Niles walk out of here with towels in his hands when there were animals left behind in cages?"

The park ranger told her after that they may have been for particular critical emergencies. She said, "Oh," and began to extinguish the flames.

Another lightning strike hit the frame and set more fabric on fire, spreading from the charge itself.

Niles made his arrival at the other entrance, climbed the stacked cages, and began extinguishing the flames.

Beyond the open canopy tent, where the large cages and enclosures were located, Lance tried to calm a young elephant that had broken out of her pole fence. As he comforted the two-and-a-half-year-old elephant, he strove to lead her away from any burning debris and trees near the fenced area. Then he tried to lead her several times to a tree that wasn't burning, but he couldn't move her in the intended desired direction.

He made an attempt to feed her. Then he used the elephant's trunk to guide her. He employed a harness to do the work for him, but there wasn't any success. Then Lance grabbed one of the watermelons and sprayed it with a scent from a spray bottle in his backpack.

After Lance returned to the elephant, the watermelon was handed to the young elephant, and she began to take a strong interest in it. So Lance slowly led the elephant to the tree, set the watermelon aside, and tied her up with a body harness after the elephant allowed him to do so. The elephant helped herself to the watermelon.

Lance said, "We're not going to get into the habit of using scent on a routine basis or you'll be found irresistible with your very own pleasant breath. We should call you the sands of time, based on your hesitation to be led anywhere!"

As the fire had begun to be eliminated in the enclosed canopy tent, no resulting factors allowed the fire to spread to different tents.

Minutes later, Niles began to tear down the bare frame structure of the enclosed canopy tent riddled with remains of fabric lingering from it.

The pole fence, which was broken down, was repaired by Lance as he reestablished a new wooden pole and rails as quickly as he could.

Jodi and Mason drove a truck with a water trailer around the perimeter to put out fires in the brush with the help of the park rangers. As Jodi was using the hose to douse a tree between the trailer and the brush, a lioness broke from her run and abruptly stopped fifteen feet from her.

As Jodi was taken by surprise and her heart began to beat rapidly, she dropped the hose and froze in fear. While Mason witnessed the event unfold as he stood by the trailer, he looked behind her and saw another lioness approach and stop on the opposite side.

Suddenly, each lioness bolted toward each other. Making the choice to dash toward Jodi, there wasn't any understanding in her mind whether she was considered prey by the two cats.

Mason grabbed her with both hands around her shoulders once the lioness to the left of her had passed her. Then Mason began to lead her to the partially open row of brush, which was in front of her, running east and west of the lionesses.

Both of the wild-cats aggressively began to lash and tear into each other. As Jodi and Mason tried to put distance between them and the lioness as they turned east, one wildcat diverted her attention toward Mason and lunged out with his paw along his leg and boot.

The other lioness continued to retaliate toward the cat, and they returned to their clash. Jagged wounds and deep cuts proceeded to ensue on both cats as they viciously thrashed each other.

Any assistance Jodi could offer was given to Mason as she helped him hobble away. As they made it past the rows of brush, both of them turned north and proceeded to move away. It was only after twenty-five feet of distance Jodi and Mason had made between the lioness and themselves that the lioness who attacked Mason decided to pursue both of them again.

Both of them turned around to see the immediate threat as the lioness began to pick up speed. After she had crossed half their distance, Niles fired a Verney Carron 700 Nitro Express Double Rifle into the air toward the lionesses right side beyond her.

Her attention was turned to Niles as she thrashed and swiped with her paws. He shot another round directly in front of her before the lioness, and it continued to stand its ground.

Then Lance sent a tranquilizer dart into the lioness while each of the park rangers showed up for support. The wounded and exhausted lioness took flight in the opposite direction of Jodi and Mason's path through the lane between both lines of brush. The two rangers tried to track the wounded lioness down to administer any prompt and necessary care for rehabilitation. Using their weapons, Niles and Lance walked the other lioness.

With her arm wrapped around his shoulder, Jodi walked Mason to the open canopy tent and gave attention to Mason's leg.

She used a pair of scissors to cut Mason's pant leg open and revealed any harm that might have come to his leg. As she pulled the pant leg back, she noticed three long deep gashes running several inches down his leg. Immediately, Jodi applied an antiseptic to clean the wound and then dressed and wrapped it. The two other conservationists returned from the outer boundaries and asked if Mason was hurt. She told both men the news of the deep long cuts Mason had undergone. As a result, they helped Mason into a car and drove him to the hospital, followed by the Hummer to Mwanza.

*****

They wheeled Mason in a wheelchair and admitted him to care for his wounds. As he undressed and put on a hospital gown, he got underneath the covers before Niles and Lance returned to the room.

Then Lance scandalously said, "I can't believe you would take an opportunity like this to meet someone. What a way to get social interaction with an eligible woman, especially after reaching the decision to gradually run away from a lion so you would be admitted into a hospital. Now we'll see if there is anyone who is a taker."

Mason gave him an evil eye and said, "Are we going to forego amputation too? Or do I get to lounge around a long time, just to rummage through hospital supplies?"

Lance said, "You should be honored. If you have good table manners, don't mistake your table salt packets as barbiturates, and the nurse always refurbishes your preferred brand of sugar packets. You'll fare reasonably well."

"I suppose every man who lays those criteria out when they search for a suitor at a hospital by embellishing on them won't bring upon himself any further medical trauma," chided a nurse who overheard the discussion and walked into the room.

Lance said, "It's crucial that no unnecessary unauthorized instruments are ever used in medical procedures, such as those used during an appendectomy, for example. One never knows the unpredictable reaction that could take place if anything were to go wrong. Such procedures should never take place. It's no different than a bank vault being opened by a thief with simple ease by using time increments from a video on a web page. The consequences are left in the hands of a thief who was not only authorized but unqualified to access the vault and robbed others."

Then Lance remained silent for a while and then said, "Then there's the conversational piece based on whether floor cleaner has enough initial cleansing agent for a woman with a sponge mop in her kitchen."

A clipboard flew toward Lance and slammed against the wall above his head shortly before he stooped beneath it.

Then Lance said, "I didn't bring up the matter about pool balls being placed into a rack at a billiard into the picture." A cluster of more clipboards were thrown and hit the wall above his head.

Minutes later, the doctor took the temporary dressing and wrapping off and concluded his assessment. He asked when the injury happened and how it took place. He asked whether there was any weakness or numbness and if Mason could initially move his joints near the cuts. He also asked if he had any other medical conditions, such as circulation problems or diabetes, to require additional treatment to prevent infection. Then he ran a physical exam, starting with looking at the edges of the gashes and the wound.

He tested nerve, artery, and muscle function in his examination. The wound was inspected for embedded objects, and then he examined the overall condition concerning possible blood loss or anxiety. Since the cuts ran deep, the doctor required stitches to repair the tissue and eliminate scarring. After the nurse brought proper suturing instruments into the room, he'd proceeded to stitch up his patient.

Later, following the procedure, the nurse returned and saw Lance leaning against the hospital bed, appearing as if he had something else to say. The nurse said, "Keep it up and I'll question you about various types of medicine."

Lance giggled and said, "Medicine! Medicine...go ahead. A wildlife conservationist seldom has a tendency to shy away from knowing more than one type of medicine within fields."

The nurse said to herself, "Malarkey."

Lance drove the stake even deeper and said, "You know, your own line of work is similar to your crisper that's put to use in your very own refrigerator."

The nurse stopped as she was walking out and sighed. Then she looked back at him, disturbed, and said, "Well if it wasn't widely known, some of us women are refusing the habit to buy takeout each night but use our crisper to our advantage...not that we're into that sort of thing constantly."

Niles said, "To his defense, he has no kitchen talent at all."

Appearing as if she had an opportunity and an edge on Lance, she momentarily remained silent. Then she said, "So is that the reason why men work so well at decorating cupcakes and cakes with decorative frosting piping tips?" Wearing a subtle grin on her face, she left the room.

The two conservationists giggled, and Niles said, "Boy, did she send you out the door with a brown paper bag and no lunch."

Lance said, "Okay, Mason may now have a greater knowledge of how she stocks her crisper and takeout in her refrigerator and what he could get her for their anniversary." After a couple of seconds, Lance made the remark, "You're the one who's been slap-hammered again!"

After Lance left the room, Mason said, "No, it would never work out between us. She's feisty, and it would never work out for the both of us." Seconds later, Mason questioned, "Do you think women might have lost their tendency to find or search for a suitor as so many previously in an unhealthy way may have at times in the past?"

Niles said, "That may be based on the grounds where awful men may very well have used a woman or she didn't understand what the heart of a man holds or how he behaves."

In another patient's room, Lance visited with an elderly man who was diagnosed and had surgery for major internal bleeding. The elderly man said in the middle of his conversation, "Who would have known that the redheaded woman was an undercover detective in Chicago, and she colored her hair with a coloring marker? I never dreamed, by the kind of fight she put up, that she would have never afforded to assume marriage."

Lance said, "What about those who are offended?"

The elderly man said, "Oh, now, what happens as you age is you don't value nor take to heart critical or judgmental matters so much. When you get older, your reaction to criticism is different and you come out of it as nothing more than a mere experience as opposed to a mishap or life-changing experience."

Lance said, "You think they'll break new ground over that?"

The elderly man said, "Right," and laughed.

"You know, I was serious about the decorative frosting piping tips innuendo," said the previous nurse who had spoken to Lance earlier.

"It was all a combined effort by the cake design industry to keep baby blue frosting out of the wildlife conservation and the medical profession," said Lance as he pulled out a rubber ball and bounced it.

The nurse whispered, "You think he'll find someone?"

Lance whispered, "Yeah."

She said, "He's the kind of guy a lot of gals are searching for out there because he's sweet, which is hard to find. He'll make her out to be a princess, which she already has been made aware of, and a very happy one too.

"They may have quite a share of a lot of similarities and differences between each other, so it leaves an impression between their relationship if they want to make it work."

"I have to get back to work. Allow the hospital to know if he rises for long periods of time on his feet."

"Gotcha."

Lance left the in-patient division and returned to the waiting room. He sat down beside Jodi and said, "I was in Mason's room for a few minutes, and they wanted to fix my hatchback on account of what I said."

Jodi said, "What exactly did you say so they would conclude that you needed such a procedure?"

"Emissions malfunction."

"Exactly. If you would have changed the muffler and checked it during routine maintenance, you wouldn't have to pay for such a costly procedure."

"And how is it my transmission has a lifelong warranty, but emission lasts only so long?"

"Because when you pay higher prices for a car after you have invested in one in this world, you must consider in light of it all a particular thing. Nostalgia, sweetie. Pure nostalgia."

*****

Weeks later, outside the grounds of an anonymous poacher camp before dawn, the lead conservationist, wearing exercise attire, stood jogging in one place. Mason approached him with his cane and a stopwatch and made eye contact with Niles.

"Are you ready?" said Mason.

"Yes, but remember, Lance mustn't know about this."

"Right."

Niles got down on his hands and bent knees to prepare himself for a race.

Mason gave the signal to Niles after starting a stopwatch, and Niles began to run toward the poacher camp.

There was nothing he carried, except a small double-edged dagger. As he approached the camp, he sprinted down a shallow hill, which gradually brought him to a large enclosed canopy tent.

Niles cut a slit into the back of the tent with his dagger and slipped inside. A small stack of wooden boxes sat inside as Niles circled around and exited the opening of the tent. As a strong agile runner without regard for his age, his legs carried him well without any hindrance.

His course took him through three more canopy tents in single file, embellished with a variety of merchandise inside each of them.

A few other makeshift buildings with easy access spotted the grounds throughout the camp as well.

As he placed one step after the other, Niles continued to breach buildings without security as he deliberately sounded off break-ins occasionally, including the sleeping quarters of the poachers.

A loud drumming sound from a large galvanized steel trash can lid in Niles's hands hammered the frames of a few bunkbeds as he got carried away while he ran through the long structure.

He climbed up the ladder inside the next building, crossed over the boarding lying on the rafters of a rundown storage building, and watched the poachers below who tried to search for him. They gradually broke off through the building like solitary sea-life that navigated on their own throughout the ocean.

As he pressed on the outside the building, the ground sloped up against a line of shanties, which ran in single file away from the hill. Niles leapt on the top of the roofs and caused racket from his feet as he stomped the tin sheeting.

His mind returned to the past to moments prior to cross-country racing where he participated as a contestant. Minutes before the start of the race, a young Mr. Wilson in his mid-twenties had spent his time building up contestants who were responsive and receptive to encouragement by lending their ear to hear his exhortation as a motivator and a fellow cross-country racer.

Moments later, the starter sounded off, and the competitive racers were set in motion. It wasn't too long before the first mile was put behind Niles in a clearing as he entered a scattered woody area.

Approximately forty feet ahead of Niles, two other runners headed through the moderately thick trees. As they continued into the woods that ran deep as opposed to wide, they captured the sound of something unfamiliar with the whistle of the branches and movement of the breeze. A coiled timber rattlesnake alarmingly startled the two runners as they closed in on it.

One runner told the other to circle around the tree to the right, avoid it, and continue the race. The runner listened and ran around the tree and carried on with the race. The remaining runner turned around and saw Niles nearing the spot where he stood. Then he walked around the tree to his right and hid behind it.

As the distance closed the gap where the runner was hiding, Niles came to the point where the timber rattlesnake had been lying on the ground.

As he tried to pass beyond the point, the hidden runner took Niles by surprise and shoved him to the ground. Niles altogether didn't suspect the presence of a snake beneath him as he landed on it. He didn't count on any strikes from the timber rattlesnake; nevertheless, they were at work against him as he lay above the snake.

Once the runner returned to seclusion, he ran on and joined the rest of the runners.

Within minutes, a few other runners came to Niles's location after they had left behind obstacles and a few alternate routes. They found a young Mr. Wilson lying on the ground with blood running from his arms and body, but the presence of apparent danger was no longer near him. The runners were left unaware of what might have affected the young man who lay on the ground.

A call to emergency dispatch was placed for the assistance of a fallen runner, and he was taken to the hospital.

As he lay in the hospital bed, Niles vaguely remembered the procedures he went through to set him on course to revitalize him. The insertion of an IV needle in his left arm struck him odd because he was unfamiliar of its origin. Faces of the hospital staff unknown to him stood out in peculiarity as well.

If there seemed to be one thing that happened to capture his interests, it was the administering of medicine that began to deliver him from a crucial circumstance. As he slowly began to be renewed over the next hour, and care and proper treatment for his diagnosis was carefully observed, he browsed from his technicalities according to his viewpoint, which was carefully watched rather than techniques. It wasn't redundancy or ambiguity that drew intrigue, and it wasn't categorized as stifling criteria, which he occasionally held toward other people. This was a mold that appeared literally cracked and broken to another world of new possibilities concerning medicine, caretaking, and observation. All those aspects were actively not part of his study as an undergraduate.

As Niles's mind returned to his current situation and present surroundings, he cut into a wide berth, circled on the ground around a few occupied rondavels, and broke into and exited them as well.

He stormed into a newly built affluent small Grecian house on the camp.

How the Grecian house could go overlooked by the observant for a poaching operator's center of operation according to its build was questionable. As Niles entered the dining room hall and came near a long dining table with the poacher's operator seated on the other end, Niles stood still while he took a long swig of whatever was found in the chilled ice.

Due to the curious nature from the servant who approached Niles, the servant insisted on asking Niles the reason for his reaction to the drink. "What is it?"

Niles quipped curiously, "I don't know, but I ordinarily never question what's in a bottle found in chilled ice."

Then Niles leapt onto the table and began to run toward the operator and upset everything on the table.

As he approached the operator, who stood and objected strongly toward Niles, the conservationist jumped off the corner of the table, causing the operator to lean back in his chair and topple backward to the floor. Niles quickly made his exit on the other side of the house.

A smaller twenty-by-twenty-foot enclosed canopy tent lay ahead of Niles's route after the Grecian house. A number of armed poachers inside concentrated their efforts to play chess on several square tables. They sat quietly behind a few tables and studied their next move. Other armed poachers stood a few feet away from the tables and spoke to each other as they sipped coffee.

After he made another quick entry into the tent opening, Niles burst through the entrance, leapt onto each table, and quickly tore through the backside wall.

A few of the poachers made quick work of the backside wall immediately and shot rounds through it. Then they quickly shuffled through the rear side wall and spread out to hunt Niles down.

Niles had already taken a firm grip of a trash receptacle, climbed on top of it, crawled onto the corner roof of the tent, and lay upon it. Below him, he observed the men spreading out around the confines of the tents. Moments later, after the tent occupied no more occupants, he climbed down to the ground and headed toward the next tent.

Inside the tent, Niles stood at the entrance and watched a number of poachers doubled and tripled together while they unusually observed night-vision technology in the dark and walked throughout the tent. In front of Niles stood more than a dozen tables with the technology standing against stacks of crates.

Niles froze and chose not to inch forward any farther but to avoid the possibility of being recognized with even a hint of detection or movement as the technology was utilized by the poachers.

Once he was certain he was not being watched, Niles placed on one of the night-vision goggle units to blend in undetected after he removed his fedora hat. Gradually winding slowly through the groups, he made his way around them with great difficulty.

He occasionally ran into a few of the poachers as he worked his way through the tent and explained that he was none other than a legitimate contributor.

Two poachers who stood apart from the crowd in the corner picked Niles out from the midst of the crowd as he wound his way to the other side wall. They walked to the middle of the sidewall where he was headed and waited for him.

He came to an abrupt halt and stood silent before the poachers as they looked at him with suspicion. Seconds later, both men unexpectedly placed their arms around him and began to welcome and pat him as they spoke their native tongue as fellow poachers. They failed to realize that Niles was a wildlife conservationist doing his own kind of surveillance with night-vision goggles.

While they chuckled and laughed voraciously, the two poachers walked away from Niles into the center of the crowd. Niles kept a close eye on them as well as the others to determine when the proper time would be to leave the tent.

Many seconds later, he found the opportunity to pull out his short double-edged dagger again and cut a slit in the side wall behind him. By backing through the slit, he made his exit and disposed of the goggles below the slit.

He put his fedora hat on and broke into a steel building. Upon his entry, he faced a great number of crates ascending toward the ceiling right from the start in the darkened building. So he leapt up and began to pull himself to the top of the first crate and saw the heading that he would need to take over the crates.

In order to reach the right stack, he had to select just the right ones by size and height. Scampering to the left and continuing to climb a number of crates, he carried on, estimating how to reach this towering stack.

He reached the middle column, which held the only opening that allowed him to cross between two higher stacks of crates. From that point, he could make a slow gradual descent over a good number of crates with many turns.

As he jumped on one crate, which rested partially over the edge of another crate, it slipped due to a lack of being secure upon the stack. When his foot came to rest on the crate, it tilted and bottomed out below into an open gap in the stack.

Another lower crate, which jogged out a few inches, allowed Niles to secure his fingers during the fall from a reasonable drop below.

He picked up from where he left off from that point and climbed to the top where the two high stacks sat safely.

As he stepped gradually lower on the other side to the ground, more light permeated the cracks upon the stacks. He dropped off the last crate and approached another door.

What lay beyond the steel building was a lot filled with trucks, livestock transports, Jeeps, and cargo trucks.

After he finished searching for the presence of others in both directions outside the outdoor building, Niles ran to the first row of vehicles and stooped down along the side of a Jeep.

When he saw no danger in any direction, he carried on by winding through a few vehicles.

Only after reaching a quarter of the distance through the lot, open fire pinned him down beside another Jeep. Shots were being fired from his left as he hunched beside a vehicle. After several seconds, he abruptly began running to break himself free from the encumbered spot and gunfire. By keeping low as he ran, a subtle hint of his fedora hat could only be seen above the frame of the low vehicles. Spotted gunfire occasionally grazed the body frame of the open-top Jeeps, placing Niles in danger as metal penetrated and bounced throughout the vehicles.

Niles made brief stops occasionally while he questioned whether eminent or immediate danger would surface as he inched closer to open grassland.

Niles looked out ahead between the two rows with a line of cargo trucks parked off to his left side. After deafening silence encompassed the grounds, Niles crossed the short distance to the cargo trucks along the last remaining Jeeps.

Sudden gunfire made strikes against him again, but he gained the advantage by staying ahead of their line of fire. Under the enduring harsh conditions, he reached a place of shelter beside the cargo trucks. Then his break came through as he dashed the rest of the distance toward the open grassland. He passed the last truck and climbed the shallow sloping hill on the grassland.

Two poachers stopped by to the front of the cargo trucks, aimed their assault rifles at Niles, and fixed their target on him. But they were too late. Their adversary had already begun most of his descent down the other side of the hill. The poachers stood still and tried to determine just exactly what should have been done.

*****

The following day prior to dawn once again, the two conservationists stood outside another poacher camp.

Donning the same athletic apparel, Niles warmed up for another run. Mason rummaged through electronic equipment in the back of the Jeep. He pulled out two Talk-About two-way radios from an aluminum truck toolbox.

He tossed one of the two-way radios to Niles and said, "This time, it may be much more crucial and critical as a case and the real thing." Niles placed the two-way radio in his fanny pack.

Once again, both of them prepared for the sound off at the starting line by using their imagination. Niles crouched down and prepared to get ready.

He started to run when the sound off had begun.

Any run of each invasion into a poacher's camp felt like the preliminary entry of a race as Niles went underway. As he circled toward the left to a small enclosed canopy tent with his small double-edged dagger, it never crossed his mind whether he would be out of harm's way during his morning intrusions on poacher camps until now.

He cut into the fabric and slipped inside where a five-by-five-foot crate sat on the ground with no lid on it. The desire to satiate his curiosity overwhelmed him as he drew closer to examine its contents.

Ordinarily on a run, he left the evidence of any poaching aside so he could return to the camps later to infiltrate them as part of the team.

What Niles found below, however, were the condemning remains of more than one hundred rhino horns piled in the crate. It undeniably appeared to be critical evidence to seize the camp without any delay.

Actively working in haste, he ran to the next metal building beyond the tent and investigated it. He found two helicopters, which further disclosed inside enough proof the purpose and strategy of the camp. These measures had been so rarely seen by Niles's team.

Niles radioed Mason to inform him about the poaching violation and air transportation on the camp.

While Mason stayed with the Jeep, Niles would inevitably return in a matter of minutes. As Niles sought to return to the Jeep, he kept a close eye on what transpired in his surroundings.

Mason called the park rangers and the authorities. While the calls were made to each of the correspondents, Niles returned and changed into his routine clothes for work.

The men placed calls to their colleague and reached other wildlife protection services and organizations.

After forty-five minutes, the park rangers, followed by the authorities, arrived to investigate the camp. A ranger informed Niles and Mason that Lance would be absent from the investigation because he was out on another wildlife trafficking assignment, looking into other poacher activity.

Moments later, Niles drew a simple map, which he quickly sketched for the group so that everyone involved had a mutual understanding of where the evidence was located.

The services broke up into groups and began to pervade the campgrounds. Mason remained behind because of his injury.

Two teams covered the tents with the verified evidence as part of their investigation. They slipped into the tear to remain undetected as opposed to entering the tent opening so the services could see for themselves the rhino horns in the crate.

Two rangers quietly stationed themselves behind the tent opening while two poachers stood outside at the front of the tent. The team decisively made further analysis and reached a count as they waited on further radio communication from the two other teams.

The first team transmitted the location of the rhino horns. The second team found both helicopters, and they disabled them from any further use while assigned guards were positioned there as well. Breaking deeper into the camp, the third team engaged another structure occupied with a good number of poachers.

The poachers in the structure were placed under suppression with gunfire. The third team held down the presence of the poachers at the rear of the tent while they crouched behind anything they could find. The team tossed a few tables on their side to build cover, but shrapnel made rather good penetration of them and cost the lives of the services, which were taken in a short time. The casualties made by the team were few as opposed to the poachers, so Niles and the few park rangers and authorities who remained fell back and left their wounded and dead behind.

The first two teams gave confirmation to each other to penetrate other structures and to advance toward any involved at the site, even if the element of surprise from gunfire was gone.

Niles broke off from the remaining poacher hunters and ran around a canopy tent; however, he came across three intimidating armed poachers. In a dominant persuasive attitude, one of them demanded Niles immediately drop his firearm. He relinquished his firearm by dropping it to the ground.

The poacher hunters who left him took another course and joined another team. They made it their objective to storm as many structures as possible so a garrison wouldn't form against them.

While many of the poachers were made another number when it came to casualties, the rest of the scarce numbers fled on foot out of the camp and were left by the authorities and rangers to be hunted down by air and land transportation.

Two of the three poachers dragged Niles backward on his heels to the other side of the camp away from the location of rhino horns and helicopters. There on the edge of the boundaries were a good number of cages, which were practically any size, filled with a range of carnivorous wildlife.

The poachers fooled around among themselves while they entertained the thought that Niles should be introduced to a cage accompanied with wildlife.

They opened the door to a cage and threw him inside with a honey badger that didn't take kindly to its territory being invaded. Niles quickly got to his feet and leapt to the top of the cage.

The jaws of the honey badger caught him on a boot and thrashed around on it ferociously.

With his other foot, he kicked with his heel to free himself, but the badger didn't budge while it was struck in the muzzle and head. He tried to work himself free repetitively, but the honey badger seemed to endlessly thrash and sound off with snarls and growls.

A bar that lay upon the top of the cage was within Niles's reach, so he maneuvered it around with his fingers, trying to move it to an acceptable spot above the cage wires. After clinching onto the bar with his fingers, he worked it through the wire and started to pry the upper jaw of the honey badger off without trying to harm it.

After trial and error, he made repetitive continual efforts to free himself from the badger's upper razor-sharp teeth. It was not apparent whether the long teeth of the honey badger had sunk deep into Niles's boot, causing any relative harm.

After sweat and adrenaline began to transpire, Niles worked the badger's teeth free at last, and then he removed his boot from the bite of the honey badger. Then he swung both legs up and tucked them close to himself.

But the honey badger immediately rose to its feet and tried to clinch him along his posterior.

It nearly bit him, so Niles was convinced to hug the cage as close as he could up above.

The honey badger continued to leap up toward him several times. Although he had a suitable, firm grip, his fingers began to grow weary.

He took the bar, swung, and poked a hole in the cage's water dispenser and saturated the dirt inside the cage. As the dirt permeated more with water, the surface became slicker and more difficult for the honey badger to stand on its hind feet.

His fingers became so weak while he remained hanging on the top of the cage. His fingers slipped through the cage wire while they were hanging from the top of the cage.

Niles toppled onto the badger but rolled off as quickly as he could to avoid being attacked. After being compressed to the ground in the mud, the honey badger scrambled to get its footing and turned toward Niles.

Working frantically, he opened a side door facing another similar side door on another cage. Niles unlatched each of them to reach what lay in the next cage. He swung each door open and made an attempt to pull a square shovel through the doors, but the blade wouldn't fit through the hole.

Niles's deep concern provoked him to double-check just exactly how the honey badger was reacting. It remained in a threatening position as it now stood in the mud.

Placing the bar through the wire and prying the wire back in places helped enlarge the opening so he could slip the square shovel through it.

Hastily, he turned the square shovel and kept the jaws of the honey badger preoccupied and away from himself.

Biting and snapping at the instrument, Niles pushed and pushed it away as it snarled at him. Two out of the three same poachers returned to the cage and began to laugh at and heckle Niles. In their proud attempt to humiliate him, they made sport and laughed at the demise he was facing from a predatorial animal. They carried on intimidating the animal, too, so that the honey badger put up a stronger fight against Niles.

What they didn't see was a Jeep that was parked behind the honey badger's cage and the proceeding cage behind it as well. Mason walked from the Jeep to two tall large doors and swung them open.

He released two lions that speedily raced toward each poacher. Each of them was overwhelmed with so much fear that neither of them bothered wielding their firearms but decided to do the first thing that came to their minds: panic and run.

One poacher gained a little of a head start, but an attack was ensued from behind the lagging poacher with the lion's jaws lunging into the back of the poacher's neck, and he fell to the ground. The remaining lion hunted the other poacher as long as he kept up flight off the grounds of the camp.

Mason scrambled to the cage and removed the padlock from the front door. Once it was made apparent to the honey badger that an opening appeared before him, he shuffled out of the cage and freed himself into the wild. The two conservationists ran out behind the honey badger cages and enclosure, climbed into their Jeep, and sped into the camp to trail more poachers.

*****

Out in the spotty bush, a three-year-old zebra grazed on short grass during the dry afternoon. It distractedly searched for leaves, which were more plentiful as the zebra wandered into another part of the savanna. As the zebra grazed for a short while in a grassy area, it sensed the presence of an intruder in its location. Looking with its peripheral vision, the young zebra searched through the territory to capture any intrusive activity.

The zebra wasn't able to locate any apparent threat according to what lay behind the brush. Its eyes continued to watch for any motion throughout its surroundings, but there didn't seem to be any activity. While it stood exceedingly still as it continued to search for any movement, it jogged its head to the left and right for any evasive creature.

In a split second, the sound of a shot fired, and the zebra was struck in the left thigh with a bullet. Stumbling on its left leg, the zebra brayed loudly as it staggered in its wounded state. It tried to adjust to its debilitated state as it circled in one place. As it was affected by trauma from its affliction and suffered from injury, its senses and equilibrium overlooked a lasso that swung in the air and wrapped around its neck.

It made an attempt to free itself as it yanked on the rope to gain some leverage. The shooter circled around from behind a thicket to another separate thicket and fired another round into the other hip on the immobilized zebra. The circumstances posed a critical threat for the zebra to further end ongoing suffering.

After removing a tool from the saddle, the shooter unfurled a long makeshift knout whip, swung it, and lashed out at the zebra. He struck the harmed zebra with the whip's fall hitch, which wrapped around the legs and were pulled on as the thong was looped around the horn of the shooter's saddle. The wire and hooks embedded into skin as flesh and gashes were left behind along the legs. The knout whip was swung again, and cuts were inflicted onto the hocks of the legs. As the zebra tried to maintain stability from its wounds, it dropped repeatedly to its hindquarters.

In the grass fifty feet away, Lance and a park ranger lay low and witnessed the heinous act performed prior to the event. Glancing through his binoculars, Lance watched carefully to see what the two poachers would initially continue to do each step further. The park ranger put a camcorder to use to provide further evidence for the crime. The ranger began to reach for a rifle beside Lance to bring the illegal wildlife trafficking to an end.

Lance said, "No...I know it's heartbreaking, but we need a little more filming!"

The park ranger's hand slowly began to pull back from the rifle, and he continued filming. A third strike was made with the knout whip after it swung in the air and struck the hind legs again. It tore into tissue and muscle approximately in the same injured spot.

Lance handed the ranger the rifle and said, "All right."

The ranger aimed the rifle at the shooter and struck him square in the ball of the shoulder. He dropped the knout whip and turned his horse to see who could be in the grass.

All he saw were tall stems of grass swaying in the wind without any trace of anyone.

The park ranger had run for his Jeep while the poacher who held onto his lasso dropped the rope from his hands and fled on horseback through the midst of the spotted thicket.

Both men who pursued the poachers couldn't understand any such treatment given to a zebra other than torture because they understood the only reasonable way to bring a zebra down was shooting it in the shoulder or the head.

Lance decided to apply the same method of gunfire upon the poacher from the brush. He searched through the branches and aimed a rifle at the poacher behind a crowded thicket.

A nonlethal hit was made immediately against the poacher, and he dropped to the ground. The poacher returned repetitive fire from his rifle into the brush and endangered Lance, but he was left unharmed.

With no reliable lead regarding where the poacher with the lasso rode off to, the park ranger's search unsuccessfully was left to a coin toss for him to choose for himself. He zigzagged through the thickets in one direction in order to locate the poacher for forty meters.

So he circled behind a thicket and drove west-southwest and confronted a herd of elephants with their young scattered twenty meters away.

The park ranger's Jeep came to an abrupt stop and circled back behind the same thicket. Then he drove west-northwest from the thicket in the direction the poacher must have ridden.

Lance pursued the poacher on foot, and the poacher's vitality had begun to fail him. After the result of being pierced by a few bullets, the onset of exhaustion and bleeding set in for the shooter.

As Lance pursued him along the far opposite side of the brush, he continued to use growth as his cover. He kept a careful eye on the shooter through the brush and continued to gradually shuffle between spots and inch closer behind the brush.

It all became short-lived when he met a male giraffe that lumbered toward him a number of meters away. With movement that worked each side of its legs separately, the giraffe approached Lance who spotted it with a steady intimidating pace.

The question Lance asked himself was whether the giraffe would act with curiosity or whether he saw Lance as a threat. Lance stopped shuffling and immediately fell backward before the giraffe in close proximity while he frantically scraped with his feet to ensure finding traction so he could get on his feet.

An attempt to persuade the giraffe by signaling it to go away didn't improve the situation either.

Lance naturally made an opportunity, once he was to his feet, to try to break free from the giraffe and zigzagged through the line of spotty thickets to lose the giraffe.

The shooter spotted Lance and the giraffe and saw what made complications for Lance as he was chased by the giraffe. The shooter simply stood still and grinned at his circumstances.

As Lance and the giraffe zigzagged and circled thickets, Lance's path met the neglectful shooter where he stood unsuspectingly, and both men collided. They immediately rolled away from each other as the threat of being trampled upon by the giraffe was imminent.

It was mere seconds after they abandoned the spot, and both men ran in opposing directions that they came close to being trampled by the giraffe's hooves.

But the giraffe kept up its speed because it was determined to chase after Lance.

The shooter once again sought seclusion immediately, found a spot, and picked up where he left off watching the outcome of the giraffe's chase after Lance behind a thicket.

Lance continued to evade the giraffe by running and crisscrossing between thickets.

After a few minutes, Lance shook the giraffe and circled back to search for the shooter. The shooter was preoccupied with watching through the thickets to avoid Lance and the giraffe. Then the shooter walked around slowly to the other side of the thicket where most of the action could be seen and looked for Lance from behind the thicket.

A few seconds later, Lance, armed with his rifle, approached the shooter in a slow gait. Being entirely unaware of Lance, the poacher continued to look for him in the open area between the thickets in front of him.

The park ranger continued to drive in the same direction as he weaved through the thickets to spot the poacher on horseback. After the park ranger drove one hundred meters, he caught a glimpse of the rider, who was unaware of him, approximately forty meters away.

A drastic deep ditch or channel appeared in front of the Jeep and erratically brought the chase to a halt. He quickly backed the Jeep, turned right, and made the effort to drive around the channel. The terrain became very turbulent to cross over as rocks presented an obstacle throughout the terrain. The narrowing channel seemed to gradually wind endlessly, but he inevitably found level ground.

Carefully accelerating the Jeep, the park ranger tried to make up for lost time.

"Well, now, it seems that the market had been predisposed with produce, just before they entered their steed into the quarter horse finals—you seem to be surprised. They had been anticipating your arrival for over an hour," emphasized Lance.

The shooter glanced over his shoulder and instantly drew his firearm to shoot Lance. The barrel of the Lance's rifle went off, and the poacher toppled to the ground.

Most of the shot penetrated the shooter's rear right shoulder. After he coiled, partially from injury, he attempted to fire his gun again. He wasn't allowed, however, to make an attempt because a second shot interfered with him.

The park ranger caught up with the rider, and the park ranger shot several rounds at him with his assault rifle.

Having the good fortune of avoiding being hit, the poacher returned fire, causing the park ranger to hunch in his vehicle. Large rocks acted as interference as a disadvantage along the park ranger's path. He steered to the far left behind the rider. Before any interference ended, the rocks put one hundred meters between the ranger and the rider.

The park ranger looked at his surroundings, speedily shifted in a higher gear, drove farther left, and rode up a small rolling hill to pursue the rider. The terrain provided a more reasonable smooth path, which amounted to nothing more than a few spotted rocks and small animal burrows.

But it also provided a view of the rider as the park ranger could pick up speed to approach him. When he reached the third hill in a continual series of rolling hills, he made a direct descent to the rider in his direction.

Once the park ranger had reached the rider, he cut in front of him and diverted his horse to the right. As a result, the interference caused the horse and Jeep to rub and make contact between each other's sides.

The sudden interference's sharp turn caused the rider to collapse from the horse and land inside the Jeep.

Galloping on without any hesitation and injury, the horse rode on without its rider.

In the blink of an eye, the park ranger straightaway brought the Jeep to a halt and rose out of the driver's seat.

He confronted the poacher, who seized him and threw him down to the Jeep's bed. After the poacher drew his firearm, a couple of shots fired as they wrestled each other. But the park ranger came out of it free from any harm.

After the long tussle that broke out, the park ranger fought his way above the poacher so the poacher would be pinned down. Then the park ranger confiscated the poacher's firearm, unloaded the clip, and threw the poacher over the tailgate.

But the poacher held onto something himself after its removal secretively beneath the Jeep as he began to wait below the Jeep on the ground.

Intimidating remarks and contempt left the poacher's lips without any lack of restraint toward the park ranger as he revolted verbally against him.

As the park ranger watched the disposition of the poacher over the tailgate, the poacher began to arm the M-67. The pull ring was pulled as he held the body and the safety lever. Then he pulled the grenade and the ring assembly apart to remove the safety pin from the fuse assembly, and then he allowed the safety lever free in his hands.

Maddening paranoia and hysteria occupied the poacher as the park ranger noticed his intention to take both of their lives.

The park ranger jumped to his front seat where he took cover from the deployment of the M-67.

A small explosion resulted from the blast; however, the fragments from the explosives penetrated along both body and frame of the Jeep.

The poacher was declared dead immediately. But the park ranger remarkably survived the result of the blast.

After the park ranger untucked himself over the console and driver's seat, he sat up. The park ranger collected himself and took a number of deep breaths from the danger he found himself in the middle of the afternoon.

*****

Lance and the park ranger visited a large shack with poachers without invitation.

Cards for poker and drinks for takers cluttered small round tables. Most of the members of the group continued to engage each other in conversation as they entered the shack, while others stared at their uninvited guests.

The park ranger said, "Pick up your chips, games, and drinks off the tables!"

One of the many Tanzanian poachers seated near the back of the room, close to Lance, made an attempt to stand up and act aggressively toward Lance.

But Lance eyeballed the poacher, pulled three of his shotgun shells out of his pouch, reached for the poacher's hand and placed them in the palm of his hand. Then after several seconds, he struck the poacher across the forehead, causing him to crash to the ground.

The unfortunate but necessary circumstance persuaded the poachers to keep the peace and were compliant to remove the items off the tables.

Then the two conservationists began to turn the tables over on their sides. As they looked beneath the tables, they investigated for any unnecessary weapons or objects, which would make the presence of the two men unwelcome.

The park ranger said, "Now, there's no question whether you're involved in wildlife trafficking! You have decorative items for attire made out of teeth and claws! You're carrying tools for poaching on you! So the eyes of the world can see it, I want to know from the video on this Chromebook—the affiliation of these two men, who are torturing animals, who might be with you."

Another poacher bitterly said, "What is it to you if we want to be rich as an heir or if we invest our time in wildlife trafficking?"

Lance said, "It's because your gold-clad wallets, which are encrusted with rubies, and the pelts that you're busy snaring don't happen to fit in your washer wringer. That allows you to further play with your runaway imagination toward fantasy and poverty."

The poacher scoffed as he said, "It doesn't hurt to try and have a go at it."

"We can also turn these chairs over and leave you sitting on the ground too," said the park ranger.

The poacher turned away neglectfully according to his reaction without a care or trace of attention.

As the touch screen Chromebook was slowly passed around to each poacher, each viewed the torture of the zebra on the technology. Each one of the poachers were hesitant to meet the requests of the two conservationists. No one spoke up to inform them of any information or contacts about the crime. Both men looked around the room and were convinced each poacher was withholding the truth.

Along the opposite wall from the entrance, two woodburning ovens sat against the wall.

Lance walked across the room and happened to lean against it.

He looked down to his left and saw a scorpion resting on the stove near the corner of the room. He glanced around the room to see whether anyone was watching him.

Then Lance placed his left hand over a charcoal grill to determine any presence of heat. A reasonably intense degree of heat could be felt from the grill.

Lance removed the cooking grate with a pair of pliers. Using a set of tongs, Lance picked off the grill a reasonably warm briquette, carried it to a poacher, and placed it in front of his face. Last of all, Lance held the poacher down in his seat firmly.

As the poacher jumped out of his seat from the impressive heat from the briquette, he yelled in a panic and ran out of the shack. Confused and baffled, the poachers looked around the room to understand who may be trouble.

The poacher sitting closest to Lance turned his head toward him and saw Lance using his pliers to hold the scorpion by its tail. What the poacher found rather alarming was not necessarily the scorpion but the grin on Lance's face. After a few moments, he chose to take refuge elsewhere outside the shack as well. Lance said, "From what I recall, they weren't asked to vacate the premises. This doesn't seem to be working like I pictured it. Can you hold them down?" he gave the ultimatum to the park ranger.

The reaction seemed like a unanimous vote that passed as a bill, causing all but one poacher to leap out of their chair and fall to the wooden floor, flailing face down. The only remedy they could find noteworthy was exiting the shack too.

Last but not least, the only Tanzanian man left in the shack altogether chose not to breakaway. A strong sense of dread had taken all the others who left due to fear.

The man who remained seated in partial darkness held onto a walking stick and had a share of jewelry with gems hung from his neck. He gazed at the two men suspiciously.

The Sukuma man said, "Are you going to torture me in the town square with a warm charcoal too?"

Lance said, "If you want to know the truth, the charcoal may have maintained a higher degree of heat toward more sensitive skin. As a fortune seeker and a mystic, could you tell us about the tortured zebra?"

The mystic said, "How do I come out of this a zebra killer? You don't even know my affiliation with these men. I may be merely a friend visiting them in some rundown shack."

Lance began the video, placed it in front of the mystic's face, and said, "You might introduce us to those who are involved in the brutality. You might find yourself someday empathetically riding on a meat wagon among the stench and aroma of mutilated wildlife as sights and smells from the disturbing scenario find themselves based on insidious conduct. You might freely want to provide the facts— freely—based on those who resort to poaching and lack freedom from the disease. But if you unmistakably want to have freedom, see how wildlife lasting freedom comes with a price because you may never know what freedom is."

The mystic cast a glance out the opened door and saw Hummers and Jeeps parked with drivers in the seats. They were none other than the authorities and park rangers.

Lance said, "Sometimes you just can't skip, glance, or overlook directions that need to be followed."

The mystic said, "I'm not here to chalk up reluctance toward your search party. I am familiar with these men. They have disbanded from Kasian, if you're familiar with that leader of a number of gangs. His poachers have relocated to Northern Mozambique from Southern Tanzania. But they make frequent visits throughout Tanzania. I've been told they are the likes who mutilate the bodies of wildlife in various locations from time to time."

*****

Niles, Mason, Lance, and the park ranger made a visit to a wildlife veterinarian for the zebra to undergo treatment at the medical facility. There the zebra could be observed for its severe wounds under rehabilitation.

With a degree of concern, Niles mentioned, "They said we would be told if there's a need to move the truck. It appears they are becoming busier."

Lance began his routine banter with Niles again. "You get bent out of shape if the ground isn't found on a cord, Niles! You can't even come to terms with it."

Niles said, "I like to use appliances that are up-to-date! I like to use state-of-the-art technology! If they can revise how they stick you in the finger with a lancet when they draw blood, I'll gravitate toward the latest choice between them both."

"Then there's always the different cuts of meat and how you cook them," mumbled Lance.

The park ranger said, "My grandmother used to say, 'One of the most important factors to remember as a baker is—if you slightly brown a dish of food, it comes out with just as much flavor as opposed to browning it.'"

Mason said, "So, according to Niles, we should keep the oven but throw away all the old appliances."

Lance said, "Now let's not get carried away. The mailbox still remains a necessity whose lid swings open, and it also comes with a red flag as a feature. You don't see it opening itself on its own! Do you?"

Niles said, "You don't plug in a mailbox to beat eggs at six in the morning."

Lance quietly said, "Boy, if I were you, I'd buy an entirely different mailbox as soon as possible."

Seconds later, Mason said, "I don't know whether the zebra's leg will pull through this situation. Zebras can lose a leg to a crocodile. But it was left with two bullets and scathed by a knout whip with wires and bards."

Lance said, "I'm sure the zebra will come through it all."

The park ranger said, "They've moved from wire snares and trap nets to insurgencies and terrorist organizations. Many of them make it out to be a reasonable and honest way of living. They have no restraint depleting species to extinction. They take part in it to come out of poverty."

Mason said, "If they would transfer a great number of species to public lands or enclosures elsewhere, such as zoos or other parklands, and build the facilities to hold great numbers, they would be in the business of preserving many. Simply preserving a few numbers at each zoo won't do it. More numbers provide the preservation of species in greater volume and value, no different than horses or cattle."

Niles said, "I certainly would like to know whether we're part of an undertaking that's too late."

As Lance looked to the next row of chairs in the waiting room, he noticed a woman who behaved rather questionably in the way she carried herself. He stood up, walked out to the front desk, and inconspicuously asked to borrow a plant. Thirty seconds later, he walked with the plant to the woman's row and sat down next to her.

Lance clearly put on an act and said, "Have you ever realized that determining the right plant as decor in your home can be a difficulty in its entirety? You need to get the right amount of sun for them in your house, which can be such a knuckle buster."

The woman gave him a cold shoulder and said, "I wouldn't know anything about it."

"You'll also discover they're just as temperamental as your own hair. Soil can become all broken and dried up. Your hair can also have the same tendency. You give it two years to improve, and it doesn't appear any better than mere results of an election before the primaries."

The woman agreed only for the sole purpose of not starting any argument.

Carrying on with his performance, he said, "It's no different than being overwhelmed by cellophane, which is put to use for wrapping. But it's a question of whether you can work through all those crinkles, which is too much. And it'll want you to relocate to another house."

She rose to her feet and began to walk away toward the front desk. Lance set the plant on a chair beside him.

He noticed in the woman's back pocket a sheet of white paper with an emblem printed on the top of it. After Lance pulled papers from his shirt pocket, he examined the duplicate emblem on the papers from a past lead connected to poacher activity. He showed the papers with the emblem to the other three conservationists and told them about the papers in her back pocket.

Lance said to the three men after they saw the emblem, "So where did the bunny rabbit disappear to when he nearly was run over?"

Mason answered, "In a magician's hat?" The two other men didn't answer him.

"He relocated into a combat helmet! Ha, ha, ha," humored Lance.

Niles said, "You're losing it! Follow her!"

As Lance carefully watched and followed the questionable woman, the three conservationists trailed from a distance behind him. They left behind the rehabilitation center.

Outside the building, the four men walked up some shallow steps, stooped, and watched her behind half a concrete wall. Her stroll came to a halt as she stood still fifteen meters from the wall. As they looked over the top of the wall, the men watched her for the longest time as she faced the opposite direction.

Then Lance said, "Why are we standing here doing nothing? I can see this concrete wall in any major city throughout the United States."

No one replied to his question.

Afterward, Lance mentioned, "Why is this presenting a difficulty for us? We can't take out a questionable woman. If it were any other man with a switchblade, AK-47, or grenade, it would make a difference."

Looking to his left down the shallow steps, Lance saw Mason walking slowly toward the woman. So the two remaining conservationists mimicked Lance in their actions.

Mason slowly took one gradual step after the other.

After meters became far more a shorter distance, followed by a few inches, Mason quietly approached the woman.

He reached to pull out the paper from her right back pocket. He grasped it with his fingertips, and slowly, he began to pull it from its place. Once the nerve-racking event was finished, he quietly inhaled deeply through his nose to remain unnoticed.

His curiosity took hold of him, however, and he decided to look over her shoulder.

Lance whispered, "Just what exactly is he looking for?" Mason's eyes opened wide when he saw a detonator in her hand.

He picked her up from behind, above his head, and began to run toward the concrete wall with a dumpster in front of it.

Mason cried out, "Bomb!" while he approached the dumpster.

Lance cried out, "Whoa!" with surprise.

The three conservationists quickly descended the steps and headed for the dumpster.

So, Lance and Niles took hold of the metal impact lid and opened it.

She was tossed quickly inside.

They closed the lid to impede any possible impact. They also wanted to avoid hazardous matter acting as a projectile.

Mason jumped on the lid to hold it down.

The detonator had been activated, followed by a blast as a result of her act of malice.

At once, Mason was sent, to some extent, into the air and crashed on a truck hood nearby.

Inertia rolled Mason off the hood and onto the ground.

Mason was surrounded quickly by his close acquaintances who checked the condition of his health.

The park ranger said, "You know, one might argue that you could have avoided the lid, but then there might have been explosives and hazardous matter that could have struck us and the clinic."

Niles said, "You drew something stronger than a cork out of a bottle. You shielded a bomb for us."

"It didn't come very easily with a light grip on the lid of the dumpster. You got bucked off a zebra!"

As he walked into the waiting room, Lance told the lady at the front desk, "Would you call a doctor or the medic for our friend, Mason, outside the rehabilitation center? And the authorities so they can remove the dead female terrorist from the dumpster?"

Lance approached the surgeon who stood in the waiting room ready to give a diagnosis for the zebra. The surgeon told Lance to go home and to inform the three other conservationists to go home as well, because they wouldn't know the results until later. The expected results were only what someone may have guessed from many surgical procedures such as those the zebra was going under. Lance said, "All right, thank you, Doctor," and he told the three other men the news outside the building.

*****

Two days later, a pair of helicopters landed on the outside of the conservation camp. Four park rangers visited with Niles and explained that they had found a bushmeat plant in connection with poachers.

A park ranger said, "The camp is in an isolated part of Tanzania, remote and far away, so we anticipate travelling by helicopter." Niles chased down the two other conservationists, and they headed for the designation point.

After a few hours, once they reached the location, they landed one helicopter in partially dense forestation. The other helicopter landed sixty meters behind the first helicopter.

Lance, who rode in the first helicopter, waited for the two rangers to direct plans for the next step.

A few moments passed by, and Lance indicated that something was suspicious outside the helicopter. A respectable distance from the helicopter, boughs and bushes appeared to be violently breaking and rustling.

"I believe we've landed in an unsuitable place," said Lance.

Suddenly, there was an abrupt crash through the trees, and a bull elephant charged out in the open toward the side of the helicopter.

The tusks of the bull elephant were so dangerous, to abandon the helicopter meant to be impaled and trampled to death. But the threatening situation didn't help solve matters as the bull elephant toppled and overturned the helicopter on its side. Sitting to the right of Lance, the ranger was riddled with broken glass embedded in his hands as he lay against the side window. The other ranger in the rear tried to hold on as best he could as the helicopter rocked in all directions.

After kicking out the window, Lance crawled out of the helicopter and was under the surveillance of the bull elephant immediately.

Lance leapt off the helicopter while the elephant continued to turn and push it aside.

Then the bull elephant charged Lance.

Again, Lance tried to put a gap between the bull elephant and himself. While he cut through gaps between bushes, he took many turns and bends to lose the elephant.

A cluster of dead and fallen trees came into Lance's reach, which he decided to attempt to throw the bull elephant as he scrambled through the middle of the broken-down growth.

Then, he faced a maze of branches and boughs, which were spiky amidst a jumble, to avoid danger. He climbed over boughs and branches extending upward and trunks as impediments.

The bull elephant reached the pile of trees, stopped, and looked at Niles working through the fallen trees. The agitated bull elephant jerked his head around to intimidate the intruder who didn't meet his approval.

Moments later, the bull elephant picked up speed and charged toward Lance through the shrubs, branches, and brush.

As Lance danced like a broken spool around a spindle, he tried to work as fast as he could through the pile as the bull elephant drew closer.

Surprisingly, the elephant inevitably overtook him and left no room for Lance otherwise, but he grabbed hold of the right partially broken tusk used to attempt to gore him. He tried to avoid the tip at all costs.

As Lance gripped it, the elephant tried to gore him into the ground but afterward decisively tossed him off his tusk.

Lance tried to reach and get more of a firm grip on the tusk while he kept momentum. The elephant made numerous attempts to jab but not shake Lance off his tusk as he maintained a reasonable grasp to hold on.

Then the bull elephant swung his head upward and violently tossed Lance a few feet forward through a bunch of brush.

Opening another window of opportunity, Lance avoided the bull elephant from the gap made between them and ran away.

Before the bull elephant could completely move through the brush and pinpoint Lance, Lance had already disappeared and couldn't be spotted among any of the spotty brush.

The other conservationists discovered the bushmeat camp, and over time, Lance effectively had caught up and found the poacher site.

"We're not about to take them into custody nor are we about to spare lives on this assignment. They're rogue criminal poachers. Those are the terms," said a park ranger who gave a pep talk to the group.

"Understood," said the conservationists.

The conservationists began to storm the poacher's lodging quarters and canopy tents. Then they toppled the empty lodging quarters and set the remains on fire. Then they stationed themselves in front of another twenty-by-forty-foot tent, positioned themselves, and waited for a number of poachers to emerge from the tent.

Both groups engaged open fire as the conservationists predominately reduced a good number, and the poachers fled and escaped from the tent.

Lance broke off from the group and entered a spacious building to the left of the tent. The five conservationists, including Niles, stormed and found a large meat locker with carts full of bushmeat in the rear.

He wheeled the carts out to the open floor while a few carcasses hung from inside the locker. Then Lance went outside to a parked cargo truck, grabbed two gasoline cans, returned to the building, and doused fuel on the most flammable materials he could find. He lit them on fire and left the building.

Stationed behind the tent engaged by the five conservationists, Mason waited as the group of conservationists flushed through a building behind it. The men stormed the building and found a butcher floor laden with workers throughout the tent.

As Mason randomly cornered poachers who came out in the open, misfortune seemed to overtake him as he ran out of ammunition. Then a poacher out in front of the tent's entrance crept up behind Mason from thirty feet and began chasing Mason with a knife.

Meat was being processed inside the tent as the conservationist's stormed inside and kicked off an invite of aggressive progressive attacks by the poachers as they attempted to draw weapons and fire upon the conservationists. A poacher fired upon one of the park rangers triggering the first hit lethally, but the rest of the poachers bore down behind the butcher equipment.

Sprinting as fast as he could, the poacher wielding the knife caught Mason and tackled him to the ground.

He wasted no effort to plunge the knife with both hands toward Mason, but Mason obstructed his arms as they came down on him.

For the longest time, he made every effort to fend off the poacher but wasn't succeeding.

Lance circled around the building near the entrance and discovered Mason under a drawn-out struggle.

A spinning machete soared through the air as it was flung toward the poacher on his knees above Mason.

The wrestling poacher uncooperatively worked and pushed his knife with one arm and held Mason with the other.

But a clear target was made out of the poacher.

The machete sank into the poacher's back, striking vital nerves, and causing him to fall immediately.

Lance stated to the poacher after he retrieved his machete, "You see, you need one of these. That knife won't get you anywhere." Showing one flat side of the bloody machete to the poacher, Lance demonstrated how effective it was in comparison to his knife. Then

Lance slapped the flat side of his machete across the poacher's face, and the poacher toppled to the ground.

Lance helped Mason off the ground and asked whether he needed more ammunition. Mason exhaled and said, "Yes."

Then Lance asked, "So where did you leave off?"

Together, Lance returned with Mason to the bushmeat tent.

Lance stooped down before the side wall of a building's joint canopy and cut two slits in the fabric to the ground. They entered the tent from the side and saw a surge of fire taking place. Near the entrance, a number of poachers sat crouched, napping between the equipment, small crates, and supplies.

Mason found a vacuum flask, and after it was read, he pointed out to Lance that it contained liquid nitrogen.

The both of them agreed to fill two metal pails by using gloves and goggles and approach the sleepy poachers as Lance crept to the side and Mason to the rear.

The conservationists remained quiet as the poachers dozed amidst the equipment.

The two men swirled the pails as they quietly approached the poachers from both directions.

Once they closed the gap, they splashed liquid nitrogen over the poachers.

A cloud developed and permeated throughout the whole tent, causing the poachers to quickly evacuate as they dispersed outside the entrance while liquid nitrogen burned them. The four conservationists who were securing a position out front near the entrance were stunned to see the sight of the poachers taking flight out of the front of the canopy and taking no part in the gunfire.

The four conservationists investigated the parked vehicles and any remaining property for evidence. After the authorities arrived and the investigation proceeded, the four conservationists waited for a flight home.

*****

Participating in a getaway, the company of four with a guest from the conservation camp were visiting Bismarck Rock at Lake Victoria in Mwanza. They rowed out to the tall smoothed-out granite rocks standing out from the water.

As they gradually paddled around the attraction, Lance said, "Who exactly did you ask to supervise the camp while we were away from home?"

"We got reliable help!" said Niles, who was sharing a rowboat with Lance.

"They'll send all our supplies of gunny sacks and olive oil to a border country, and we'll have to do with both cauliflower and wild rice," jokingly poked Lance.

The elderly stout male guest with gold-framed glasses said, "That, my friend, is the behavior of riddled paranoia and fear. What a little boiled water and whole grain rice won't do for you."

"I got it. You can put any topping on it, including hominy, and it would taste far better—impeccable flavor," said Lance.

Niles rubbed his eyes while he couldn't believe what he'd heard. Niles was left with mere astonishment because of Lance's suggestion while their guest tried to work around putting any topping on the suggested food.

Lance saw his confusion but only added about Niles, "You've never seen this man choose exactly what he wants to eat. He had servants in his household while he was growing up, and he couldn't bring himself to cook a prime rib while he wrestled with the cap on a vitamin bottle."

"I explicitly put the temporary help in charge of watching over the camp so the gunnysacks and the olive oil would get through any critical moments during our time off!"

"Get out of the boat and climb the rock. Do something noble for a change."

"How is that going to make anything noble?"

"You'll obviously dive into cold water," said Lance gambling with a grin.

"Niles frowned and said, "What part of it is cold?"

Niles pushed his oar against Lance's shoulder, and he fell out of the boat into the water. Then Niles continued paddling as if the event had never happened.

Behind Niles's boat followed Mason in his boat, and he offered an oar to Lance while he swam toward his boat in the water, but Lance simply grabbed it and threw it toward the front of Mason's boat.

"So you haven't been fortunate with your post-academics until now with your second degree. You enjoy the field. Your curator who worked as an adviser in your line of work hasn't delivered over so many years so that you might have the good fortune to place you on your feet," said the guest while the four men were led by Jodi up on the shorter rocks in the direction of higher ones.

"It's not a bother as opposed to—" said Niles.

"You want to exist as a team! I would implore you to understand that the window of opportunity, at times, will lie with you by participating with others. But I'm also aware of what it can do to you. It's a fine line to follow. I look forward to seeing the results of your trek, which you can reach by locating opportunity when it knocks."

"We don't know whether you're reaching a higher level as a result of putting your trust completely in a contact or not. Anything can happen based on what occurs at a camp. But where archaeology leads you could be anywhere or nowhere at all. He's turned us around six times in the middle of air flight, behaved like a despondent at times at certain grounds during projects, and abandoned them many times after that," said Mason.

"All I get from it is the harrowing circumstance of confusing sriracha sauce with saline solution for your eyes!" shouted Lance.

"That's what they call groundbreaking news for Applebury from a microbiologist and a nuclear physicist's point of view according to Lance," kidded Niles.

Moments later, Niles looked at Lance in the face after partially crawling Bismarck rock to the top and said, "I knew I should have kept a close eye on your mini fridge."

Lance raised questions and said, "If you want to bring the authorities into this conversation, go ahead. If you think I looted your tent for artifacts, be my guest! You'll go so far as to believe that I looted the museums you've contributed to with your awkward findings."

"I know I'm in good company when the pool size you expect to jump into, Lance, is above the tower into a kiddie pool. Try springing off the diving board into an Olympic—-sized pool," said Jodi.

"Hey, we're standing above crocodile-infested waters over twenty-five feet high on rocks, and from what I understand, the toaster oven back home has never been misused! Now I have a question for Mason, who can confirm for us whether our friends in the world of nature aren't any more right at home in their habitat as opposed to another environment. It's no different when it comes to sriracha sauce and Applebury," bantered Lance.

Niles said, "Lance, these friends of yours in nature, who traverse a hundred miles, even a thousand, to answer the call of migration follow through with such a great feat when it comes to stamina. But you always naturally find all your articles of clothing in the right place?"

The guest said, "Look. The sea turtles of the deep are clad with a protective carapace. Undeniably, they are at great odds when it comes to vulnerability as one no different who might make the same kind of trek themselves. But after it's all over, they have faced some of the most adverse conditions as they enter into a world where they are free."

Lance said, "Good, we'll charter a plane from Tanzania to Nigeria so Applebury can search for some of the finest Terracotta in Nigeria."

Mason said, "During this round, I think he has the advantage on you, Niles, because all we have to go by is Applebury's record. It's no different than malpractice work by a doctor. Don't let it grow and flourish like a horribly disreputable incident, which can be so frequent in a doctor's field."

Lance said, "Remain with the Tabasco and Worchester sauce, Niles."

The guest said, "What are your thoughts, Jodi?"

"I think there's even a far greater line up of friends in nature who have far greater invulnerability *and* means to protect themselves than a sea turtle."

Lance veered and moaned and said, "She just had to go searching for a far more exquisite snow globe, didn't she?"

Throughout the duration of the night, Jodi and Lance danced to traditional African folk music and its rhythm at a resort where they stayed with the three other men.

*****

At an employer's large office suite on a Mediterranean estate out on the grasslands, a Tanzanian woman named Lola was asked by another Tanzanian woman, who was the manager, to clean part of the estate. After the manager had finished advising Lola what duties she needed to perform, the manager left, and Lola cleaned the suite for the first time.

She began cleaning priceless collectibles on the desk and alternated some of them with other choice collectibles wrapped in paper from boxes in storage. Then she polished the surface of the desk.

A wide bookcase was cleared in order to polish the shelves stocked with books. Before they were put back in their original place, she heard a parrot inside a cage, mimicking speech with a number of words. She looked around to see if she was being watched possibly by an owner, manager, or employer of the estate. As she moved her eyes around the room, Lola caught sight of several reasonably hidden cameras.

She didn't allow herself to be alarmingly suspicious in front of the cameras as she placed her polishing rag aside. Summoning enough courage to set aside work, Lola behaved inconspicuously as she walked over to the cage on the other side of the office and listened to the parrot.

The parrot spontaneously said, "I grow bothered about how to hide this key!"

The statement captured Lola's attention on account of its peculiarity.

"Here's the poaching ledger!" said the parrot.

She continued to look ahead so she didn't give away the appearance that she was possibly up to something while she listened closely.

"The book will hide the key."

Lola almost turned to look at the cabinet behind her, but she continued to watch and listen to the parrot.

Candidly, the parrot said, "There's a price to pay the parrot."

Intentionally breaking away from the parrot, Lola left the office suite, ran from the estate, and drove away in a company mini truck.

Several hours later, she stood outside the estate as the three conservationists drove on the property and allowed her to explain to them what the parrot disclosed to her.

Niles asked, "Are you sure you're safe to return to work? Or are you going to quit?"

Lola said, "No, I can do this, even if they threaten my life. My manager may stand behind me, even if they become suspicious."

Mason said, "That's very brave of you."

Lola said, "I'll stick it out. Keep me in your prayers." Each of them mindfully kept the conversation at a minimum so she could leave the estate.

The estate front door opened slowly to the office suite as Niles's drawn pointed sidearm entered the room. He quickly looked across the inside of the room from the entrance to the far wall to check for any unwanted guests.

He remained near the right wall, then strode to a door in the far wall, and walked through to investigate other parts of the estate.

Mason entered the office suite after Niles entered the door in the far wall and immediately began to investigate the office desk.

Meandering through the door behind him into the office, Lance said, "Nobody ever offers you chocolate chip cookies on a platter at the front door anymore."

Mason said, "It's probably because you're so accomplished, Lance. You've picked up lift in the wind and got your Chinese kite caught in a tree."

Lance obnoxiously said, "Yeah, you're right. Who could make sugar cookies during the summer and have them turn out just the right size like I can?"

Mason said, "Imagine that, especially when you use the same baking method like everyone else."

The parrot said, "Use the same method like everyone else!"

Both men's attention was caught as they heard what the parrot mimicked.

Mason resumed to continue his search through the desk drawers.

Lance, however, kept his eye on the parrot and reflected on what the bird had spoken.

Then Lance mumbled to himself, "I talk to myself."

The parrot said, "I talk to myself."

So Lance walked across the room toward the parrot's cage and listened to the parrot.

He tested the waters of the parrot and said, "Shut up, Polly," to study his response.

The parrot repeated his reply again.

Then Lance stopped and waited for any further reply.

The parrot didn't make a response.

After a few moments passed by, he replied, "The book will hide the key."

He said it twice, grabbing the attention of both men.

Lance quietly asked Mason to search through the books in the bookcase for a key.

The bird carried on and said, "Here are the game meat and pelt proceeds and hire payments."

Moments later, the parrot proceeded to speak. "Left middle drawer—a stack of paperwork."

Lance whispered to Mason across the room, "You're unable to find a key?"

"I'm searching as fast as I can."

Lance searched for paper and a pen on the desk to remember in writing the parrot's replies so they didn't take any chances and return to the cage.

Mason said, "I found it!"

They examined the key and couldn't identify what it belonged to.

Mason tried to place the key into the locked drawers of the desk, but he had trouble finding a keyhole that fit any of them.

Lance began to move chairs out from under the table near the far wall.

As Niles returned from the other estate's room, he saw what Lance was doing.

Lance said on account of Niles's reaction, "The table needs to be moved."

They removed a large, round, decorative rug. Once the table was removed, Lance removed a cut secret compartment of wood from the floor, uncovering a safe.

Lance retrieved the key Mason found in the bookcase and discovered it was the right key and opened the safe.

As they opened the safe, Lance said to Niles, "They moved a large table and chairs to gain access to a safe inside the floor?"

Niles said, "They're determined to keep it a secret."

Together, they examined all the documents and accounts they'd found in the safe.

"Everything is here," said Lance.

"If they ask us how we came across this information, what do we say?" asked Mason.

Niles said, "Tell them instead of leaving the snake charmed, you charmed a snake handler to help open the safe for us." And he walked away.

After a few moments, Lance turned to Mason, placed his hand on his shoulder, and said, "Just remember, it's okay to use our antivenom anytime you want in the not-too-distant future," and he stood up and walked away with the documents. Mason didn't know exactly what to think about what was said to him.

As he walked out the front door, Niles ran to the Jeep and placed a call to the authorities. As a result, they could take into custody the owners of the estate on poaching charges.

On the winding road that led to the estate while he placed the call, Niles saw headlights approaching from some distance toward him. He told the officer the danger of remaining on the line and got off the phone quickly. He ended the call and honked the horn to get Lance and Mason's attention.

The two men exited the estate, left the wraparound porch, and ran to the Jeep. Niles hastily persuaded them to find a place to disappear with him so they would take cover as a vehicle approached the estate. They hid from view behind shrubs in the garden behind the estate and watched the vehicle as it approached.

Mason asked, "Will the authorities arrive soon?"

Niles said, "Yes."

Two high-priced Duesenberg Model Js arrived on the estate, and its passengers got out of the vehicles and entered the estate.

The three conservationists remained behind the shrubs for twenty minutes until the authorities arrived with the rangers accompanying them. At that time, the authorities were allowed to know exactly where they could be found. They presented and informed both groups of officials what exactly they had found and any other evidence.

*****

A few days later, Jodi, Niles, Lance, and Mason prepared to attend a conservation convention. The plan was to join a large crowd in informal wear.

Attending the function in her favorite finest apparel was Jodi, who put on the last touches in her tent. She couldn't be any more ecstatic.

She walked to Lance's tent and said, "Knock, knock."

She entered since he had finished wrapping up the last touches with what he was wearing.

Jodi said, "Aren't you glad tuxedos aren't about to be worn?"

Lance said, "Other surrounding reserves attend a convention, and they never wear a tuxedo. I don't mind occasionally wearing a tuxedo, but the cleaning routine has a—"

"Umm, it's kind of flashy during those special occasions like these."

"Okay, I'm ready."

"Are you going to give me a proper send-off for the evening?"

"Yes," said Lance, and he took out a white handkerchief and blindfolded her.

She said, "What are you doing?"

Lance said appreciatively, "I'm going to show how much I appreciate you based on more than merely being special and not simply being someone who fills in all the nooks and crannies."

"Oh no, what are you up to?"

Then he proceeded to tie pieces of cloth around a few of her fingers.

"What are these?"

"These are going to be timeless reminders. Imagine they're rings…in regard to a woman, like you, doesn't live life in a complex way, but simple, by eating snacks out of a vending machine," said Lance as he glanced at his mini fridge.

"Balderdash…we all know your mini fridge is the only vending machine we have around here!"

"And while you occasionally do munch on a snack, I'm able to place a new ring on your finger as a reminder to remember we have each other while you help yourself to anything you'd like."

"This why you don't celebrate birthdays for your animals around here."

"You're going to make it a requirement for me to sit at the kids' table, aren't you?"

"Oh, I don't know. Where should I have you sit?" said Jodi as she put up a bold, daring front.

"You'll have me sit in a booster seat, won't you?"

He wrapped an arm around her waist, pulled her toward him, and gave her a lasting kiss.

Niles walked to the entrance of Lance's tent as Mason joined him.

"Have you proofread my speech?" asked Niles of Mason in front of the tent.

"Yes," and Mason gave him the speech.

Jodi and Lance exited Lance's tent.

After looking down at Niles's polished attire, Lance felt unsure about his clothes and started to reenter his tent.

Jodi grabbed his arm and said, "No, what you're wearing is fine."

Lance said to Niles, "So how long is the speech? I'd like to arrive home sometime tonight."

"That's okay, when you become scarce prior to the beginning of the speech, we'll place a grave marker out for you and name a conservation magazine for you in your honor."

The four attendees drove by Jeep fitted with a top to the convention. After they arrived, they took their assigned seats in the front row.

The opening ceremonies had started, and the first conservationist spoke about the affairs and present-day work in conservation. After the introduction, Niles was invited to engage the crowd at the lectern with his prepared address.

"I'd like to start by giving thanks to the Tarangire and Ruaha National Parks for the prompt action on the part of their work toward poachers and supporting our work in the conservation field. There have been many contributors, too numerous to mention, toward our uninterrupted durability and prosperity as a conservation site. My staff and I would like to express our deep appreciation for the way they back small conservation wildlife, which they help keep in our area on our preserve.

"One of the other interests that has surfaced over the months has been the debate concerning whether or not there should be more captive breeding in our zoos to establish life. The point I would stress would be zoos could allow wildlife preserves and national parks as well as the wild to naturally establish wildlife out in their exclusive habitats, which may need to be supervised temporarily with the help of protective fences or boundaries. This form of existence conforms to the healthy vigor of any animal life and can determine whether any good manageable establishment of breeding can be procured."

His discourse carried on for a few minutes as their attention was captured by his informative purposes and ideas.

"Next, there is some remarkable news that my staff and I discovered that we could wholeheartedly welcome. We have the capability of working with an archaeological institute that has assigned us to an undertaking, which we can be involved in ourselves in accord to its development."

The crowd applauded the mission that he introduced in his speech.

At the back of the audience, three seated men listened closely to all the words Niles had just spoken. After he made certain particular remarks, key points, and statements, they rose to their feet and exited the convention center.

Seated in his wheelchair on stage to the right, Lance saw a man watching Niles deliver his speech. Lance rose to his feet, walked up to the lectern, and candidly spoke to Niles.

"What is Applebury doing here?"

"Take it easy," said Niles who tried to appease Lance's anger while he was busy glaring at him.

"I will not take it easy. That man has led you astray on eleven assignments, and you want to be mystified by him again? When are you going to allow your unsaturated mind to face the fact that he has his own people who can handle his own archaeological work?"

"This is all legit based on grounds that are founded upon indisputable matters."

"No, no, the answer is no! When are you going to hammer it all out correctly in your mind when a decision is reached?"

"You don't understand."

"You're gone! You are absolutely gone!"

Lance's attention roamed off stage as he searched for Applebury while Applebury remained briefly where he sat until he headed in the other direction out of fear of Lance.

The infuriated conservationist made an attempt to pursue him but was thwarted by Niles as he restrained him physically.

"Let this one go," said Niles, but Lance broke free and walked off the stage. He reached a door in the right wing and entered a long room with a long counter that had science equipment on it in the center of the room.

On the other end of the room, he found Applebury behind the counter's end.

"You!"

The attention of the man had been firmly gripped.

"What kind of prize did you stick beneath his nose this time? It's not enough that you come up empty-handed without a trace of anything in the past!"

"I can back Niles during the expedition and at the excavation site on all levels! You haven't even given it a chance!"

Lance began to run along his left of the long counter as he chased Applebury, but Applebury wheeled himself on the opposite side of the counter.

"Come here, you little sea dweller! You don't even have a shell to crack open to any vital parts!"

"Can we be reasonable and theorize a plan that grounds both parties in a mutual agreement?"

Once they closely reached opposite ends again, Lance realized he didn't make any headway, so he chased him again from where he left off and began to circle half of the cabinet again.

"You know the track record you carry! Explain to me how you escaped that one!"

After both of them had finished a rotation around the counter, Lance repeated to chase him around the counter, crawl over the middle of the counter, crashed into the science equipment, and lunged for Applebury.

The curator proved to be too quick, however, and completed circling to the end of the counter.

Lance stood to his feet, glared at Applebury, and tried to catch his breath while he said, "You're the one who has made a fatal choice to boil himself at the bottom of the cauldron."

Lance was decisively convinced to leave the room, while Applebury wheeled himself quietly and calmly to the other end of the counter.

Applebury was left behind all alone in the science room while Lance made his departure.

*****

During the night at the conservation camp, Lance lay down on his cot with his eyes closed while he lingered, shy of sleep. He felt someone tug on his clothes and opened his eyes. He discovered someone wearing a Chinese festival mask while they stooped over him in a disturbing way.

He let out a loud scream and climbed to the back of his cot. As a result of being backed up against the back wall of his tent, he fell in between the cot and the tent.

"Are you going to take me to China if you go?" said Jodi beneath the mask.

"China? Who said we're going to China?"

Jodi took the mask off and said, "For the archaeological trip!"

"Oh no...none of us are going to China, and I'm not going anywhere!" Lance paused for a moment and said, "Who told you there might be a chance that anyone's going to China?"

"Oh, you're going!"

"Oh no, I'm not!"

"You have to go!"

"I'm not getting sedated to go on some excursion for some thoughtless trip, not knowing where I'm going for who knows what!"

Then Jodi put the mask on, moved gradually closer, raised her arms, and let out a bloodcurdling scream.

Lance's eyes gaped wide open with petrified fear, and he scrambled out from behind the cot and tent and ran outside.

He stumbled on the ground while he sought to get to Niles's tent. Niles was reading a newspaper on his cot. As Lance entered the tent, he said, very bothered, "Tell her to take off the mask. You've got to tell her to take off the mask!"

"Nope."

"Come on...the mask...you've got to tell her to get rid of the mask!"

"What kind of mask? African? Indonesian? What type of mask is it?"

Lance grabbed Niles and shook him violently.

"The mask...you've got to tell her to get rid of the mask!"

Niles rose from his cot and walked outside his tent as Lance followed him. They happened to meet Jodi outside; she was wearing the mask.

"That's it! That's the mask!" reaffirmed Lance.

Niles gently removed the mask off her face.

"And tell her we're not going to China."

"We're not going to China," said Niles.

"And tell her I'm not going anywhere either!"

"You're going with us."

"Oh no, I'm not!" Niles began to walk away while Lance continued to carry on.

Jodi stood still and giggled at Lance on account of how it appeared he had no other choice.

*****

The next day beneath the open canopy tent, Niles worked with a TV so it would operate on the counter.

The news anchor said, "A remote tribe from Kenya acted in hostility a day ago by killing a couple of tribal members from another large tribe from Tanzania. The authorities have taken nobody into custody because of insufficient evidence."

Niles said to himself, "That tribe may run in conflict with the camp if it strives with the Kenyan tribe."

*****

A few days later, Niles and Lance spent the afternoon visiting the Tanzanian tribe by sitting with their elders.

"I know a few of your people were killed by the tribe in Kenya, and nothing will bring them back to life. You must understand that vengeful actions will stir strife in the land. It won't answer the solution to their death. If you believe in a power greater than we are, then you know what he said, 'Vengeance is mine; I shall repay.' Retaliation has never solved or presented a solution. Let him handle vengeance on your behalf. Do not handle it by your hands," said Niles.

"We have already determined to seek vengeance on our adversaries, but we will give what you have said some thought."

Niles and Lance left the tribal village, disheartened over the disposition the tribe was left according to the condition of their hearts.

*****

A week later, the news anchor broadcast that those held responsible for the deaths of the tribal members were killed by another tribe in Kenya through a rebellion. Niles taped the broadcast and paid a visit to the Tanzanian tribe. He brought a portable TV and VCR and showed the broadcast to the entire tribe.

"You see, there is no longer any tribe in Kenya to take retribution against. They've died in the hands of adversaries."

The tribe sat in bewilderment and began to scrutinize themselves for the retaliatory interest to rise and seek vengeance above all.

After Niles returned home and nightfall came, he could rest in his cot and be at peace in his heart because the tribe had taken no rash actions. Niles enjoyed the rest of the evening.

*****

The following day outside the conservation camp, Jodi was on a swing beneath a tree. As she swung back and forth gently, she saw Lance approach her with a clipboard in his hands. They made immediate eye contact as Lance stopped a few feet from her.

"I'm not going."

"Yes, you are."

He proceeded to walk past her a few steps and then doubled back and pushed her into the branches above. She returned below, swinging erratically and screaming, with leaves and branches braced on her head.

Later in the day, as Mason walked along the outer boundaries of the camp in the high temperatures, he discovered a wandering donkey.

While he looked into the condition of the animal, Jodi joined him and said, "Ah, a donkey."

"He must be missing from someone's property. I guess will give him a place to stay until someone claims him," said Mason.

Niles approached both of them as they led the donkey to the pens to the east of the open canopy tent and said, "Where did you find him?"

"Out in the brush," said Mason.

"Could have been picked off by wildlife very easily." Lance walked to the group with a bucket and pitchfork and observed the creature.

"No...no, we are not keeping a stumpy, drowsy—"

"He's cute and beautiful," interrupted Jodi with a hint of sarcasm.

Then Lance took his time to finish his sentence and said, "Wasteful!"

"Wasteful?" objected Jodi.

"We can watch over him until we find its owner or find one for him," said Niles.

"You're convinced it'll be safe existing in those kinds of enclosures?"

"We're responsible for any loose domestic animals, and we provide adequate shelter for any of them."

"You don't know that."

Niles kept eye contact with Lance while he actively continued thinking. Then he stepped forward toward Lance and said, "You're going."

"No, I'm not."

Mason and Jodi led the donkey to an enclosure and gave it the proper food and water in the donkey's new temporary home.

*****

An hour later, Niles walked to the picnic tables where Lance sat and joined him. Lance worked on paperwork.

"You're going to regret it," stressed Niles.

"Oh no I'm not!" resisted Lance.

"What will you do when we discover something and you're left out in the cold rain?"

Lance softly said beneath his breath, "Gah, you're annoying."

Niles objected and said, "I'm annoying? You're the one who won't be able to live with himself when we come home with an artifact!"

Lance stressed, "When! When!"

"You're going to lose."

"I have one word—Applebury!"

After Niles shook his head, he rose from the table and thought hard upon what he'd like to say. "Would it persuade you to go if I told you the location?" said Niles.

As Lance continued to refuse to take his eyes off the paperwork, he said, "Nope."

Niles left the open canopy tent.

*****

A week later, Jodi, Niles, Lance, and Mason rode in a Jeep to the airport. As Jodi was sitting in the back seat with Mason, she whispered a question to him.

She said, "What convinced Lance to go along on the archaeological trip?"

"Niles told him he would never live it down if he wasn't there to oversee the archaeological expedition and see if it turned out to be a failure."

Jodi grinned and returned to enjoying the scenery. They arrived at the airport and took a five-and-a-half-hour direct flight to Ben Gurion Airport, Israel. Upon arrival, they travelled by shuttle to their accommodations on the second floor, Terminal 3, from Gate 23.

After the part accessible by Jeep would be made, the remainder of the route to the location site would be made by camel in the following days.

As they walked through the airport, Lance said, "Why did that man try to sell the sleeves off his shirt to me?"

Niles said, "Because he may very well be in poverty."

"He was selling jewelry. He had an assistant with him, and he didn't have a stand or the authorities may have arrested him. His wife was near him in a seat. She wore some of the most expensive clothing you'll ever see."

Mason said, "Perhaps he's cutting out the middleman and providing a clothing store to suit her expectations."

Seconds later, Lance mumbled, "If he starts pulling clumps out of his own hair, he could restore the hair to those who lie in state amongst museums and tombs."

Outside on the street, the three conservationists stepped into line to board the shuttle.

Offering all the kindness in her heart and a desire to make an honest living, a poor woman offered Lance a small brass bowl.

Lance said, "No, that's quite all right, but what's the price for the brass bowl?"

The woman told him it was nine agorot.

Lance said, "I'll give you fifty shekels, and you may keep your brass bowl. You have a good day."

Filled with an abundance of joy and great cheer, the woman thanked Lance and walked away.

Lance earnestly mentioned enquiringly to Niles and Mason who stood in front of him, "Do you think the price we paid for the shuttle will be as reasonable as the bargain she offered me for the brass bowl?"

Niles said, "We'll see."

Lance said, "What happens if the suspension is no good?"

Mason said, "It all it depends on whether you drop something fragile while you ride and put a dent in it."

Niles said, "And hit your head."

Lance said to an old man behind him, "Did you hear what they have in store for me on this ride? And I'm supposed to ride with them on this transportation. You see, most people would ask if I was about to take it. But all I have to do is turn the ride around due to the shuttle's suspension performance and tell everyone how much of a past these two men have." Lance trudged on the shuttle and muttered to himself, "Now if I can only understand where the man who sold his sleeves came into the picture."

Once Niles and Mason found a seat in the front, opposite to each other, they engaged in small talk with the driver. Lance sat alone in a seat close to the back on the right-hand side.

To break the ice concerning what kind of business brought him to Israel, the tourist seated next to Lance asked him, "And what is the nature of your stay here in Israel?"

Lance grinned and tried to say with the utmost sincerity based on being taken hostage, "You could say it's primarily based on merit founded on principle, I guess."

The tourist said, "My son and I are going to some ruins in the Negev around Avdat Park. We've decided to spend a few days in that area."

Lance said, "Ah."

Once the vehicle was placed into gear, the shuttle pulled away from the curb to get to Tel Aviv. Having shared a significant extent of busyness in the coming days ahead, the tourist continued to carry on endlessly without any interest concerning whether or not Lance gave him his attention.

Another shuttle inched closer into the left lane behind the conservationists' shuttle. Its speed picked up and moved next to the conservationists' shuttle.

A native on the shady conspicuous bus had an assault rifle strapped to his right shoulder and walked to the doors of the bus. They opened, and the native fired at the conservationists' shuttle driver. Stark fear and anxiety filled with deep concern struck all the passengers on the conservationists' shuttle.

The driver crouched on his seat while he tried to maintain eyes on the road. The passengers immediately considered the shuttle suspect as they looked amongst the shuttle's passengers to determine who was on the vehicle as they hunched down in their seats or in the aisle. As they drew conclusions, they noticed nearly all of them were armed with weapons.

The assassin who stood in the open doors angled his assault rifle higher pitilessly and shot a round into the driver's head. The driver lifelessly slumped down into the steps of the shuttle.

Mason took the wheel immediately and did what he could to manage the steering.

By veering strongly into the assassin's shuttle, Mason kept firm against their vehicle, while Niles broke out a few of their windows on both shuttles with a large tool. Then Niles reached out and seized the armed native.

After Niles tried to restrain the weapon in his hands, Mason detained the native's firearm, and the throng behind him gladly acquired it by passing the assault weapon to Niles to defend their shuttle.

While the steering wheels acted like a captain's wheel that handled at sea, Niles broke the rest of any glass out behind Mason and fired on the assassin.

As the assassin steered free from the shot, he absconded behind metal in front of the first seat. The shuttle of the assassin's driver maneuvered their vehicle violently into Mason's wheel well and fender, deliberately thrusting Mason's shuttle into the concrete barriers.

There was instant impact damage and debris broken from the shuttle. The shock tossed Mason over the dead driver down into the steps of the shuttle.

Niles grabbed the wheel and navigated as best he could until Mason could return to the seat. After Mason returned to his seat, he made certain that his seat belts were put to use to drive the shuttle.

"They don't seem to want to return fire!" emphasized Mason.

Another attempt was made on Mason's life with an assault rifle, but Mason demonstrated his ability to collide twice with their shuttle before he was shot. The forceful blunt blow hit the door of the assassins' bus and caused them to veer from their lane.

As Mason pulled back into his lane from the contact, one of the assassins was left hanging dead inside the shuttle.

As Lance sat in his seat with a scowl on his face, while he glanced at Niles in the aisle with an assault rifle, Niles could only imagine what was on his mind. So Niles questioned Lance and asked, "What?"

"You've made it fully understood to me how much of a lousy vacation this has been until now!"

Niles frowned and sighed at Lance.

Kindling fury from the act of Mason's deliberateness, the rest of the group of assassins emptied out their assault rifles into Mason's shuttle.

So Mason engaged the brakes as fast as he could and distanced the shuttle far behind the assassins' shuttle.

It was mere moments when the assassins' shuttle depressed their brakes and nearly caused an impact into Mason's fender. Mason swerved to another lane to avoid them altogether. Unfortunately, he found himself on the other side of the assassins' shuttle.

As he endured another blow from the shuttle and witnessed the screams and harm that it brought to the passengers, Mason said, "This didn't work to our advantage for Lance's Lancaster to be left behind."

While Lance overheard what Mason had to say during the two conservationists' conversation, he simply shrugged his shoulders at Niles. By stepping up abruptly once again, Niles fired at the shuttle driver and killed him to put out the continual trepidation of afflicted passengers.

Mason's shuttle swerved off on a turnoff, accelerated, and deviated on another highway to shake the shuttle. It was mere moments before the shuttle joined them from an off-ramp and continued to pursue them.

Mason said, "I can't break free from them when I don't know the city."

Niles pointed his firearm through a passenger window and shot the driver, and their shuttle was without a driver.

The group of assassins stooped low on-board in a huddle and discussed what they should be prepared to do.

It was only until one of them asked, "Who's going to drive the shuttle now?" Then each of the men turned to one another without an answer.

Next, Mason broke through a roadblock as he made a second opportunity to breach from their course with their vehicle. The road, however, turned into a broken ramp, which rose more than four feet off the ground.

Niles fretfully said, "What are you doing?"

Mason said, "A busted shuttle and an unbuilt bridge are going to set us free!"

Rising off the ramp, the shuttle became reasonably airborne, fell to the ground, landed, scraped its front bumper, and rocked intolerably and vehemently.

The difference made in Mason's driving left little to be said as the highway beside Mason, which rose on an overpass above his shuttle from a distance, took the assassins' shuttle in the same direction.

Lance stressed loudly to Niles, "You are going to get the ever-living Teflon pan coating kicked out of you!"

With unexpected unpredictability, Mason joined the same highway with the assassins from an on-ramp while his shuttle lingered slightly. Abruptly, Mason's shuttle fiercely veered into the right rear bumper of the assassins' shuttle.

The assassins' shuttle was pushed aside and pivoted to face the concrete barrier. Mason made no hesitation to press on ahead with his shuttle.

Without making a second bluff in their attempt to chase the conservationists' shuttle, the assassins quickly backed around on the highway and pursued them once again. Naturally, it took time to accelerate enough speed to catch the conservationists' shuttle. As the speed on Mason's shuttle grew, two other cars squirmed their way around the assassins' shuttle, which hindered their route.

As the cars closed in on Mason's shuttle, the assassins' shuttle hammered the second car into the concrete barrier. Plenty of damage was left behind as the car gradually came to a screeching halt.

The assassins' shuttle barreled forward and rammed into the back of the first car driving next to Mason's shuttle. So the assassins' shuttle was able to forcibly make room to push the car out of the way and move to Mason's side to attempt to nudge against Mason's shuttle again.

As the assassins' shuttle compressed against the side of Mason's shuttle, the company of assassins broke any remaining glass in the windows and seized three passengers.

They heaved Lance and two other passengers through the windows and pulled them onto the floor of their shuttle.

Then the driver, who wasn't reluctant in any way, pulled away from Mason's beat-up shuttle, and they sped off.

Niles said, "Stop along the side of the highway."

Mason said, "Boy, that's putting some use into a battering ram."

In the assassins' shuttle, three men had pointed their firearms at Lance.

Niles lightly mentioned, "I wonder how their debut album is going to do on the charts if they keep this up."

Mason said, "I believe it has already reached platinum, Niles."

Niles pulled a walkie-talkie out of his pocket and quietly radioed Lance.

After hearing Niles's transmission, Lance slowly pulled out his walkie-talkie and returned the message.

Lance said, "What is it, Niles?"

Niles said, "Where are you headed?"

Lance said, "I can't determine that! Just don't follow us! There are two more civilians, but the terrorists don't appear too experienced! I'll catch up with you!"

The assassins drove south toward the desert region of the Negev. The overwhelming heat and arid conditions were attributed to their surroundings as they drove deeper into the desert.

After an hour and forty-five minutes, Lance saw a moment where an opportunity presented itself to remove the magazines off a few assault rifles, which rested in one of the middle seats of the shuttle. After he scooted in their direction and gradually removed them, he used a pocket knife to cut a slit into a seat cushion and placed them inside. An agorot coin out of his pocket was flung, and Lance came into contact with the face of one of the terrorists who stood near the front of the shuttle. The terrorist questioned one of the assassins further to the back of the shuttle.

"And what's with the agorot tossed at me? Don't you know how to place it in your pocket?" said the sarcastic terrorist who was struck by the coin.

"You broiled monkey, what do you know about how I use my money? Come here and say that to my face, you gutted pig!" said the smug second assassin.

The second assassin lifted his assault rifle toward the terrorist at the front of the shuttle. Three more assassins farther to the rear of the shuttle raised their assault rifles to shoot him but discovered their magazines missing. They anxiously searched for them amongst the seats but found nothing. So they decisively reached a decision to do what they settled on together as they continued to scowl toward the accused assassin.

They demanded him to lay out the reason their magazines were missing.

"I took one from the rest of the ammo because I was out of rounds," said the calm accused assassin.

"But you have had the same magazine the whole time! Where are the magazines that were in our assault rifles?" said another fierce assassin.

"I don't have them!"

They snatched the assault weapon out of the accused assassin's hands, fired on him with his own weapon, and he slumped to the ground.

Then they concentrated on Lance at the back of the shuttle on the floor.

One of the three assassins said, "Why do we need to continue on with him? We don't need him! Get rid of him!"

Out in the heart of the desert, the shuttle bus came to a halt.

Lance was thrown out of one of the broken shuttle windows and upon the impervious soil. There he was left, abandoned and alone, as the shuttle sped off without driving on any approximate recognizable road.

He found himself standing on brown, rocky dirt, near wadis (dry riverbeds) and craters.

Lance didn't waste his time for a brief moment, and he took to the higher elevation immediately and started to pass through the desert. He climbed toward a curved ridge and followed it into debatable territory.

After Niles and Mason made the arrival at their accommodations, they bore down in their room and consulted each other on Lance's apprehension and their assignment.

"The amount of time he could be disposed with them is anywhere from four hours to days," said Niles fretfully as he set the two-way radio on the table.

"It never takes him that long. He's never made that tendency," said Mason.

"I don't want to get the authorities involved, not yet! What we can address during the time given to us is verifying the steps that involve the site. First, we'll confirm the Jeep rental for our designation after—"

They laid out several rather large maps on a small table. The first map showed the winding roads to the designation they needed to reach to the south by Jeep. The second map represented the site as depicted according to sources, which Niles and Lance were willing to accept according to its rendering. It would suit its objective for the assignment.

The oppressive heat began to take an impact on Lance after several hours in the desert. He came upon a lookout point and saw there would be several more hours before he would circle down below. But with no sign of any settlements or trace of life, there appeared to be nothing to alleviate his parched condition. His slowed pace carried on as he settled in his mind to gradually break down the route into manageable distances.

Throughout the time spent crossing the lower valley, Lance came across a dry wadi, which had a sloped risen embankment. This may have been a reminder for him to simply take the high ground.

After the dry conditions had already begun to set in against Lance's favor, a dry bed in the dirt seemed to rain on his parade the wrong way.

He fell forward to the ground and rested to build his energy. After twenty minutes seemed to vanish, he looked up toward the embankment and decided to crawl slowly toward it to see what was ahead in the valley. The remainder of the distance he crossed came gradually as he crawled up the embankment.

It wasn't exactly what he saw ahead of him that captured his attention but what lay below him. There were trickled traces of water still flowing across a sandy bed looking exceedingly refreshing to himself. He removed his Outback Aussie hat from his head and used it to catch some of the water. He pulled out a small water test kit from his cargo pants and used it to check the quality of the water. A number of minutes later, he drank up and kicked back in the ceaseless heat.

Fifteen minutes later, he rose from his shuteye, crossed the wadi, and carried on his route toward hilly desert. After walking at least twenty meters, he erratically jumped aside in the air and scrambled to the right.

A Palestinian viper struck out with its fangs, nearly clenching him on his leg. He secured his footing and quickly shifted to avoid it.

The viper maintained its raised poise and slinked forward to advance against Lance. So Lance began to run away from its reasonably impressive speed and offered the viper more than sufficient room between the both of them.

Before dusk, Lance located a large opening in the side of a cliff. The opening's width was four meters with a height of five meters and its concave length nine meters.

A lip extended two feet up from the ground with a rounded smooth surface upon it. As Lance examined the inside of the large opening, he concluded that the rocky layer inside needed to be removed for his resting place. Lance found a stick sufficient for walking and used it to move the rocks around to detect possible critters. While he rummaged through them, he disposed of the big rocks outside of the large opening.

A minute later, after toiling, which seemed forever, Lance lifted a Palestine viper out of the opening with the body resting on the stick. With as much caution as he could muster in his gait, he carried the viper away from the opening to a separate isolated grouping of large rocks. He returned to the opening, crawled inside, and recuperated from the desert heat.

At the rise of dawn, Lance climbed out of the opening, walked to the top of a ridge, and searched for any residences or dwellings that he could see with his binoculars.

Approximately nine kilometers straight ahead appeared to be a settlement. He strode down with the use of his walking stick and randomly chose a method to journey ahead toward the rocky terrain below in a valley. The course offered such difficulty at times that he had to double back long distances after a few attempts.

After he cleared a sandstone hill, he made the choice to critically regard any direction ahead before he would close an existing passage. He had to determine the critical factors, facts, and use of logic based on what was necessary.

He set out to move on as he traveled down a small canyon.

At the bottom, where it was free of any breeze, he heedlessly walked near a Palestine viper. It lashed out to strike after resonating its disturbing hiss. Coincidentally, the viper fortunately had allowed enough time for Lance on this occasion to be fended off with Lance's walking stick. The long piece of wood appeared to have life of its own as Lance skimmed the tip quickly across the ground as he tried to ward off the advances of the viper. Lance did reasonably well as he drove the viper back into the desert brush. Then Lance cautiously returned in the direction he was originally heading.

Forty-five minutes after he crossed the bottom of the canyon, it appeared to Lance that he had made the correct course after he made an ascent up a scalable ridge. Once he was upon the rock plateau, a plain dotted with acacia trees permeated the landscape. He found shade beneath the trees and a breeze as he walked beneath them. After he crossed the plain of acacia and came upon a high, rocky, steep hill, which he was determined to reach, he spent an extensive amount of time finding a route up the steep hill.

After half an hour had passed, he attempted to confront the endeavor by putting his best foot forward. His steps took costs calculating where the unmarked path would take him up the rocky climb.

As he reached a slightly large rock, he grabbed hold of it, and it began to tumble over him, leaving him partially bruised.

It started a threatening rockslide that caused him to take the brunt of many blows. Instantly, he tried to get on his feet again and find crucial footing along the cliffside. As he struggled to successfully move, he avoided the end of the rockslide.

While he held to the side of the cliff, he watched the slide grow in intensity with slightly larger-scale rocks tumbling downward, toppling into one another. A long, spacious recess was created by the rockslide, permitting Lance to cautiously carry on up the steep cliff.

An approximate seven-and-a-half-meter incline lay ahead of him before reaching the top, coupled with a sheer rock face under certain conditions.

Rock climbing was involved in the remainder of a slow climb.

After he reached above the top edge with one hand followed by the other and a foot secured on level ground, Lance came to the surface of the steep hill.

He brushed his hands off, took a brief break, and looked ahead across the plain, which led straight to a settlement.

It was his understanding according to the distance that the settlement presented itself closer and now appeared more like a trading post and less like a number of residences. Its shape gave way to numerous outdoor canopy tents set up as markets that sold goods, whether it was animals or products. He spent another forty-five minutes crossing relatively flat land to the trading post. There was reasonably no trace of adverse conditions that worked against Lance any longer except for the opposing strong heat.

The distance waned away, and there were only a number of meters between the trading post and Lance. Lance observed a road that lay through the middle of the tents, which were marketplaces that sat on either side. Once he walked across the road between the markets, he saw the parked shuttle that had a part in the kidnapping. Two market stands behind him across the road stood the four terrorists who were involved in the kidnapping.

Lance walked toward the opposing side from the terrorists and purchased a golf iron from one of the stands.

He proceeded to walk toward the terrorists who were standing in a line in front of one of the markets. As he raised the club, he made sure he had a firm grip on the rubber grip.

Then Lance immediately struck the first terrorist, beating him with the golf club on his head and back.

As the first terrorist fell to his knees, Lance advanced against the next terrorist beside the fallen terrorist preceding him. The second terrorist also fell to the ground after being put down by blows throughout his body. Lance used one stroke to deliver a blow to the third terrorist, and then he caught up with the fourth terrorist a few feet away who made an attempt to flee. As the fourth terrorist tried to run, he was surprised by Lance with a stroke to the knee, which caused him to double over to the ground. Lance returned to the third terrorist, who summoned up enough confidence to rise to his feet, but Lance struck him twice on his backside that left him undeniably sore.

The terrorist who was first struck looked up at Lance while he sat up on the ground and said high strung to Lance, "Why did you do that?"

"Have you not read? 'Blows and bruises remove evil. Beatings cleanse the inner parts.'[1] How about we move to some serious injuries?"

The terrorist raised his shaking hand and cried out, "*No, no, please, no!*"

Lance left the terrorists, walked back to the stand with the golf iron and returned it to the salesman behind the stand.

Lance said, "This club no longer holds its shape. Would you like it back? I'll even reimburse you for it."

"Sure," said the salesman enthusiastically.

"You have a remarkable set of number seven irons at your stand. I achieved a lot of holes in one with mine." As soon as Lance returned the golf club, he turned toward the terrorists and noticed security investigating them. Lance thanked the salesman and asked him for information on a mode of available transportation.

---

[1] Proverbs 20:30, CEB, Bible Gateway.

The salesman said, "I'm sorry, I can't help you."

He moved on to each stand along the road, and the answer remained the same. It wasn't until he reached a woman who gave him another answer.

She said, "You won't find transportation here. We'll take a bus because there's too high of a susceptible chance for anyone to steal it here."

Lance asked, "How about an animal to ride?"

"You have to ask the man in the next stand."

After he approached the man's stand, Lance asked him, "Do you have an animal to sell for a ride to the next town or city?"

The Bedouin man said, "I do…but I'll sell you the transportation based on the amount of expenses I pay over a year and not for itself. To see whether or not you can guess the right price, food, water, and supervision." The Bedouin raised a paper up to his forehead with the price on it after he told Lance what he had wrote on the paper. He asked with a remarkable grin, "What is it?"

Lance squinted as he recalled the last horse he rode not long ago. He estimated a guess and said, "$1,200."

The Bedouin's mouth gaped open and he said, "No one has ever given the approximate cost for expenses before!"

"I don't intend to keep the horse."

"Very well, the horse is yours, but where are you taking it?"

"May I return it to any connection you may have in Beer Sheva?"

The Bedouin came alive and said, "Ah, Beer Sheva, the land of great opportunity, so many it's hard to count. Absolutely, I will give you the connection's address."

He provided another paper with the contact and said, "Your horse awaits you in Shivta, the city of ruins, just up the road. Bless you. Bless you."

Lance nodded his head and said, "Bless you" and walked out of the market on the long dirt road.

He stopped to buy food and a bottle of juice from the last stand prior to leaving the trading post.

Ten minutes from the market, Lance removed the top of the bottle, and he took a swig and swallowed. An immediate involuntary repulsion insinuated, and he vomited the drink from his system. He tried to stomach the food but only ended up expelling it.

After traveling the long dusty road for a total of fifty-five minutes, he reached Shivta, an ancient city, along its western gate. As he passed through the western street built up with stones to the two inner pools many meters inside the city, he turned right to meander northwest to the animal pens many more meters.

There he walked through a break in a wall and saw a boy who watched a horse in a predominantly enclosed hold. As soon as the boy saw Lance, he immediately began to object to his presence.

The boy said, "No, this horse is not for you! Go away! It's someone else's horse!"

Lance tried to calm him down, pulled out the horse's papers, and held them in front of the boy.

Suddenly, the boy began to sob strongly. "No, I won't allow you to take my master's horse! I am watching it for him! I won't allow you to take him!"

Lance walked closer and showed him the documents, but the boy refused to put the pieces of the puzzle together. The boy continued to wail. "You're taking my job away from me. He wanted me to watch the horse until he got off work."

Lance said, "It's not about buying and keeping it, it's about using it temporarily. You'll be right back here, watching the welfare of the horse in a few days." Lance remained silent for a few moments. Then he encouraged the boy and said, "In the meantime, you can fend off opponents as opposing forces try to take the ruins from you."

Filled with disappointment and a little irritability, the boy pushed Lance in the stomach and said, "You better bring him back!"

Lance placed his arm around the boy and said, "I have something to tell you. There was once a lush meadow with a very tall and spacious iron fence with a gate holding a reasonably priced horse inside it. Outside was a boy who was expected and required to supervise the horse in a rather endless acreage inside the iron fence in the middle of nowhere. Throughout the course of the day, his employer never furnished him with food or drink, nor was he allowed to do anything, so he wandered after the horse during his free time.

"Elsewhere, amongst the ruins in the wilderness, was another boy who watched a prize stallion that never ventured away from its open pen. The boy was confident that his stallion was there to stay. The boy's employer furnished the boy with plenty of tasty meats and drinks or whatever his mind could possibly imagine. Rest assured, it was provided for him. He discovered that all he had to do was take responsibility for the horse while he was allowed to follow a heart filled with content.

"Last of all, there was another boy who was required to watch an old, weary, and spooked horse in the middle of the desert. He spent countless exhaustive hours chasing after the horse so he wouldn't lose sight of it. The time spent supervising the horse was ever continually burdensome and painful. The thought of furnishing sustenance for the boy didn't even cross his employer's mind. The boy experienced nothing but sleepless days and nights filled with discontent. Now, tell me? Which of these boys was better off and happier in the long run?"

"The second boy," said the boy with a calm and quiet spirit.

"Now do you believe the horse that you supervise will return to you?"

"Yes."

"Do you believe your employer will allow it to end up missing?"

"No."

"Do you think that you will continue to watch over it happily?"

"Yes."

"Good. Now that the threat of opponents has gone away, you can keep the papers until your connections in Beer Sheva return your horse to you."

The boy walked toward his horse, stroked its forehead and the bridge of its nose, and said, "You'll return here with me once again, won't you, Champion? It won't be a long wait, and then we'll take rides into the wilderness like we have before."

Lance placed a saddle on the horse, untied it, took the bridle in his hand, and mounted the horse.

Lance said, "You'll find him in good shape after I've returned him to you. I'll be gone only briefly."

The boy stepped back and waved goodbye to Lance and Champion, and then they rode out of the pen, north to Beer Sheva.

As Lance rode twenty minutes into the desert, he passed a large ATC six-by-six-foot military truck with a few flat tires parked fifteen meters off the side of the road.

He stopped on the road beside the inoperable military truck and came across a scraggily, somewhat weary, and lightly coherent man in the driver's seat.

After Lance dismounted Champion and tied him to the truck, he climbed up the step and asked the engrossed man, "Are you about to be struck by a meteor shower anytime soon? In fact, are you sure they're not about to strike anywhere near this location?"

With a slight measure of incoherence, the slow-to-speak man turned to Lance and said with a slight despondent smile, "Ah…no, that's not what's about to happen, not now anyway."

Lance reflected on his reaction and said, "May I join you?"

"Sure."

Lance walked to the other side of the truck and climbed into the passenger's seat.

"My name is Lance. And yours?"

The man said, "I have a name. My name is for me. It's what I use it for. But what I can't understand is if I use a name and I am who I am, why can't I secure opportunities and other things for myself in my life?"

Lance saw the man's downcast spirit, and he understood the troubled matter that weighed on the man's mind.

Nearly in his sixties, the man continued to casually carry on with his discourse, which he explained to Lance, his audience.

"I've lived ever since my youth with what I understood or perceived to be a compliant, faithful life, without gravitating toward being stagnant or being someone who plateaus throughout their life. Neither have I suffered from regression, backsliding, or drifting, and it seems as if I have come to a place where some of the passages are not at God's disposal so I might have life. Am I a moth that simply beats its head on the glass of an oil lamp but continually remains attracted or drawn toward the light? What should I do, remove the glass from the oil lamp? Is there a candle I should gravitate toward?

"I'm not living to have every question answered, nor do I care to. But why does it seem as if he has discontinued remaining steady with his feet on the ground when it comes to promises? He's renowned for accomplishing great feats that I've always trusted he'd follow through with and never pass by when it comes to opportunity. Others have asked why evil prevails in the world, which I know the answer to. Am I the only one whom he doesn't trust? Answer in a timely manner or simply leave me to work through any matter at hand. Am I out or down for the count?"

Lance said, "Well, I'm not about to tell you to be faithful only to an equivalent that you can strive toward in your life's accomplishments and so forth." Lance stalled for a few seconds. Then he said, "Perhaps you don't need to seem as if you're pushing the envelope but head him off at the pass by joining him where he expects you to meet him and seeing whether those opportunities you're searching for do take place for you after all. It might also involve his identity in regard toward who he is, according to his manner as God, based on how he behaves as a father toward his children *and* a bridegroom toward his bride."

The man bore an ecstatic happy smile as he stared at Lance and said, "Well, I never thought of it that way before. Heading the father or the bridegroom off at the pass explains a whole lot to me. I'll certainly look at it that way and see how the results turn out for me!"

"You'll eliminate the glass from the oil lamp or head for the flame on a candle pillar that way. It may do you a whole lot better as opposed to your current method."

The man raised his fist in celebration and shouted, "We've crossed the very barricade we built against ourselves, and we've been reassured that we can meet our responsibilities head on!"

Then Lance joined him with a little humor and said, "If you can add ingredients such as spices or anything hot to the recipe, do it!"

"Dig deeper when you cut out the dark spots and the eyes of a potato. Cut the time factor down or the middle man out of the situation!"

"Well said. Always know if you're going to depend on a fishing float, it isn't always the best option. Always follow through completely in your execution. It should make good ground. Now...are you in need of a ride to the next city?"

The man said confidently after giving it some thought, "I'll be fine...really."

Lance smiled, stepped out of the truck, and removed a canteen from the horse's saddle. Then he offered it to the man through the driver's window.

Lance said, "Here, you'll need this."

"But what about you?"

"I have another. Are you sure you'll be all right?

"Never better."

Lance patted him on the shoulder and said, "Until next time." He untied and mounted Champion and headed for the city in the late evening.

Roughly seventeen minutes later, he entered Beer Sheva and located the address where the horse was to be left. After he left the horse at a ranch, he contacted a car rental and arranged reservations for a Jeep to drive to Tel Aviv. He began an hour-and-fifteen-minute drive to Tel Aviv to his destination.

Fifteen miles prior to coming to the metropolitan area, he radioed Niles back at the hotel on his two-way radio.

Lance said into the receiver, "Niles! Niles!"

The radio transceiver fell onto deaf ears as Niles and Mason were sleeping in separate beds in the room.

Lance glanced stringent at the two-way radio and then glanced back at the road.

Unexpectedly, he shouted into the two-way radio, "You none other than rapscallion, agitated, decomposed, hoodwinked, congealed gravy!"

Niles sprang up in his bed and fell to the floor beneath his flat sheet. Then he threw the sheet aside and hastily rushed to his two-way radio on the nightstand and quickly answered Lance's response.

"Lance! Are you in trouble? Where are you?"

Lance said sarcastically, "I just thought I'd help you out on your research paper. I didn't catch the batteries in your flashlight losing their charge at the most inconvenient time, did I?"

At that time, Mason woke up and listened in on the conversation as well.

Niles said, "How are you?"

"I'm fifteen miles from the hotel. Do you think you've handled all the proper arrangements that require critical attention?" asked Lance as a straight shooter.

Niles sarcastically said, "Yes, Lance, we've cast off any shadow of doubt on your incentive to grace us with your presence from all your fortuitous charm to qualities resembling livestock as you make your nefarious arrival."

"We work with wildlife, Niles. We work with wildlife."

*****

A half an hour later, as Niles and Mason further reviewed the maps, Lance came out of the bathroom, drying his hair with a towel.

Niles and Mason looked over their shoulder at him, and Niles straightaway probed him and said, "How did you get in here?"

"I got a card key from the front desk. After all, the room is in *my* name!"

Mason said, "You have your own card key, don't you?"

"Yes, in addition to the joint doors," said Lance. "What's with the decorative pillows? You know what I think about those accommodations. And what were you thinking when you asked for this minibar? Do you think it was going to empty itself after you stocked it with your selection of snacks that you brought with you, especially after you've left it warm?"

Niles vehemently said, "I had nothing to do with the minibar selection, no different than the furnishing for your room or our own!"

Lance saw Niles's denial and decided to carry on and said, "And the selection of fibers you chose for your towels. I would have chosen coarse as opposed to fine any given day! And you're busy studying maps with Mason!"

Lance started to return to his room when Niles objected and said, "Where are you going?"

After a few seconds, Lance responded, "I'm going to perforate more holes into my toaster pastry so more heat can ventilate because the setting on the toaster was too high."

Niles gritted his teeth, growled, and clinched his fists.

Lance tossed the damp towel that was wrapped around his neck into Niles and Mason's room, and it landed on Niles's face.

Lance promptly closed and locked the joint doors behind him.

*****

Before dawn, after Jodi had arrived at the hotel and had her own room booked, she stepped out of her hotel room and shuffled to Niles and Mason's door. She discreetly knocked on the door, and Mason opened it.

"You know if Lance is awake?" asked Jodi.

"I don't know. I was just brushing my teeth. Do you want me to check Lance's room and our own?" said Mason.

She strode toward Lance's room, pounded abruptly on the door, and shouted, "Are you up? Are you up? Are you up!"

After a few seconds went by, Lance appeared out from Niles and Mason's hotel room door. After a few moments passed by, Jodi noticed Lance standing out front of their hotel room.

She pulled out a hotel card key and held it in the air.

Placing it through the slot on the door, she entered Lance's hotel room.

Lance cried, "No! No! No!" and ran to catch up with her.

"Show me these towels you've unearthed in Nile's room on your rendezvous across a passage you call a hotel room!" shouted Jodi.

"Show! Go ahead. Place Niles's towels under lockdown, but be very aware that fine threads get into all those pores of yours before you attend the ballroom!"

"So who did you pay to stock your minibar for you—Pepperidge Farms?"

Lance gazed at her and said, "Peanut shells present a difficulty for you to open, and you want to interrogate me on my minibar?"

"All right, let's see these impervious peanut shells from your minibar. Perhaps since you have an odd choice in food, you were expecting chocolate-covered peanut shells rather than chocolate-covered peanuts!"

Jodi quickly intended to investigate what was stored inside Lance's minibar.

Through the glass door of the minibar, the shelves were filled with all kinds of fish, meats, wild game meats, and goods found from Israel were furnished as well.

"So, why—in your mini-fridge—do you have literally every hooved animal and sea creature as an entrée on this planet? Does its origin come from what you scraped off your delivery pizza?"

"Well, if you look closely at each of these creatures, you won't find them covered in practically diamond-encrusted chocolate like the peanut shells on the bottom right-hand shelf."

As Lance began to walk toward the front hotel room door, he looked over his shoulder at Jodi with a surreptitious look and headed for *her* room.

After a while, she watched him leave and then she yelled out, "No! No! No!" and ran toward the door and stopped outside the hotel room. There she saw him standing at her front door and grinning at her.

"I want to see you get past the lock!" said Jodi.

Lance fished a hotel card key out of his back pocket and quickly opened up her hotel room. Right away, she checked her back pockets and realized he took it when she wasn't watching. He cackled as he entered through her door and closed it shortly before she scrambled to the door.

She pounded her fists on the door and insisted he open her door. Then she heard him say, "Now we're all aware of how much a woman keeps a close eye on her belongings as opposed to a man, don't we?" As he continued to laugh as she tried to persuade him to open the door, he remained inside her room for a short time and searched throughout her room. "Ah…what sort of odds and ends do we have at this sidewalk sale and yard sale?" After a few seconds, Lance hollered, "I happened to find something that's mine as the rightful owner!"

"Oh no you have not!"

Niles and Mason carried on, leaning against their front hotel door and watched the couple for any odd behavior.

*****

In the morning on the road, the direction of their assignment brought them south to the region Lance had driven to arrive at the hotel.

The short span to the Jeep's dropping point was a shorter distance than they expected, and they found the camel keeper who would provide camel rides for them.

As all four of them mounted their camels for the second route, Lance's camel became spooked and rode a mile before it tossed him off its back. The camel paced away and didn't appear it would come to a stop anytime soon.

Lance stood up, brushed himself off after landing on his back, and started to return to his three confidants.

It was a mile before he caught up with Jodi's camel.

"Give me the water," said Lance.

"The water?" objected Jodi.

"Where's the water? Give me the water?"

"You want the water? You've merely walked one mile and you want the water?"

Lance climbed on her camel's saddle and sat behind her. Then Lance tipped Jodi over the right side of the camel and held her by her legs while she was upside down.

She screamed lightly and said, "What are you doing?"

"Where's the water?" he said lightly.

Jodi broke out in laughter, giggled, and presented no desire to answer his question.

"Where's the water?"

She carried on with her laughter while she hung off the side of the camel.

"I'm going to drop you, and then the camel is going to turn around and bite you."

She proceeded to giggle.

So Lance let go of one leg, lowered her closer to the ground, and waited on her. She let out a scream, giggled more, and said, "No!"

"Where's the water?"

"Left side pouch sack."

He returned her to the camel's saddle, and she gave him a slight nudge for pushing her over the side of the camel.

After he quenched his thirst, Jodi and Lance joined Niles and Mason and continued to ride to the archaeological site.

*****

Once they'd traveled an hour, they came to a depression on a slope where a few people were unearthing ground at an archaeological site.

Lance dismounted and said to the people, "It appears as if you're searching for something."

A man said, "Oh, we're just looking for archaeological relics in these small square ruins in this foundation. I'm the person overseeing this project. We had been finished for years with the excavation until we removed this square slab to unearth another segment in the floor. We discovered some sufficient ceramics and vessels from Jeremiah the prophet's era.

"Amazing," said Niles.

A second later, he explained, "We were on our way to investigate an archaeological site ourselves. We're a team who's involved with M. Applebury, a curator out of Chicago. Did you need some help?"

"Would you like to help us finish unearthing our findings and pack them into crates?"

Niles looked at the others and said, "I believe we would."

The team remained to help extract the ceramics, vessels, and any other discoveries they encountered.

After one ceramic was lifted out of the square sunken depression, they examined it on a table to see what it held for contents. A few of the ceramics discovered held cloths, while others held jewelry and silver from the ancient era. Then they separated the discoveries into storage containers and put the ceramics into packed crates.

As the leader helped lift one of the last crates onto his truck, he said to Niles, "Why don't you come lodge at my house tonight? It's most likely too late already for you to search out the archaeological site you plan to visit. Come stay with us."

"I'll discuss it with the others on our team. I'll see what they think," mentioned Niles.

Niles raised the question with the others, and they gave the answer, "Yes," to their team leader.

"Grand!" said the archeological site leader.

As they completed the handling of any remaining pieces and secure a fence around the site, Niles asked Lance for his two-way radio, and they provided it to the leader. Then the leader's team led Niles's team to his house.

The leader and his wife treated their guests to their large one-story house and to dinner during the evening.

"What have you heard concerning this site?" said Niles as he showed him a map of the team's site.

"Yes, I assumed that was the location you discussed and were going to investigate up north from our house. It's an ancient Roman structure with stone slabs all around it. I have a map that documents far better and shorter trails to get there."

The leader showed Niles the map, and he said, excited, "This will help us significantly!" And he drew a copy of the map.

The leader's daughter carried an iguana to the dining table and set it on Jodi's shoulder as it calmly flickered its tongue and gazed at her. Shrinking back in disgust, Jodi didn't make a move while she looked away from the iguana.

Lance picked up a cat from the floor and, with a grin on his face, began to stroke its back. She saw Lance's grin out of the corner of her eye and frowned at him with rivalrous disgust and then sarcastically smiled back once she began to stroke the iguana.

"Where do freightliners fly out cargo if we find anything in large quantities or size?" asked Niles.

The leader handed him a card and said, "This is the most reliable local freight carrier found nearby." He paused for a moment and then said, "You should be able to rely on them if you need any freight relocated."

The leader's wife asked Niles, "Have you met someone special in your life like Lance and Jodi have?"

Niles said, "Location and not having the exposure or the right lady who completes the jigsaw puzzle have been getting in the way."

Mason said, "Sweaty palms, fidgety vocal cords, feet that can't walk a straight line, cooking habits."

"Stop," complemented Niles.

Lance said softly to the archaeologist leader's wife, "I thought these guys had a fantastic chance of meeting someone because they're so keen with one of their five senses."

Niles emphasized, "Remember, Lance, any fond interest of yours does pick up on that overwhelming ambiguity you're notorious for." Lance drank from his glass.

"So what have you earned in your education or experience in your work?" asked the leader's wife.

Niles said, "I have a bachelor's degree in wildlife biology, environmental sciences, and agricultural science, a bachelor's degree in archaeology, and a doctorate in veterinary medicine. Mason and Lance have earned the same degrees as well. Lance has had extra field experience in archaeology."

Jodi said, "I have a bachelor's degree in business administration as a missionary."

The leader's wife mentioned to Niles, "Your mothers must be very proud of the careers you're involved in—missionary work, conservation, and archaeology."

Niles said, "Actually, my mother wasn't entirely supportive while I grew up."

"Ah, that's too bad. I couldn't live with myself for one moment without backing my children who I gave birth to. How about your mother, Mason?"

"She didn't support me either, no different than Niles."

"And you, Lance?"

"I was an orphan. The staff and administration were always there to back me."

"You, Jodi?"

"My parents believed in me and still do to this day."

"Oh, that's good. I wouldn't have it any other way," said the leader's wife as she patted one of her children.

Niles said, "We're thankful for the lodging this evening and the meal."

In the late evening, the leader's wife began to show them to their sleeping arrangements. Niles and Mason were led to rooms inside the house while Lance made the choice to sleep on the roof.

As Lance lay and enjoyed the night sky, Jodi walked up the ramp to the roof and said, "May I share some time with you?"

Lance nodded his head.

She bolted up against him and buried her head in his chest, causing him to wheeze.

Lance winced while she snuggled by his side and smiled.

Jodi said, "So what was it like growing up in an orphanage? Did you ever feel the desire to have parents, especially since they were absent from your life?"

"I don't know whether I would have traded it for the freedom to do the things I could do independently as an orphan. I sure had a lot of freedom, a lot of alone time. It allowed a lot of objectives to be brought to completion."

He turned toward Jodi, stared at her, and said, "So if you could have any animal, what would it be?"

"A ferret."

"A ferret?"

"They're cute."

Lance spurred and trivialized the thought and said, "Ferrets are temperamental. Choose another animal."

"Rabbits."

"Rabbits?"

"Yes."

"They sit in one place over a long period of time, nibble food, and wiggle their nose."

A few seconds passed, and she said, "Well, I certainly don't want a lizard."

"If you reach a decision, let me know."

"You already helped me bring together a wildlife barnyard."

"I have a favorite for you in mind."

"Oh…well, I'm sure you may be unaware whether one of them would be my favorite."

"I guess you'll leave me no other choice but to rifle through them one by one."

Then she moved his head close to hers and kissed his lips, closed her eyes, and laid her head to rest. They eventually fall asleep together on the roof.

*****

Early the next morning, Lance woke beside Jodi, who was asleep on his left side, and one of the leader's daughters was on his right side.

"Why is there a tendency for children to gravitate toward me?"

Suddenly, Lance overheard the sound of a motor engine starting in the front yard. He gently moved Jodi and the daughter aside and rose to his feet. Once he walked to the edge of the roof, he saw a couple of peddlers handling the relics, which belonged to the leader.

"Hey! Stop!" shouted Lance.

He ran back to his shotgun scabbard, put it on, and headed down the ramp after the peddlers. Jodi woke from Lance's shout and the vehicular noise and stumbled to her feet. She followed Lance down the steps.

The peddlers leapt into their truck, filled with stolen relics from the leader's truck, and sped down the road. Deeply concerned about the heist of the relics, Lance and Jodi climbed into the leader's truck and pursued them.

As Lance accelerated the truck close to the back of the peddler's truck and left the steering wheel to Jodi, he climbed from the leader's truck onto the peddler's truck. Taking a great risk, he balanced himself toward the cab on the side panel of the cargo box.

He pulled out his shotgun and shot a round close to the back window and shattered the back and front window.

After Lance made a loop with a nylon strap in the payload, Lance clutched the passenger with his hand, looped the nylon strap around his neck, through the cracked window, and pulled back on it. The passenger thumped against the passenger window while Lance pulled the nylon strap as tight as he could.

Seconds later, Lance made sure there was no more slack in the nylon strap as he opened the passenger's door and swung it open by hand. The passenger fell backward out of the cab as the nylon strap was set free and dragged behind him.

Lance crawled into the passenger's side cab, shut the passenger door, and set his shotgun aside.

"Pull the truck over! Pull the truck over!" shouted Lance.

The driver pulled out a Middle Eastern antique knife, lashed out, and cut a long gash across Lance's forehead. But the knife was so unkept it was too dull to cut a gash in his skin.

Lance lifted his legs and then thrust and pinned the driver's head and chest against the driver's side door. But after a driven struggle, risk became a hazard on Lance's part, and he was pushed away from the peddler. The driver attempted to lunge his knife into Lance, who was backed against the bottom, backside of the bench seat, with the peddler leaned over him.

Lance moved away toward the passenger door, however, to avoid the peddler. After several seconds, Lance pushed the peddler to his side without any advantage.

Then he raised his shotgun as it rested against the dash, aimed it toward the floorboard, and shot a round into it.

The driver let out an excruciating cry as he slumped over the steering wheel.

Filled with rage and fury, the driver climbed over Lance and made an attempt with both hands to lunge and stick his knife into him again.

He tried to avoid it, however, by lifting his hands in front of the peddler while Lance held him up.

As Jodi drove her truck along the passenger side of the other truck, she shifted into neutral and leapt into the cargo box of the peddler's truck.

She balanced herself in the cargo box across the tops of the crates, careful to avoid crushing relics. Then she opened the cab door and took the driver's seat.

She pushed the driver with her foot into the half-opened window and the rest of his body into the passenger door.

Fed up with the peddler's constant squirming and making an attempt to gain the advantage with the truck and himself, Lance began to fester in sheer disgust with the thief.

Reaching beneath the bench seat, Lance found something flat, which he recognized.

Then a loud scream came from the driver as he cried out loud as a sawtooth-back machete penetrated the driver's abdomen and jabbed slightly through the roof.

After he moved the legs of the peddler aside while they draped from the roof, Lance sat in the middle of the bench seat while Jodi drove back to the other truck. With an abundance of anger over the ensued struggle, Lance looked toward the peddler and found his backside pointed toward him. So Lance gave a quarter turn to the peddler in disgust so that the peddler's backside would face forward away from him.

After they tracked down both trucks, they started to head back to the leader's residency.

Outside the house, the leader and Niles waited for Lance and Jodi to return. The two men spotted Jodi and Lance throwing dust behind the leaders' trucks and shortly returned to his driveway.

After they climbed out of the truck, Lance said, "Well, you got a free truck out of the event…and two fewer peddlers."

"I'll need to deliver my findings in a quicker time frame as soon as possible."

They walked to the back of the payload and lifted lids on all the crates to see if there was any damage.

After close examination, it appeared there was no damage to the relics.

"I think we'll move on to the archaeological site," said Niles.

One of the leaders' helpers who had made their arrival prior to Lance and Jodi volunteered to drive the truck with the relics to a curator as soon as possible.

"I'll drive you to the intersecting road because there are many paths you may get lost on, regardless if you have a map of your own," said the leader.

The leader and his family drove Jodi, Niles, Lance, and Mason to the intersection through the wilderness.

From there, Niles's team was on their own.

Their travels led them for another forty-five minutes to a large rectangular area of ruins recognized as a Roman temple with many rectangular flat slabs to the front of the formation. Standing around the site were a few partially broken pillars. The site was predominantly bare and desolate.

They climbed off their camels and studied the site.

Lance walked to the front of the temple and examined the site while Jodi and Niles followed him. Then they slowly doubled back and walked beside the side of the temple.

Lance turned around and said, "This is what worked you over so badly with Applebury? This is what you anticipated? Do you realize it appears we won't find anything here? How many times did I tell you the number of strikes that man has against himself?"

Lance turned away from Jodi and Niles and walked to the edge of the temple. Unexpectedly, the sand began to sink beneath Lance's feet. His right leg bowed, and he wasn't able to pull it out of the sand.

Jodi cried out loud, "Lance!" as she tried to help him, but Niles held her back for fear she would be trapped herself as well.

"You'll sink right along with him!"

Lance stuck his arms out into the sand, but the settling sands continued to swallow him. It took only a few seconds before he had sunk over his head and disappeared beneath the sifting collapsed sandy depression.

Jodi began sobbing and weeping in Niles's arms.

Mason quickly hunted for a rope, handed one end to Niles, and removed the slack from it as Mason began to dig down in the depression.

They found no trace of him.

Mason discontinued his search, and they all sat back and mourned their friend's loss.

Minutes later, Niles and Mason walked over the tall edge of the stone floor of the temple and studied whether anything could be found. Jodi crouched down on her legs and wept deeply.

They studied the temple for an hour but made no significant discoveries.

Then Niles wandered to the front, right corner of the temple, and studied the flat slabs that made the front walkway between both corners. By good fortune, out of the corner of Niles's eye, the inner corner edges of one slab in the front right corner sifted sand out randomly from beneath itself.

So he took a handful of sand, poured it on the edges, and it disappeared beneath the cracks. He summoned the two others and showed them the results of the slab.

Then Niles fetched a few crowbars, and they began to pry the slab upward where it rested in the sand to unseal it from the temple.

Niles said to Jodi as she helped push the slab up, "Keep on going, girl, we need all the leverage we can muster." They freed the edge of the slab from the desert sand and circled around to topple it to the ground on the other side.

It opened to a set of stairs that led to an underground chamber. Niles took a small flashlight from his belt and traveled down the stairs while the other two followed him.

They descended below where no light could be traced at all. After he turned on his flashlight, he traveled toward the side of the temple to dig from large piles of sand leaning against the wall, which had seeped in from the surface. Jodi and Mason helped him move a lot of sand.

The three of them found nothing.

There was no trace of Lance, and their hopes remained ruined. They began to slowly walk toward the other side of the temple.

Against the other wall stood numerous statutes standing in single file nearly toward the back of the temple, resting untampered from the outside world. While Niles led Jodi and Mason with a weak beam of light through the thick darkness, he stopped briefly and looked around quietly while Jodi and Mason waited behind him.

"Where does this lead or end?" said Niles.

Instantly, a lighter ignited in front of Niles who stood shy of Lance in front of the group.

The three frozen wanderers staggered and screamed out loud. Then, after they calmed down, they joined together and took deep breaths.

"Oh, Lance, you're alive!" said Niles, collecting his breath.

His girlfriend simply stood still for a couple of moments and said nothing. Then Jodi ran to Lance and gave him a strong hug and cried.

But Lance stood emotionless, lifted his finger to his lips to indicate they should remain silent and then waved with his finger to follow him.

He turned around and proceeded to walk forward to the far end of the temple. His lighter set on high and Niles's flashlight faintly illuminated the floor around them as they continued to a short ridge across the floor. There, resting upon it was a piece of wood approximately a meter long tied to a four-meter wooden pole that Lance put together.

He lit the end of the wood as a substitute torch, raised it up in front of what appeared to be a crucifix which lay against a group of innumerable rows of other crucifixes and wood for the same purpose. There didn't seem to be an end to the back wall, only darkness covering what lay beyond rows of crucifixes. And up above was a sign posted on the crucifix.

"We need to see what's on the sign," said Niles.

Moments later, Niles stood on Mason's shoulders, and Mason stood on Lance's shoulders while they leaned against the cross.

"Just a few moments, and I'll be able to interpret the sign," said Niles as he read his own small set of dictionaries that could interpret Middle Eastern languages.

"One thing for certain, you're coming down a lot quicker than you went up!" grumbled Lance.

"I hoped we would have won the argument about getting a ladder, Lance," said Mason.

Niles said, "We don't have time for a ladder. Anyone could easily discover the site, and I don't want to take that risk.

"It says, 'Jesus of Nazareth, King of the Jews.'"

Abruptly, Lance doubled back on his feet from exhaustion while Niles and Mason came crashing down to the ground.

After a few moments, Niles and Mason rose and brushed themselves off. Mason said, "Well, what now? Are you going to claim it, remove it, or leave it here?"

"I don't know," said Niles.

Lance, who was still on the ground, sitting up on the palms of his hands, said, "Are you sure the world is ready for it?"

"No?"

Lance stood with a hunched back and groaned lightly.

Niles prodded Lance lightly as he said, "Well, I guess Applebury hit the nail on the head after all."

"Once! Like a gardener who killed all his plants eleven times and had success with the twelfth spring season."

Mason lit up the horizontal beam with Lance's torch after he borrowed it and whispered, "Look…blood."

Niles said, "I can't believe they were willing to save lumber for crucifixes as opposed to burning them for the sake of guilt."

Seconds later, Niles said, "Let's move it."

After a few minutes, Mason hauled the bottom end of the cross while Lance and Niles each moved a corner of the crosspiece across the chamber toward the entrance. And Jodi led the way as she illuminated their path with a few torches.

They reached the steps and Niles said, "Don't let it touch the wall of the temple or allow the sign posted on it to be disturbed."

Their arms began to tire as the cross weighed down on them as they slowly treaded the steps and began to exit the temple. They cleared the ceiling overhead by inches, stepped out into the sand, and set the cross upon one of the front slabs. After they carefully rested the cross on the stone slabs, they collapsed to the sand and caught their breath.

Unexpectedly, four men armed with assault rifles held up the team and let it be made aware of their desire to confiscate something belonging to the team.

"Well, you don't necessarily need to carry this finding on much farther. All we need to do is require you to load it onto our truck. How about that?" said a poacher.

"This will open up an entirely new opportunity to one of Charles's collection pieces, an undiscovered breakthrough from the past where an infamous person supposedly died for others," scoffed another poacher. "You can introduce me to your shotgun as well."

Nothing could breach the scowl that broke across Lance's reaction as he turned over the cross and treasured Lancaster shotgun.

The poachers self-contentedly watched as they required the team to place the cross on a sizeable flatbed and load it onto their truck.

After they confiscated his shotgun, they carelessly tossed his cherished collector's item into a toolbox on their truck.

"Why would you want to confiscate a crucifix at all? It has no connection and initial interest to you and the world," said Lance.

"There's always something you can lay claim to as a trophy, and this was it for you. Sorry to disturb your efforts as an archaeological team, lady and gentlemen. Shalom."

The poachers drove away from the conservationists.

As they stood speechless for a minute, Mason said, "Well, this is just ripe. Where does it leave us to get another crucifix in its place for a find?"

"We won't claim any crucifix other than the one we found," said Niles.

"They scratched my Lancaster too," whimpered Lance.

The airline address the lead archaeologist had given him was removed from Niles's pocket, and he made the decision to track Charles's men through the reputable and reliable freight line.

"We need transportation," mentioned Niles.

They mounted their camels, which was their only resort, and rode to the lead archaeologist's house.

Once they arrived at his house, they questioned where transportation might be found that they could put to use. He drove them to a business that could furnish a truck. Afterward, they set out for their next destination.

They made their arrival, entered into the warehouse to the airfield unannounced, and stood a far distance from an office with a stack of crates between one another.

Shy of the security and inventory office, they quietly observed above the crates to see if a delivery in the form of a cross had been delivered to the warehouse. They neither saw a crate the size of a cross or a truck that was loaded with it. They reached a mutual decision to refrain from asking where and whether the crate the poachers stole had been delivered to the freight line.

Lance told the rest, "Remain here."

He walked toward the office and stooped to waddle into the office.

As he hunched and moved from side to side, Lance maneuvered behind a security guard seated in the corner and reached for a series of clipboards on the wall. Then Lance waddled to the right side of the security officer as the officer turned to his left to check over his shoulder. It was only seconds before the security officer turned to his right to check over that shoulder while Lance moved behind him to the officer's left side. After deciding he saw nothing, the security officer returned to the work at his desk, and Lance discreetly left the office with the paperwork hanging from the clipboards.

Lance began to return to the team but saw in a distant aisle the truck that was used to confiscate the cross in an aisle across from the team.

There was no sign of the cross on the flatbed truck. After he climbed on the truck and opened the toolbox, looking for his shotgun, he found nothing.

He decided to see whether he could spot it in the cab.

It was nowhere to be found.

He circled to the front of the truck and knelt behind it as the poacher approached the driver's side door.

In the hands of the poacher who confiscated the items from the conservationists was Lance's shotgun.

Lance climbed onto the flatbed and leapt upon the poacher against boxes behind them, seized his shotgun, and began to butt it against him.

The poacher collapsed to the concrete floor and said, "I can see you give little regard for your shotgun. Never mind how I scratched your prize possession."

"I know what's good for my shotgun, not you!"

Niles spoke cautiously from above the crates to Lance, "Do you have a remedy for loud noises, Lance?"

Lance scaled the crates again to join the others and pulled out the papers he found on the clipboards.

"It's supposed to be shipped to an overflow warehouse," said Niles.

"Where is it?" asked Lance.

Minutes later, Niles began sprinting below along the crates while the others followed. They crouched and hurried themselves by the front of the security office, ran through a few turns around stacks of crates, and to a large open space on the floor to the other far side of the warehouse. There, they discovered an open warehouse door.

"It's not inside the warehouse!" said Niles.

As they looked out of the warehouse, they saw a large forklift with a long flat crate placing it onto the hatch of an open cargo plane.

They drew closer to the partially open warehouse door, squatted, and used Lance's binoculars to look closer at the freight.

"It's our crate!" said Lance.

The forklift drove away, and the cargo plane began to taxi toward the runway.

Lance said, "Follow that plane!"

They all began to run from the warehouse toward the plane, but as they inched closer, Charles's men marked their territory with rounds from the cargo plane. All the team members could do was to try their best to avoid getting shot.

Lance clutched his shotgun and fired off several shots, causing the poachers to seek cover deeper into the plane. While Lance ran to the far right, the rest of the team continued to move toward the freight in the open hatch of the plane.

As the poachers began to gradually reappear again in the hatch, Niles and Mason took their pistols and fired to drive them back and away from the crate. Under pressure, Niles stressed to Mason, "Avoid busting up the crate with your firearm under any circumstances!"

Then a few of the poachers propped junk car doors in the back of the open hatch for possible protection they may offer and continued to fire.

A bullet nearly grazed Jodi's foot, and it caused her to drop to the ground.

Niles and Mason fell to the ground and continued to fire rounds off at the poachers.

While the poachers seemed to be closing in with their gunfire on their potential targets, a Jeep driven by Lance broadsided the hatch of the cargo plane from the right and crushed the poachers on the hatch door and behind the car doors.

One poacher inside the plane to Lance's right side tried to discharge a few rounds against Lance, but Lance's reaction was immediate. His delivery was sudden and sure by striking at close range. Then Lance climbed out over the Jeep to the right and faced another confrontation with another poacher.

Lance ended up crashing onto the crate carrying the cross itself.

Niles and Mason climbed across the Jeep and into the plane while Jodi climbed into the driver's seat of the Jeep. She drove the Jeep off the hatch door, parked it, and ran back into the cargo plane.

Niles and Mason faced six more poachers toward the very front part of the cargo bay who lacked any kind of response as opposed to the previous poachers out on the hatch. There was little left from their careless reactions in their response to the dynamic Niles, Mason, and Jodi had as they advanced against the poachers.

The team refrained from further use of their weapons, and they depended upon subduing their opponent because there seemed to be no further threat among them.

Jodi ran to the cockpit among the pilots and put her foot down with one of the men and then persuaded the other in the same way.

One poacher made an attempt to subdue Lance as they wrestled.

Niles found himself in a difficult position with both of his hands full as two poachers pulled at his arms and tried to seize him.

The two remaining poachers began to dislodge the crate from a few ropes holding it down and releasing it loosely from its tension so it would break free down the track and work its way off the cargo plane.

A crank wound up by the rope refrained it from coming entirely loose. But it began to slowly drag outside behind the hatch.

Over a period of time, Lance got the upper hand on the poacher who grappled with him. He seized the poacher by a thigh and the chest, turned him upside down, and thrust him hard to the ground on top of his head. Lance left him entirely convinced not to pick up where he left off with Lance.

Lance turned to one of the two poachers on Niles's right hand and struck him in the face to set Niles's arm free.

The poacher stumbled back as Lance pulled out two cartridges labeled "Rubber Projectile" and loaded and aimed his shotgun at the other poacher's knee. In intense pain from being unloaded on with the rubber shot, the poacher leaned against the inside of the cargo bay and found a long crowbar to pick from the metal strip on the fuselage. He held the crowbar high above his head awkwardly and prepared to swing, but Lance gave him an intimidating look with his eyes and cockeyed head.

The two conservationists mercifully picked the poacher up and threw him out of the plane. Niles raised his pistol above the poacher as he rushed from the plane, fully convinced not to attempt to board the plane.

Scampering out of the back of the plane, Lance attempted to pick up the crate from behind and gradually gained ground by maneuvering it. But the weight caused him to collapse beneath it.

He quickly crawled out from under the crate, turned around in exhaustion, and said, "If he carried it, why can't I do it?"

Preoccupied with the wound tangled rope around the crank, Niles nervously worked the nylon to set it free.

Mason kept at work, fixated in a physical struggle with the last poacher just shy of the cockpit.

Jodi asked Mason, "What should I do?"

"Make sure the pilots keep it taxied and assigned to their seats!" said Mason.

Another Jeep with two men arrived out beside the rear of the cargo plane. Unsurprisingly, they both were recognized as additional poachers as the driver ran hastily inside the cargo plane. The passenger had the appearance of being highly energetic in his personality, but something else fueled a high in him.

His entirety was stooped in crime in a pool of stimulant drugs, which caused him to be heaped up on hyperactivity. His physical build left an impression, but he apparently put it to use with no sense of self-control, which presented trouble for the team.

The brute rushed in with a frenzy as well as unstable emotion into the cargo plane and threw Niles out of the hatch. Then the brute stopped and looked at Niles antagonistically with a freakish grin on his face and laughed.

"That's never happened before," said Lance to himself.

The driver of the Jeep made an attempt to confront Jodi, but she turned around and saw the threat immediately.

With prompt quickness, she struck a crowbar against the top shoulders and chest of the poacher, inflicting heavy blows and injury on him.

It was more than enough to capture the attention of Mason and the poacher who wrestled but came to a complete stop to watch in shock and deep respect for her display of self-defense she placed against the driver.

Once the driver collapsed, Mason and the poacher who were contending with each other looked at one another and carried on wrestling with one another in combat. They both thought if that could be done to one man, what potential would it leave her to do to others?

As the brute covered ground and scurried toward Lance, he tried to strike the brute with his shotgun, but it was seized by the brute's open palm, and he shoved Lance to the ground.

"Why behave the haphazard you are when it's the world of fighting, and you're not putting up a bold front? Keep it up and see what it possibly resorts to," said the brute in an intimidating way.

Aimlessly swinging Lance's shotgun resulted in shoving him back onto the ground while the weapon was simply tossed over the brute's shoulder. Lance stood to his feet but was reluctantly struck in his gut. The brute carried on the same action several times.

Lance kicked his gut as hard as he could, but there was no effect on the bizarre and rash man.

"It would make it much easier if you'd saved your strength and stayed alive," said the brute.

Lance allowed the large brute's comment to sink into his mind for a few moments, and he reflected on it while he remained completely silent.

Lance reached behind his back, removed a snub-nosed revolver, and discharged it beneath the brute's chin.

The brute stood frozen for at least a few remaining seconds from the 9 mm embedded into his facial bones.

Then Lance walked slowly to his shotgun, picked it up, returned to the brute, and guided him off the side of the crate. It was there that Lance pushed him to the ground where he remained.

"Don't keep me from loading a crate onto a plane...and don't toss my Lancaster," mumbled Lance.

Then Lance shouted at Niles, "Aren't you done loading it onto the plane?"

Niles stepped to the edge of the hatch door and said, "Forgive me, I haven't been allowed to fully admire all the wonderful surroundings one might enjoy this evening!" Then Lance returned to the crate and began to push it toward the plane.

Niles yelled, "Keep on pushing it this way!"

Niles finished freeing the tangled rope around the crank and handle and began to wrap the rope by cranking its winch.

With both of their efforts, the crate was dragged across the asphalt close to the rear of the plane. Together, they lifted the end closest to the plane and pushed it with care onto the hatch floor. Niles continued to crank it farther inside and secured it to the cargo bay.

Mason continued to fight the poacher who tried to subdue him.

"Are you done?" asked Lance.

"No," said Mason in his resistance.

As he walked by Mason and the poacher, he entered the cockpit, clenched the shirt of the remaining pilot, and pulled him into the cargo bay. Without any reluctance, Jodi got hold of the other pilot and evicted him like a bad tenant. The exact same thing occurred to the other pilot as they removed them off the back of the plane.

"Mason!" hailed Lance.

Lance captured the attention of both Mason and the poacher.

"Fly," said Lance.

Then Mason led the poacher to the passenger door, shoved him out, and locked the door behind as though they had never been familiar with each other. Mason sat behind the control wheel and sped up as he made a turn onto the runway. Niles and Lance finished closing the hatch so there would be no more uninvited guests.

They made a flight to another airport outside Israel where they had two legal pilots selected to fly their freight. From there, they made their flight to Chicago in the United States of America.

*****

After they disembarked from the plane, they met with Applebury, who furnished a location in a museum for the crucifix. A body of preparators of the museum staff carried the cross onto an assembled stage behind a showcase and inserted it in a foundation furnished for it in the floor beside two artificial crosses belonging to the two historical vagabonds.

After several minutes, the crucifix had drawn a healthy crowd, and applause was given for the discovery.

Two young men walked up to the showcase after the crowd dispersed later and began to mock the exhibit beside an old man.

One of the young men slapped his hand on the old man's shoulder and said, "Can you believe with your own eyes that they have a cross here?"

The old man turned to them and said with reproach, "Well, if you want to turn your back on what it has to offer, that's your problem!" And he calmly walked away.

*****

The team took a plane back to Tanzania. There, out in the savanna, the four of them enjoyed a picnic far away from the conservation camp.

"I still don't understand how the both of you knew freight could be allowed to pass through a reputable airfield and warehouse, aside from the crooked parties involved, and didn't allow the crucifix to slip through their hands under the direction of Charles's men," said Mason.

"It's because I'm privileged," said Lance, full of pretend pride and sarcasm.

Niles glared intensely at Lance and then motioned to Mason regarding his particular comment.

So both men rose to their feet, grabbed an arm, carried him a few feet to the edge of the cliff, and threw him over it.

He wound up falling down a steep drop into a body of water below. He slapped the surface of the water feet first but found a way to gain his equilibrium as he turned in the water.

As his head and body rose out of the water and he looked up, he spit out water and walked out to dry land.

"We'll see if he's privileged to participate in any leftover picnic food," said Niles.

Jodi, Niles, and Mason began to eat their meal without Lance as he made the long journey back to the picnic site.

*****

Another week passed when Lance stopped by Jodi's barnyard and backed a truck up with a large enclosed cage. He opened the cage, removed a capybara from inside, and set it free in her wildlife barnyard.

She began to mosey to the barnyard when she saw what Lance brought her. She ran inside and gave the capybara a big hug. She couldn't have been any more overjoyed. They spent the rest of the remaining afternoon spending time with the barnyard animals.

Throughout the following week, a project was set in motion to rebuild Lance's thatch hut in the conservation camp itself. A wilderness fence was also beginning to be built around the compound.

In a matter of weeks, his hut and the fence were completely built with the help of contributors throughout the area. Once again, Lance was attributed to his old hammock in his own thatch hut and found himself sleeping soundly in the warm arid breeze of the Tanzanian climate.

Works Cited

Common English Bible. 2011. Biblegateway.com. www.biblegateway.
com/passage/?search=proverbs+20%3A30&version=CEB.

About the Author

Beginning a series of suspense in their interest to wildlife conservation and archaeology, these four spirited prize hunters, presented by Daniel Nuss, culminate far more questions in their suspense-filled adventures than answers. Living in Loveland, Colorado, Daniel has spent his time creating art and writing in his pursuits. He also passes his time with family and friends throughout his day-to-day living.

CPSIA information can be obtained
at www.ICGtesting.com
Printed in the USA
LVHW110059221122
733724LV00004B/111

9 781685 266356